"It's difficult to imagine a myth riper for harvest than that of Cassandra, the tragic Greek figure who uttered prophecies no one believed. She was, to begin with, a woman, and that is what Sharma Shields, in her biting second novel, sinks her sharp teeth into the deepest. . . . The dream scenes . . . provide necessary, sickening contrast to the spit-and-polish patriotism via talking coyotes, deformed fetuses, and other grotesqueries. . . . But nothing is more troubling or more brilliant than Mildred's horrifying reaction to a trauma that implicates all of us so forcefully that it's easy to believe Shields is the one blessed—or cursed— with visions of impending ruin."

—Daniel Kraus, *The New York Times Book Review*

"Dissecting humanity's cravings for power and our fascination with destruction, Sharma Shields's *The Cassandra* is a call for us all to truly think about who we are—and who we are becoming."

—*Electric Literature*

"Shields's novel addresses the questions of collective guilt and blindness, of how flawed our love is for one another, and the terrible consequences of our cleverness. It's a well-paced story that gives the reader plenty to think about."

—*The Historical Review*

"*The Cassandra* is . . . a weird, discomfiting book of epic poetry and intimate prose that grows both more and less fictional with each passing page. Sharma Shields's novel is a relentless rush, a distressing re-envisioning . . . compelling and beautiful."

—Tor.com

"Shields writes the natural world with clear joy, and she evokes scenes of destruction with horrifying beauty."

—NPR

"Sharma Shields has weaved a true twentieth-century story around the classic Greek myth. Exploring man's propensity to destruction, she shows how humans can also challenge the power. It will not be easy to put it down once you start this well-researched and stylishly written novel."

—*Washington Book Review*

"*The Cassandra*, with its multiple parallels to the original story, might be the truest twist on the Cassandra myth ever attempted—and certainly the most relevant to our times.... In Shields's hands, this gift-made-curse sport of the gods becomes not personal but systemic. It feels less like myth or magic realism than reality itself. In a timely take ... for the #MeToo era, Shields poses critical questions: Why do we ignore the truth when women tell it? Why do we compound the injury of rape with the insult of not believing the women to whom it happens? With all due respect to Virgil, it's high time we had a Cassandra story told by a writer whose primary purpose is not to sing of arms and men."

—*New York Journal of Books*

"Fans of Madeline Miller's *Circe* will be similarly inclined toward Sharma Shields's provocative, beautifully rendered account of a World War II-era Cassandra.... Shields has crafted a clever, fierce parable about the blindness of those entranced by the powers of violence—that those people are mostly men should come as little surprise."

—*NYLON*

"[A] galvanizing variation on the ancient Greek tale of a seer doomed always to be right, yet never to be believed. Shields ... offers satirically comedic scenes and satisfyingly venomous takedowns of the patriarchy, welcome flashes of light in this otherwise harrowing dive into the darkest depths of hubris and apocalyptic destruction. A uniquely audacious approach to the nuclear nightmare."

—*Booklist* (**starred review**)

"Lyrical ... well-researched.... Shields's reworking of the classic myth— about a young woman whose warnings about a future she alone can see are ignored—is filled with grotesque and violent images and episodes of keening sorrow. Shields delivers what her heroine cannot: a warning, impossible to ignore, about the costs of blind adherence to ideology."

—*Kirkus Reviews*

"[An] alluring, phantasmagoric story.... With a plucky, charismatic narrator and vivid scenes incorporating the history of a real World War II facility, Shields's novel digs into the destructive arrogance of war."

—*Publishers Weekly*

"*The Cassandra* is a magnificent exploration of the consequences—both incredible and devastating—of human ingenuity and human intuition. This novel is full of magic and hope, even while it brings up to the light some of our darkest past."

—Ramona Ausubel,
author of *Sons and Daughters of Ease and Plenty* and *Awayland*

"*The Cassandra* is a fantastic achievement of unflinching honesty, psychic power, and sustained empathy. Sharma Shields's fearless reckoning with American might at the beginning of the nuclear age closes the distance between victor and victim, historical detail, and mythic truth. This fevered novel's seer will infect you with her visions, but her moral candor will work on you long after the dream is over."

—Smith Henderson, author of *Fourth of July Creek*

"*The Cassandra* feels powerfully—chillingly—relevant to our own political moment, even as it unfolds against the bleak splendor of the 1940s American West. It's a harrowing story, beautifully told, of patriarchy and violence intertwining to make a combustible monster; and of the woman who speaks the truth about this monster, only to be dismissed as unhinged."

—Leni Zumas, author of *Red Clocks*

"A stunning fable of hubris, complicity, and nuclear genesis, set against the raw backdrop of the wartime northwest. Sharma Shields illuminates the grotesquerie of humanity's progress and offers up an elegy for a damned world."

—Megan Kruse, author of *Call Me Home*

"Sharma Shields is one of our finest literary fabulists and *The Cassandra* is further proof—a brilliantly tightening knot of dread, a phantasmagoria of nightmares and daytime horrors that glows with powerful insights about the nation's reckless nuclear history and its corrosive chauvinism."

—Shawn Vestal, author of *Godforsaken Idaho*

Also by Sharma Shields

The Sasquatch Hunter's Almanac

Favorite Monster

THE
CASSANDRA

THE
CASSANDRA

a novel

Sharma Shields

A Holt Paperback
Henry Holt and Company
New York

Holt Paperbacks
Henry Holt and Company
Publishers since 1866
120 Broadway
New York, New York 10271
www.henryholt.com

"Richland Dock, 2006" from Flenniken, Kathleen. *Plume: Poems.* © 2012.
Reprinted with permission of the University of Washington Press.

Names: Shields, Sharma, author.
Title: The Cassandra : a novel / Sharma Shields.
Description: First edition. | New York: Henry Holt and Company, 2019.
Identifiers: LCCN 2018022670 | ISBN 9781250197412 (hardcover)
Subjects: LCSH: Secret Operations. | War stories. | Fantasy fiction.
Classification: LCC PS3619.H5429 C37 2019 | DDC 813/.6—dc23
LC record available at https://lccn.loc.gov/2018022670

ISBN 978-1-250-26062-8 (trade paperback)

Originally published in hardcover in 2019 by Henry Holt and Company

First Holt Paperbacks Edition 2020

Designed by Meryl Sussman Levavi

Printed in the United States of America

10 9 8 7 6 5 4 3 2 1

For Itha Anderson, who loved me and warned me.

The Columbia rolls on
through the desert,
unimpressed and unattached—
. . . The mighty river passes, not touching,
But not untouched.

—"Richland Dock, 2006" by Kathleen Flenniken,
from the poetry collection, *Plume*

I look back now and realize this was a free country but we were living behind barbed wire at Hanford, all to protect womanhood. I know that where women were concerned, Hanford could either make you or break you.

—Jane Jones Hutchins, 1940s Hanford worker,
from *Working on the Bomb: An Oral History of WWII Hanford*
by S. L. Sanger and Craig Wollner

Have I missed the mark, or, like a true archer, do I strike my quarry? Or am I prophet of lies, a babbler from door to door?

—Cassandra,
from Aeschylus's *Agamemnon (The Oresteian Trilogy)*

CONTENTS

1944

Afterlife

1944

TO MAKE MEN FREE

I was at the mercy of the man behind the desk. I needed him to see my future as clearly as I saw it. He held four pink digits aloft, ring finger belted by a fat gold band, and listed off the qualities of the ideal working woman.

"Chaste. Willing. Smart. Silent."

I swallowed his words, coaxed them into my bloodstream, my bones. I crossed my ankles and pinned my knees together, morphing into the exemplary *she*.

The man eyed me with prideful ownership. "Frankly, Miss Groves, you're the finest typist we've interviewed. Your speed and efficiency are commendable."

I opened up my shoulders, smiling. "They named me Star Pupil at Omak Secretarial."

"You're not a bad-looking girl, you know that?"

"Thank you. How kind of you."

"A little large. Plumper than some. But a nice enough face." The man smoothed open the file on his desk. "Good husband stock at Hanford, Miss Groves. Plenty of men to choose from."

In my lap my hands shook like tender newborn mice. Such sweet, dumb hands. *Calm down, you wild darlings.* I focused on the man's sunburnt face. It reminded me of a worm's face, sleek, thin-lipped, blunt. He was handsome in a wormish way, or wormish in a handsome way. If I squinted just a little, his head melted into a pink oval smudge.

We spoke in a simple recruiting office in my hometown of Omak, Washington. All of Okanogan County was abuzz with the news of job openings at Hanford. It was like this, too, when they started construction at Grand Coulee Dam. We were patriots. We wanted to throw ourselves into the enterprise. *Men and Women, Help Us Win! Work at Hanford Now,* the *Omak-Okanogan Chronicle* urged. I'd snipped out the newspaper article and folded it into my pocketbook, away from Mother's prying eyes. I was here in secret, and the secrecy delighted me. Goose pimples bubbled up on my forearms and I tapped my fingers across them, tickled by how they transformed my girl flesh into snakeskin.

The room we sat in was crisp and clean, beige-paneled walls, pine floors, plain blue drapes. A war poster hanging behind the recruiter's worm-head featured a young, attractive woman in uniform, crimson lips, chin nobly lifted, blue eyes snapping and firm, their color enhanced by the stars and stripes rippling behind her.

Her proud expression spoke to me. *I'm here, Mildred. I can help you.*

I smiled at her. *I'm here, too. For you. For all of us.*

Aren't we lucky, her eyes said. *If anyone can save them, it's you.*

Above her strong profile it read,

TO MAKE MEN FREE
Enlist in the WAVES Today
"You will share the gratitude of a nation
when victory is ours."

I, myself, wasn't joining the WAVES, I was joining the civilian force, the Women's Army Corp—the WACs—but the work at Hanford was just as crucial for the war effort. With the woman in the illustration I shared a gallant dutifulness. I mimicked her then, holding my chin at the same noble angle, lifting my eyebrows with what I imagined was an arcing grace. I wanted to show the recruiter that I was just as earnest and eager as she was to join the fray.

"You're squirming," the man said. He smiled with concern. "Are you uncomfortable?"

I assured him I was fine, just excited, and I lowered my gaze. I wore my only good blouse, cornflower blue, and an old wool skirt, brown. The shoes were Mother's and pinched my feet. One day I planned to buy my very own pair of wedged heels. I'd circled a black pair in the Sears Christmas catalog that I very much liked. They looked just like the famous movie star Susan Peters's shoes. When Mother had found the page in the catalog, she scolded me for marking it up with ink.

Once, in downtown Spokane, just after we'd visited our cousins, I saw her—Susan Peters!—walking in a similar pair. She was graceful, athletic. I waved at her and she waved back as though we were dear friends. I wanted to speak to her but Martha, my older sister, pulled me away, telling me I was acting like a starstruck silly boob, and I had better stop it before I did something we'd both regret.

Don't embarrass me, Martha had hissed. *Act normal for once, please.*

The recruiter cleared his throat, shuffled the papers on the desk, and continued his summary of the Hanford site. I chided myself for my woolgathering. I fought the urge to slap myself and leaned forward clutching my elbows. I hoped I looked alert and intelligent.

"Hanford is a marvel," the man said, "nearly seventy-five square miles in size, smack dab on the Columbia River. We started construction last year and we're darn well near finished, which is a miracle in itself. You'll see what I mean when you see the size of the units. These are giant concrete buildings. They make your Okanogan County courthouse look like a shoe box. We've brought in more than forty thousand workers to live at the Hanford Camp, so believe me when I say you'll have plenty of men to choose from." He winked here, and I gave a small nod of appreciation. "The work being done is top secret. Frankly, I'm not sure what it's all about—mum's the word—but everyone says it will win us the war. I do know that a top United States general is involved, and some of the world's finest scientists. Construction is being over-seen by DuPont. But even these details you must keep top secret, Miss Groves."

He handed me an informational sheet, and I read it self-consciously, keeping my back straight and my head slightly lifted so that I didn't give myself, as my sister liked to tease me, too many chins.

To accommodate nearly 50,000 workers, the Hanford Camp is now the third-largest city in Washington State:

8 Mess Halls
110 barracks for men (for 190 persons each)
57 barracks for women
21 barracks for Negroes
7 barracks for Negro women
Plus family huts and trailers
Overall: 1,175 buildings in total for housing and services
There's a lot of us, so remember: Loose talk helps our enemy, so let's keep our traps shut!

"What a bold undertaking," I told him. "What an honor it would be to work there."

His face crinkled cheerfully. "Regarding your application, I don't have many reservations, Miss Groves. Your background check is clean. You've signed the secrecy documents. The only concern raised was about your questionnaire. A few of your answers were—how shall I put it? Unique."

For a moment my future darkened. I had agonized over my application. I couldn't imagine anything amiss.

"For example," he said, lifting a sheet of paper up to his nose, "your response to the request for relevant job experience, if any, was, 'I have imagined myself in a giant number of jobs, some of them impossible, some of them quite easy, and in my imaginings I've always done well by them, impossible or no.' This statement struck some of the committee members as a wayward answer, Miss Groves. Would have been better to just state 'No relevant job experience.' Most of the women answering the charge are lacking in it, you realize."

"Yes, I understand." My eyelid violently twitched.

"And then there was your response to the question about your weaknesses. You wrote, and I quote, 'I have made a big mistake in my life and it haunts me. Sometimes when I make a mistake this large it stays with me for a long time. I wish I got over things quickly.'"

I waited for him to continue, holding my breath. I thought of Mother, of the splash and crunch of bone when I pushed her down the bank into the river. I wondered if he could see her shadow flicker across my face, hear faintly the sound of her muffled scream.

"Lastly, when you were asked if there was anything you wished to add, you wrote, 'I only wish to say how confident I am that I will be the best fit for this position. I have seen myself there as clear as day. I dream about it. I know for a fact that you will hire me. I will not let you down.'"

He looked up at me with his smooth worm's face, his graying eyebrows raised slightly. He seemed more amused than troubled.

"I don't need to tell you," he continued, "that we need workers with very sound minds for this position, Miss Groves. We need reliability and obedience. Your confidence struck some of our committee as arrogance. And one or two of the men wondered about your rationality."

"Omak Secretarial told us to be forthright and self-assured in our applications, sir. If I overdid it, I apologize."

The recruiter cocked his head. "Personally, I found it refreshing. You should see some of the anxious girls we get in here. A bit of confidence is a good thing."

I stayed silent, balancing the line of my mouth on a tightrope of strength and humility. I knew better than to tell him the truth, that I *had* dreamed about Hanford, that I *had* seen myself there. I had, in fact, sleepwalked into Eastside Park, awaking with a start beside a grove of black cottonwoods, the trees shedding puffs of starlight all around me, the wind whispering through the branches my fate. He would hire me because I had envisioned it, and my visions always came true in one form or another.

As if sensing my memory, the recruiter's face tightened. "You can no doubt imagine the outcome if secrets were shared with the feeble-minded."

I leaned forward gravely. "Our very nation would be destroyed, sir."

The recruiter's visage softened into an approving pink mud. I'd made a good impression. He sat back in his chair and smiled.

"The truth is," he said, "when I read your comments I thought, now here's someone who really gets it. The confidence might bother some of my colleagues, but these times call for backbone. For attack! We should bomb those Germans to smithereens, wouldn't you agree?"

"Oh, yes," I said, "most certainly. Bombs away."

"You're an exceptional sort of girl, Miss Groves, a skilled typist and a clear patriot. You won't meet a more outstanding judge of character than myself, and given your excellent response in person, I'm happy to stamp my approval on your form." He grinned at me, the grin of a generous benefactor. "I'm hiring you as a typist for Hanford. Welcome to the Women's Army Corps."

I closed my eyes for a moment and took a deep breath. My limbs buzzed with elation. "Oh, sir," I said, opening my eyes. "I'm so grateful."

I'd never stepped foot outside of Omak, but now I'd be a sophisticated, working woman at Hanford, joining the fight with the Allies and making the world a better place. I teared up, not sure if I should lean across the desk and shake his hand or if I should just stay rooted to my seat, trembling with destiny.

"I'm thrilled. You have no idea."

"I tell every young person who comes through here, 'Stand tall. You're a hero.'"

He lifted gracefully from his chair as though showing me how to do it. I rose, too, more clumsily.

"Stand tall, Miss Groves. Shoulders back, chest forward. There you are. Well, almost. Good enough, anyway. Of course I can't tell you the

particulars of the work, but let me just say, you've chosen a lofty voca-
tion. Selfless girls like you are one of the many reasons we'll win this
war."

At the word *selfless*, I heard in the stunned silence of my mind Mother's
dark laughter.

He offered me a sheaf of introductory papers and a voucher for a
bus ticket. I accepted these, allowing his warm hand to grasp my elbow.
He guided me toward the door and then released me.

"You'll make some young man very happy one day, Miss Groves.
Patriotic girls always do. Whatever you do, hold on to that innocence."

Imagining Mother and Martha overhearing this description of me
was almost more than I could bear. They would fall upon the recruiter
and tear him apart for his mistake.

"I'll hold on to it," I said. "I promise."

"Good girl. And good luck."

I left his office a new woman, a WAC, a worker, a patriot, a selfless
innocent—a warrior ready for battle.

OFF TO THE MOVIES

I stopped at the drugstore on the way home and bought myself a cola and a tube of red lipstick. Mother gave me a small allowance once a month. I'd used almost all of it on these two items, but I wouldn't need her money now, I'd soon be making my own. Old Mrs. Brown, who ran the shop, peered at the lipstick tube and grimaced.

"A whore's color," she said. "Tell me this isn't for you, Mildred, dear."

I tucked my chin. "It's a gift for a friend."

She handed it back to me. "You shouldn't spend your money on such things during wartime. God prefers a pale mouth. You don't want men to get ideas."

I opened my pocketbook and counted out the change. "Thank you, Mrs. Brown."

"Take care of yourself, dear girl. Send your mother my regards."

I drank my cola on the way home, accidentally smashing the bottle into my front teeth so that my whole head buzzed.

I forgot to tell Mrs. Brown good-bye.

She would scold me for leaving, but what if I never saw her again?

Silly Mildred! You'll see her again. Of course you will.

I quickened my pace, half-walking, half-skipping. It was pleasantly hot and dry and the cola was cold and fizzy in my throat. I opened up

my arms and spun about, just once. Another spin and I would lift off
of the sidewalk and corkscrew into the fat diamond-bright sky.

❋

Omak was a small town nestled in the foothills of the Okanogan High-
lands. For a couple of short months in the spring, it was a very pretty
place, verdant and alive with birdsong, but the winters were harsh and
the summers harsher, so dry that you inhaled the heat like a knife. Can-
ada was a short drive to the north. Hanford, I'd learned, was three hours
south, in a similarly arid place. This would give me an advantage,
accustomed as I already was to the ungracious environment of Central
Washington State.

The sum total of the neighborhoods in Omak were modest, and
our street was no different. We lived in a white house on the busy main
road, surrounded by other small, simple houses. What set our home
apart was the large garden bordering the yard, which Father, before his
death, tended obsessively. Throughout my childhood it teemed with
perennials, allium, aster, lupine, and coneflower, and the north-facing
plot grew heavy and green in the summer, laden with vegetables and
fruits. On the weekends, he would sell bulbs from his abundant perennials, putting out a handwritten sign, BULBS, TEN CENTS A DOZEN, and cars
would pull up all day long to purchase them. I liked to sit in the lawn in
my bare feet and watch people unfold from their vehicles, usually with
exclamations of awe or envy at my father's green thumb.

Our town bordered the westernmost edge of the Colville Reserva-
tion, made up of various tribes like the Nespelem, Sanpoil, and Nez
Percé. Our region was most famous for the Omak Stampede and the
Suicide Race, where men would urge horses down the perilous banks
of Suicide Hill, plunging into the Okanogan River and crossing in a
dead sprint to the finish line on the other side. Our neighbor, Claire
Pentz, was the rodeo publicist, and she started the race in 1935 as a way
to drum up excitement for the stampede. She said it was inspired by
the Indian endurance races, and she called it a cultural event. It was a

thrill to watch the wet horses gallop with their riders the last five hundred yards into the rodeo arena, but the year before my father died was also the year the race killed two horses, one from a broken neck and another from a gunshot to the head after she broke her leg, and then Mother refused to attend.

After that, some of our neighbors muttered, "The barbarity of the savages," but Father argued with them about it.

"Blame Claire," he would say. "She's the one who made this, all for rodeo money. And she's not Indian."

But I knew he secretly looked forward to watching the races, and he was proud of the toughness of the men here, even though he would never willingly ride a horse down Suicide Hill, or even canter on a horse bareback, being constructed of what he once described to me as "sensitive bird bones."

No one who saw me would accuse me of having bird bones, but I was sure my whole self was cluttered with them, my brain and my heart each their own nest of delicate ivory rattles that jostled and clicked together when I moved too quickly. As a young girl, I ached over paper cuts and whined when I lifted anything too cumbersome. A casual insult—*eager beaver, fathead, fuddy-duddy*—pained me like a toothache for days. My mother was made of tough bear meat: solid-fleshed, big-backed, firm as she was certain. Her shoulder-length hair was so dark brown it was nearly black, and she wore it styled closely to her face, without any of the rolls or curls that were popular at the time. Despite her complaining, I always had the impression that little bothered her—insults, mistakes, the stupidity of other people—she took nothing personally. Life, I assumed, would be easier to navigate with an unforgiving nature.

It doesn't matter now, I told myself, returning to this ordinary street in Omak on this hot summer day. *I'm going away from all of this. I'm snaking out of my old skin to become a bigger, better self.*

I reached our front lawn. The neighbor boy had mown it yesterday.

It looked neat and comfortable and I thought about sprawling out on the green, uniform blades and enjoying my afternoon here in peace, but there was Mother, sitting very still on the porch, wrapped in a thick blanket.

"Oh, Mother," I said. "Are you unwell?"

She coughed and drew the blanket tighter around her shoulders. "I have the sweats."

"Mother, darling, it's ninety degrees and you're wrapped in a quilt."

Mother scowled. "Mrs. Brown just phoned. She said you bought a whore's lipstick. She said I ought to know. The whole town heard about it on the party line."

"It was a gift for a friend. I already gave it to her on my way here. It's her birthday."

"You have no friends," Mother said.

This was true: My classmates in school had been impatient with me if not exactly unkind. And now that I was older and more confident, maybe even worthy of a friend or two, I was alone with Mother.

"Allison," I told her, recalling a girl from high school with lustrous hair. "Allison Granger, who lives a block south from here, and who I saw at the church picnic. She has three men asking for her hand—three!—and she says it's all because of her dark red tubes of lipstick."

The uneven plate of Mother's face splintered into a sneer. "You have the devil's imagination, Mildred. Allison Granger lives in Airway Heights now. I saw her mother just the other day. She told me that Allison's married a lieutenant colonel. Imagine how proud *her* mother must be."

I listened to this quietly, without comment.

"Forget it." Mother shifted in the old blanket, grimacing. "I'm unwell. I have the sweats. Help me inside, Mildred, before I faint."

"You need a glass of cold water. Let's get you out of that quilt."

"I've never been so sick. I'm dizzy."

"Here, Mother, take my arm."

"Mildred, you're the most ungrateful daughter who has ever lived."

"That's it, Mother, take my arm. Come inside now."

"What are you crying for? You're upsetting me."

I wasn't crying, not really, I was simply emoting, and that emotion ran like water down my cheeks. Next week I would leave, without saying good-bye to Mother, which I felt horrible about, but it was no use divulging my departure; she controlled me like a marionette. She would lift a finger and yank the string attached to my chest and I would pivot. I would stay, hatefully.

No, I had a plan: The morning before my departure I would post a letter to my sister, Martha. She would receive it the following day and learn that I was gone. It would be too late for her to stop me. She would come and check on Mother, begrudgingly, I knew, but I'd been caretaker long enough. It was time to live my own life. They didn't think I was capable of it. They thought I was better off locked away with Mother, away from any true experiences of my own. For a long time—riddled with guilt after I'd harmed her—I trusted them, and I served Mother dutifully. I cooked and cleaned and cared for her, answering her every need even when her requests became ridiculous.

I had done enough.

I would continue to serve her now, but in a different way. I would send money from every paycheck to them, more money than they'd ever seen in their entire lives. And when I met my husband and had my children, we would return to visit, and then I would apologize to Mrs. Brown for never saying good-bye, and she would apologize to me for being such a grumpy tattletale, and everyone would be very pleased with me and all would be well. Mother would be beside herself with the beauty of our children—her grandchildren!—and she would thank me for growing into such a responsible and independent young lady. And my sister would say, jealously, *Why is your husband not old and bald, like my husband, and why are your children so kind and generous, unlike my children?* and I would shrug and embrace her and tell her no matter, that I loved her and her old bald husband and her wretched children, and she would say, *Oh, Mildred, I love you, too, and I admire you so.*

"I need to go to the toilet," Mother said, loudly.

I had just settled her on the couch with her blanket and her pillows and a glass of cold water.

"Right now?" I asked her.

"No, next week, Einstein."

"Okay, Mother. Come on. Take my arm again."

"Are you still crying? Your moods today! You're making me nervous. What's going on in that ferret brain of yours?"

Good-bye, Mother!

I waited outside the door for her to wipe herself, for her to flush, so that I could help her back to the couch and make her a healthy lunch. I brought my hands to my mouth and tried to shove my happiness back down my throat. The tears were gone. Now I was brimming with laughter.

Good-bye and good-bye and good-bye!

"Mildred," Mother said sharply. "Are you giggling? Get in here and help me clean up. Jumping Jehoshaphat, I've gone and made an absolute mess."

I forced myself to remain solemn. I squared my shoulders and lifted my chin. I went in to help poor Mother.

A few mornings later I pinned my handkerchief around my head and put on, again, my good blue blouse and wool skirt. I went downstairs to check on Mother one last time.

"Are you feeling all right?" I asked her.

She lay on the davenport, a wet washcloth over her eyes. Her graying hair hung in tangles around her big face, and I reminded myself to give it a good combing before I left.

"I'm at death's door," she said. "But otherwise I'm fine."

"Is it a headache?"

"No, it's a splinter in my foot." She tore the washcloth off from her forehead and glared at me with moist eyes. "Yes, it's a headache, Mildred. If you were a good girl, you'd fetch me an aspirin."

I fetched her one. I was wearing my black driving gloves and worried what she'd say when she saw them, but she accepted the aspirin without comment.

"Let me get you a glass of water," I said.

"I've already swallowed it."

"I'll get you one. For later, if you need it."

"Mildred, you know I hate it when you do unnecessary things for me."

"For later, Mother." I shouldn't have said what I said next. It was some sort of mischief rising in me. "I might be gone a long time."

"Don't say that," she said, and she looked at me with a mixture of panic and derision. "Don't tell me you're going to spend all day at the movies again, watching the same film half a dozen times? You'll bring on another one of my heart attacks. I hate how you envy those silly starlets."

"No, I'm not doing that, Mother. I promise."

I didn't point out that she'd never had a heart attack.

I went to the kitchen and drew a glass of water for her and returned to set it on the coffee table. *Good-bye, old table!* This was where I had once cut out paper dolls with my younger sister. At that age Martha had gushed over my precision. She had asked me to help her and I was glad to do it. *Good-bye, kind memories!*

I placed the water close enough to Mother so that she could reach it easily without having to sit up.

Well, there, I thought. *Maybe I should give her a little food, too?*

I went to the pantry and found some saltines and spread a handful across a plate and brought that to her. She watched all of this silently, sulking.

The phone rang. Mother reapplied the washcloth to her face, waving at the noise dismissively.

I went to the phone and brought the receiver to my ear.

"Mildred," my sister said. "I'm livid. You stay right there. Walter's getting the car. We're coming straight over."

"Oh, hello, Martha," I said. I inwardly cursed the postal service's promptness. I hadn't expected them to deliver the mail so early. "So good to hear your voice. How are the children?"

From the couch Mother groaned.

"Don't act like the Innocent Nancy here, Mildred," Martha said. "I've read your horrible letter. You can't, you simply *can't* upset Mother like this. She's an old woman and she's alone in the world. And to expect me to uproot my life in this way, when I have children, Mildred, when I have a husband! It's just extraordinary! It's like I always say, if only you had children, if only you had a husband, you would understand, you would know *implicitly* what I mean."

Mother rose up on one elbow, turning her head toward me with the washcloth still smashed over her face. "Tell your sister I can hear her squawking from across the room. It hurts my sensitive ears. Tell her she sounds like a drunk banshee."

"Marthie," I said, interrupting my sister gently, "Mother says you sound like a drunk banshee."

"Hand the phone to Mother. Have you told her yet? No, of course not. It's just like you, to run away from things like a coward. You're the most cowardly person I know, Mildred. Put Mother on the phone. She'll scream some sense into you. And Walter and I will get in the car right now, with the kids, we'll be there in twenty minutes flat—"

"Mother," I said, "Martha wants to speak with you."

"No. Absolutely not. You deal with her, Mildred. As if I don't have enough on my hands. Tell her I have a terrible headache."

"She won't come to the phone, Martha. She has a terrible headache. I'm sorry. And now I really must be going." I glanced at Mother, who was relaxed again, lying flat on the couch and nibbling on a saltine. "I'm going to the movies. I'm going to the movies for a very long time. Goodbye, darling."

"You won't go through with it. You've never gone through with anything in your whole entire life."

I hung up, trembling with relief.

I kissed Mother. "Good-bye." I tried not to sound too meaningful.

She refused to remove the washcloth, but she accepted the kiss graciously enough.

"You'll rot your ferret's brain with those movies, Mildred."

Her voice was not unkind. It was not such a bad way to leave her.

And then I went out the front door, leaving it unlocked for Martha and Walter, even though they had their own key, and I went down the cement stairs and retrieved my little suitcase, which I'd hidden earlier that morning beneath the forsythia. My father had died pruning this bush—felled on the instant by a massive stroke—but it remained my favorite plant here, so brilliant in spring and so brilliant now, again, in the early fall. Beneath the bright leaves, the limbs looked like Father's thin arms, reaching skyward, surrendering. When I was very little, he'd called me whip-smart, but Mother had demurred. *She can see the future, this girl*, he'd said. He was right. I could. But Mother had told him that there was no place in the world for knowledgeable women; he should be wary of encouraging such nonsense. *Foresight won't do a woman any good*, she'd said. *It will only double her pain.* The forsythia shook in the breeze, as if to deny this memory. I backed away from it with a respectful nod of my head.

The luggage handle felt good in my palm, hard and solid like a well-executed plan. I'd packed very lightly, with only a few clothes, an old pair of winter boots, my papers, my red tube of lipstick, and my pocketbook. Within was my bus voucher. I hurried across the street, toward the station. Only a few minutes remained. I couldn't be late.

Martha was wrong: I'd never been so committed to anything in my entire life.

PERFECT WOMEN

"I'm Bethesda Green," the woman said as the bus's brakes released. She offered me her hand. "You can call me Beth."

"Mildred Groves," I said, touching her fingers. "I'm a typist."

"Nurse," Beth said, pointing to herself. She leaned her lovely head against the green vinyl of the seat back and smiled kindly at me. "You remind me of my little sister, my Annie. I can tell we're going to be good friends."

"Oh, please," I said. "That would be wonderful."

It was the best sort of omen, to meet a friend so quickly. A few moments earlier, I'd tripped over the stairs while hurrying onto the bus. A loud masculine laughter had lifted all around me, and as I straightened I met the jeering, angular faces of several dozen men. One of them had leaned toward me, offering his hand.

"You all right, Miss? Quite a spill there. Guessing you're not much of a dancer."

I'd leaned away from him instinctively, alarmed by the strong onion smell of his breath.

"I'm fine," I told him. "I need to sit down."

I'd looked around desperately for a softer face, and midway down the aisle I saw one, pretty and kind, gazing back at me peacefully. I was relieved when the woman scooted over and patted the bench beside her, as though she'd been waiting for me all along. A couple of other women had chosen the seat directly in front of us. The four of us formed an unsteady raft in this sea of men.

"You have lovely hair," I told Beth now.

She reached up and touched the auburn ends of it and smiled. "You're a sweet soul, Milly," she said. "Just like my Annie was. One of those rare open types."

"Where is Annie now?" I asked.

Bethesda brought a hand to her throat and adjusted the prim collar of her dress. "She died when she was twelve." Her face grew very cold, and I could almost see Annie bobbing at her side like a deflating balloon.

"I'm very sorry," I said.

Beth broke out of her trance. She looped an arm through my own so that our elbows formed a knobby pretzel.

"You really do remind me of her. The eyes, I think. Sad and wide. Anyway, we'll room together, you and me. I'll see to it. And we'll go out together when we aren't working. To dinner, the pubs, the hairdresser, *everything*. We'll have a fantastic time. You'll be the peas and I'll be the carrots."

"How wonderful," I breathed. "I could really use a friend."

"Couldn't we all?" she said, and laughed.

It wasn't like I hadn't had friends before, but they had been rare and brief experiences. There was one-legged Melanie Bright in grade school, whose shirts were always rumpled and who caught frogs with me in the lake until I accidentally crushed one of hers with a rock and she punched me in the nose. She thought I'd done it on purpose, and she never believed me otherwise. And there was Junie Anderson in my math class, who walked home with me to play paper dolls sometimes, at least until I foretold her mother's death. *She'll die in a car wreck.* I was certain it would happen on a rainy Wednesday evening, although I wasn't sure what month. I wouldn't let the subject go, pressing it on her urgently even when she told me to shut my mouth. I was trying to warn her. Incensed, she took up a pair of scissors, cut off the heads of all of my paper dolls, even the ones drawn in her mother's steady hand, and refused to speak to me or even look at me in math class anymore. When her mother died a year later, killed on a rainy night in a horrible wreck involving three vehicles, I was sure we might be friends again, but her hatred only deepened. Her mother had died on a Thursday. I'd been wrong about it, after all.

I was friendly with a couple of girls in high school, but they all seemed to be so much more savvy than I was, and also somehow stupider. I had dreams about all of them. Sometimes it was a daydream, where I would envision their future even as I spoke to them about the day's Latin lesson, and then I would black out, coming to on the floor, babbling incoherently about their oncoming illness or stillborn baby, with everyone hollering to give me space because I'd gone ahead and had one of my nasty fits again. The most terrifying episodes happened when I slept. I usually woke up from these nightmares wading in Okanogan Creek, having wandered a half mile from home, the bones of my shins chilled to icicles. In my waking visions those girls became women. They married too young, grew tired of their husbands, rotted with strange diseases, beat their children, or reposed in bed all day crying and wondering what was wrong with them. Only one of them seemed to have a happy life, a loving husband, and adoring sons, but I foresaw her lonely and painful death, in a nursing home where the aides were too rough and hateful, with no family nearby to check on her. I warned everyone about what lay in wait for them, but my insistence frightened them.

Leave us alone, Mad Mildred. Worry about yourself for a change.

I *was* worried. I worried about all of us.

My father noted my despair. He liked to remind me, "Ma Ingrid was the same way as you, Mildred. *Wahrsager*, she called herself. Fortuneteller. As you grow older, you'll learn to hold your tongue."

Mother, hearing such a statement, would look up from her embroidery, frowning. "Ingrid was always difficult. The whole town called her

Hexe. Some were afraid of her. I always found her too domineering and foolish."

I remembered Grandma Ingrid, that tall, ursine creature, who didn't seem silly to me at all, but awesome, terrifying. She spoke only German. Her lone companion was an Okanagan woman, a Syilx Indian. They walked every morning to each other's shacks to play cards, gin rummy, and Canadian rummy, and they spoke in brief grunts of German and Salish. They seemed to understand each other perfectly well. I almost never saw Grandma smile, except when she won at cards, and then she gloated to her friend, lifting ceremoniously from her chair to dance a slow, clumsy *schuhplattler,* clapping and striking her thighs with those ferocious palms, stomping her big feet on the pine floor. The Syilx woman, Nicky, pretended to frown at this behavior, but when our glance met I could see the twinkling merriment in her eyes. They drank small cups of beer as they played and I liked to pour the beer for them. It was the color of gold and I made a show of recoiling from its dank smell even though I secretly found it warm and comforting.

One day as I poured Nicky's beer, she told me in English that her daughter was getting married the coming weekend.

I asked if Grandma Ingrid was going to the wedding.

"Not invited," Nicky said, and I laughed in surprise.

I thought she was joking.

Grandma said something in German and shrugged. She understood every word even if she refused to speak the language.

"But you're good friends," I protested.

"We're good at cards," Nicky replied, shuffling the deck. "But Ingrid's settler blood. Like you. You are the uninvited."

Grandma Ingrid drank her beer and dealt the cards, impassive. She was an outcast, a reluctant immigrant. It was fine with her if she was an outsider.

But I was troubled by it. I had been born here but my birth was a presumption. My home was in a region that my grandparents and great-grandparents had misshaped and bullied, that my parents and peers continued to bludgeon and disrespect. When I walked, I began to hear the very earth groan beneath my feet. What did it mean to be born white in this country, to speak a language germinated not here but overseas? To infest and control but to never belong or care for, like a parasite? What horrors had we committed, what horrors did we continue to commit, to the original inhabitants, Nicky and her kin? *What have we done to their children, small and scared, like me?* My skin itched. I scratched self-consciously at my elbow. Nicky watched my face and read the confusion and unwillingness floating there and turned away from me. I stewed in my discomfort. She flicked a card to Grandma Ingrid, one to herself, back and forth. They played long into the evening, and I fell asleep on the floor near the stove, only to wake later when Grandma Ingrid dropped a heavy blanket over me.

Usually if we stayed the night, Grandma tucked me into the big bed with her, while my father slept on a pallet on the floor. On her lumpy mattress, I lay on my side, facing the wall. She spoke to me in German and stroked my hair. I fell asleep listening to those sharp whispered words, the sound of her fingers against my skull like distant slicing blades. I dreamt of dark forests, wild dogs, long-clawed hags, cottages with candy-coated exteriors belying menacing contents: cages, skeletal remains, a hot stove reeking of burnt flesh, cutting boards strewed with bloodied fingers. I awoke once from such a dream to the sounds of the coyotes screaming, an accusatory ululation that reminded me of the faceless howls in my nightmares. I burrowed into the solid heat of my grandmother's bulk, her blood warming my blood. Those girl-like screams held secrets in them, and if I listened carefully, I could harness their power.

One day in the middle of winter, when I was eight years old, Grandma Ingrid fell on the ice on her way to the hair parlor. A boy who witnessed it said the sound of her head hitting the sidewalk was like an axe splitting wood. He marveled over how she had convulsed for a few moments before going completely still. Father told me it was a blessing, her quick death. On the way to her modest service at Our Presbyterian,

Mother muttered again about "Ma" Ingrid's "foolishness," as though foolishness had anything to do with dying.

To be fair, Mother disliked her own parents, too. Although Mother refused to speak of it, my father said her parents were harsh disciplinarians, religious to a fault. They had believed the world was in peril, on the verge of destruction. Mother found their endless discussions about Revelation and the battlefield of Megiddo tedious. She noted the flexing end-time predictions halfheartedly, while secretly certain they would never directly affect her.

One night, when she was sixteen, a boy my mother loved invited her to her first dance. For weeks she prepared for the event: buying a pretty red and maroon calico fabric, sewing her own dress, polishing her church shoes, buttering up her parents so that they finally allowed her to go. They agreed only on the condition that her mother would chaperone. On the night before the dance, she pinned her hair up in curlers and slept excitably with the pins stabbing her repeatedly in the skull.

I loved the details in this story and would always ask my father to repeat it. It was mythical, a creation story about my mother's singular joylessness.

Finally the afternoon of the dance arrived. Mother combed out her beautiful chestnut curls and slipped into her pretty dress. It accentuated her waist and bust. She twirled in front of her brothers and sisters. They applauded, in awe of her transformation. She daydreamed about the boy she loved and imagined his expression when he first saw her. She supposed he would want to marry her on the spot.

Just as she was about to leave, someone knocked on the door. Her parents opened it with their usual modest hesitancy.

It was their preacher.

"It's today," he said gravely. "Gather your children. You won't need any belongings. We'll meet at the top of Golden Hill. I don't need to remind you about the speed required."

Her parents turned to their children with proud, eager faces. "Today," they rejoiced. "Today, finally!"

The children tried to mirror their parents' happiness, all of them except for my mother.

"Come now, come, get your shoes."

My mother's face reddened. "I'll meet you after the dance, then."

The blow her father gave her—hard across one ear—disturbed her hearing and balance for days following.

So she went and sat with them on the hillside in her good dress with her pretty curls, watching the sun go down over the little town and wishing savagely for the world to end the way the preacher said it would, but it didn't, it only ended a little for my mother and for the boy she loved, who wouldn't speak to her again after she stood him up. Hours went by and finally the preacher said, "God is good. He's allowed the weak and evil to remain for now, in an attempt to save them. We will continue our work." And just like that, they were dismissed. Her parents continued to worship as if nothing had happened, and they returned to the hill again and again and if they were disappointed with the absence of Armageddon, they never admitted it.

As all girls did, I wanted my mother to be happy. I tried to please her by being obedient. I helped with chores, anticipating her needs before they were spoken. I prepared meals and mended my own clothes. Talk of my visions upset her, so while I might burden Martha with them, I never mentioned them to Mother. Martha, not as dutiful or good of a daughter as I was, enjoyed lording over me what she saw as her superior sanity. She encouraged me to record my visions, and even went so far as to buy me a notebook from the drugstore. I wrote them down for her until I found out that she relished showing my words to her friends. Everyone loved to gossip about Mad Mildred, even my sister. On certain nights when I awoke in the creek bed, having sleepwalked there with the zoetrope of my mind swirling, I returned home as silently as I could and dried myself off in the bathroom. Then I slid under the blankets, shivering with both the extent of my powers and of my loneliness. By my sixteenth birthday, I knew how to keep my mouth shut.

Then high school ended. Unlike the other girls, I didn't get married straightaway or attend a vocational school. Not long after Father's sudden death, I pushed Mother into the river. She survived, but her health was shaky. I became her caretaker. The dreams loosened their grip. Alone with Mother, my brain quieted. Even the passage of time froze, and every night when I slept, an empty blackness swallowed me whole. I aged without aging. It was a relief at first, to no longer upset people, to no longer see their life peeling away from them, but when I turned twenty I began to wonder if I'd lost myself entirely, as though my own potential had in some way been tied up in the vividness of those waking dreams and nightly pictures. The death of all dreams is what it felt like, both the good dreams and the bad. This was the reason I attended secretarial school, to try to jostle that part of me back to life. I stared into the faces of the other pupils, straining to read their future, but the trick no longer worked. The women blinked back at me, curious, unafraid. They were kind to me if indifferent. Maturity, responsibility, whatever you wanted to call it, had stopped up all of our fire.

Then, out of nowhere, I had my vision about Hanford, and the next day I applied for the Women's Army Corps.

Now, on the bus, joggling toward my new life, my fire returned. My gaze flitted here and there like a dragonfly, and my line of sight shook just slightly at the corners, blessed with a renewed energy. I ground my teeth together with happiness. My jaw muscles ached.

Beth, my new friend, gave my forearm a squeeze and then withdrew her arm from mine. I was determined not to lose her friendship. I admired the dim bust of her profile against the white sky and sienna desert. The bus was hot, the windows thrown open. There was a good breeze but it was stitched with Central Washington's dry heat. The underarms of my shirt dampened.

The bus accelerated and bounced over an enormous pothole. The woman ahead of me turned to face us. "I've bitten my damn tongue."

"How wretched," Beth cooed. "Not a smooth ride, is it?"

"You a nurse?" the woman asked. When Beth nodded, she said, "Me, too." She put her hand out to us. "Katherine Berg. From Seattle. Just saw my mom in Ephrata. She thinks I'm a twit, leaving my job like I am, but I said, Look Ma, all the doctors are married in my ward, so it's pointless to stay there."

The girl laughed raucously. I didn't like her. She was mean and coarse, not at all like Beth.

"Nice to meet you, Kathy," Beth said. "I'm Beth and this is Mildred."

Katherine narrowed her eyes at me. "You a nurse? You don't look like a nurse."

"I'm a typist," I said. "I took a secretarial course in Omak. I was the fastest typist in the history of the course, teacher said."

I hadn't meant to gloat. It was fact, pure and simple.

Kathy sniggered. "You're joking, right?" She looked to Beth, motioning to me with her thumb. "She's bonkers, huh?"

Beth laughed her gay, ringing laugh and put an arm around my shoulders. "She's perfect. She's a doll."

I thought of the dead sister, her ghost buzzing like a fly in her sister's ear, the white noise of grief, and I didn't mind her presence, so long as Beth's affection toward me remained just as perpetual and constant.

Next to Kathy another girl shifted her shoulders and said, "Can you all pipe down? I'm trying to sleep here. I've got a horrible hangover."

Kathy apologized loudly but then stuck her tongue out at the girl when she closed her eyes again.

"Look at these men," she whispered to us. "We're the only girls on board. Just the four of us."

I could hear all of those men laughing and jostling around us, and I could smell them (wood, cigarettes, a raw muskiness). All of their conversations and attention pointed somehow at us.

"Look at you," Kathy teased. "Blushing head to foot. Like you've never seen a man before!"

Beth patted my hand and said to Kathy, "Of course she has. Don't be silly."

"Of course I have," I said dully, but the words were cement blocks in my mouth. "My father," I began, but then I stopped, remembering my father's effeminate shoulders and hands, the gentle way he carried himself. He was an outdoorsman, a hunter and a gardener, both, but Mother liked to say that she was more of a man than he was. A group of teenage ruffians in Omak had once bullied him about, and I'd seen that it would happen before it did, how they punched him around a circle they'd formed with their lean, tough bodies, and how he'd shrunk to his knees, shrieking for his life (and why didn't I warn him? Was I mad at him that day? Was I too young and indifferent?). This event troubled him for years. He once asked me, deeply pained, "Why did they do that to me?" I'd said nothing; I was unsure. I worried he'd thought of it beneath the forsythia as he drew his last breaths. I hoped not.

"What about you," Kathy said to Beth. "Husband hunting?"

"Not me," Beth said. "I'm a widow. My husband died of influenza last January."

I brought a hand to my mouth.

"Tragic," Kathy said admiringly.

"This is a much-needed adventure," Beth said.

That Beth had already gained and lost a husband was extraordinary. It mystified me, the intimacy of being married, of sharing a bed with a man, holding him, kissing him, feeling accustomed to all of his angularity and brawn. I grew a little nauseous, thinking about it. Maybe I was carsick. I'd never even seen my own parents touch. They slept in separate rooms all of my girlhood. I closed my eyes and breathed deeply.

"I'm serious," the girl next to Kathy complained loudly. "Please. This headache."

Kathy rolled her eyes dramatically and then blew us a little kiss and settled back into her seat.

"I'm not bonkers," I whispered to Beth. "She smells like a whiskey barrel."

Beth laughed. "She's probably hungover, too. Don't you worry about old Kathy. I won't let anyone bother you. We're going to have a golden time, you and I, Milly. Can I call you Milly?"

She'd already called me Milly half a dozen times. "Of course."

"I'm going to make sure we're assigned to the same barracks," she said, growing very serious. "It's so hard to meet sincere people these days. I won't let them break us up."

Gratitude tasted sweet on my tongue, extravagant like hard candy. I wanted to tell her how long it had been since I'd had a true friend, but, no, it was unnecessary. The friendship shocked me in its immediate affection. I gave myself over to her fully.

We curled up together like two cats, my head on her shoulder, her head on my head, and we rested, half-dozing, half-dreaming. I thought of my sister and my mother together, how worked up they must both be by now, and I stifled a sad little laugh.

"I'm so happy," I told Beth. "This is the greatest day of my life."

"I'm glad for you, Milly," she said.

I was only slightly disappointed that she didn't say it was the greatest day of her life, too.

Overhead the ghost of the dead sister dipped and danced, threaded to Beth's throat by a fine fishing line of grief.

Beth nodded against my skull and our heads melded together, our brains seeping one into the other, lava flowing from ear to ear. I dreamt we became the perfect woman in just this way.

GLASS BOOTH

In Kennewick, I placed a call to Mother.

For a few moments she wailed incoherently into the phone.

I chewed on my cuticles and let her cry. Beth eyed me from afar, standing with Kathy at the bus terminal. Even stately Beth looked small and fragile surrounded by the shoulders of a hundred men.

"Look what you've done," Mother said. "You've gone and killed me. I can hardly breathe. I'm mid–heart attack as we speak."

"I'm in Kennewick, Mother. I'm taking the bus to Hanford in thirty minutes. I called to remind you to do your exercises."

"I won't lift a finger for the rest of my life. I'm *grieving*, Mildred. I want to *die*. And you've gone and left me with Martha and her husband. He's no better than a stiff at the morgue."

"Be nice to Walter. You know how sensitive he is."

"He's a turd with legs."

A man peeled away from a wall of bodies and approached the phone booth, grinning widely like he'd just heard a lewd joke. He was broad-shouldered and handsome. He reminded me of Susan Peters's husband, Richard Quine. I'd seen Richard Quine in *Jane Eyre*. I thought he and Susan Peters made the most attractive couple. The tall man looked me up and down, leaning against the doorway of the booth as though he owned it. I flushed hot and tried to turn my body away from him, but the phone booth was tiny, and I smelled the man's exhalation, mint and cigarettes.

"Almost done?" he said. "I've got my own people to call."

I held a finger up at him, mouthing, *One moment.*

"Your sister wants to speak with you," Mother said. "But I won't let her, because she'll just scare you away with her harpy's voice."

"I left a letter for Martha with instructions. I'm sure she's already found it, because I put it with your aspirin, Mother. Please remind her about the calisthenics."

My voice shook. The tall man half-smiled at me from the phone booth doorway. If he leaned in much farther, his lips would brush my forehead. I was an ant in his shadow. Behind him, Beth and Kathy watched us. Mean Kathy snickered and kind Beth's brow furrowed with concern.

The man began to hum and he had a low, sweet voice. I worried my locked knees would turn to rubber and that I would collapse against him. I shrank back against the glass.

Martha, meanwhile, must have wrenched the phone away from Mother.

"You are a horrible person, Mildred," my sister said. "I can't remember anyone ever being so selfish and cruel. You've gone and made my grown husband weep. Think of all the lives you've ruined today, Mildred. If you have any conscience at all, you'll come back this very instant."

I wondered if the whole neighborhood was on the party line, listening.

"I love you very much," I said, "and Mother and Walter and the children, too. The instructions are all there, written out neatly. I didn't forget a thing. And I'll send you money after my first paycheck. I'll be making forty a week. Forty! Isn't that incredible? I'll send you as much of it as I can."

"Come home right this instant, Mildred. Not just for us, but for you. You know you won't do well there. Your mind, Mildred. You'll just crack."

"I love you, too," I said, and for a brief moment I met eyes with the tall man who looked like Richard Quine, and when he blinked at me I changed into Susan Peters, beautiful, intriguing, brave. I wasn't from Omak at all, but from a lovely farm in California, where you could eat fruit from the trees and wade into the ocean in a peach petticoat. "I'll always love you," I said, and the man looked away from me, and I became Mildred Lovell Groves again, disappointing daughter and sister.

"If you know what's good for you, come home this instant," Martha said. "Remember what you did to Mother, remember how you get when you're—"

The line went dead; I was out of change. I hung up, shaking, and then I tried to return to Beth, but the man refused to move. I was trapped in the little glass booth.

"Excuse me, sir," I said. "I'm all done here."

"Are you now?" he said. "What's your name, sweetheart?"

I glanced up at him and then back down to my feet, where my mother's old shoes chewed at my toes.

"Mildred Groves," I said. "From Omak."

"Mildred Groves from Omak," he said, like it was a funny joke. "Pleased to meet you, Mildred Groves from Omak. I'm Gordon Nyer from Omaha. I'd be off fighting Hitler my goddamn self if it weren't for my enchanted eye." He pointed to his right eye. It didn't focus on anything, just sat unmoving in its socket. It was a ball of glass. I thought it was beautiful, bright blue even though his other eye was a greenish-brown. "Pleased to make your acquaintance, Mildred Groves of Omak."

He thrust out his strong hand and I timidly accepted it. He drew my knuckles up to his lips. My torso tightened and I drew back even farther against the booth, half-worried I would break through the glass panes and fall into the crowd on the other side. He released my hand but continued to lean toward me with his handsome, wolfish face.

"You're blocking my friend's way," a terse voice said, and he pivoted and there was Beth, her auburn hair backlit by the sun.

"Hey, Ginger, there's no need for that tone," Gordon said. "Miss Groves and I were just making each other's acquaintance."

Beth looked at me and I smiled weakly, but she must have seen the question in my face. She put her palm against Gordon's right shoulder and pared him away from me.

"Come here, Mildred," she said to me, as if I were a frightened pup.

I came forward and she put an arm around my waist, leading me away.

"What's your name, Ginger?" Gordon called from behind us. "I like your style."

"None of your business," Beth said. "Stay away from us."

I shrank into her and we made our way onto the smaller bus, the cattle car, that would cart us into the Hanford compound. In a few minutes Gordon, himself, boarded, and when he smiled at me and waved I saw clearly the mockery of it and I crossed my arms over my ribs. I made sure not to look at him for the remainder of the trip to Hanford.

⁂

After a good twenty minutes—the bus rumbling along the smooth ribbon of freshly laid asphalt—the Hanford Camp appeared. We disembarked in an orderly line only to join another line for job and bed assignments. I wasn't bored at all, even as others complained around me. There was so much to see and smell and hear. Hanford was a sprawling compound, far larger than my hometown, a noisy, dusty, abrupt city of long, one-story buildings that looked like they had been raised overnight.

Directly behind the northern border of the camp was the Columbia River. We'd passed the Columbia at various points during our trip, tracing its path on Highway 97 from Brewster to Wenatchee and then again as we approached the Tri-Cities: Kennewick, Pasco, and Richland. It was wider than two dozen Okanogan Rivers, nearly a mile from bank to bank, so big and powerful I immediately imagined drowning in it. Its gorgonian muscularity wrapped like a flexing limb around the edge of my new home.

On the eastern side of the river loomed the White Bluffs, pale layers of sandy cliff piled on top of one another into the rock-stippled cake of a giantess. The striped faces of these cliffs loomed over the Columbia with a quiet ghostliness, and behind them rolled the hills of the Saddle Mountains. Until a few months ago, there had been a town here called White Bluffs, but the government had depopulated it in a handful of weeks, forcing residents out for little to no compensation. The Wanapum had been ordered out, too, urged north, out of their traditional fishing grounds. Boundaries reimagined and reordered, a process so sudden and unfeeling it almost seemed like an accident, as though the force determining it all was inhuman, a particularly destructive episode of weather, say, or a contagious disease. The people who had been here vanished. Richland was emptied to make room for more governmental housing. Hanford was here, instead, teeming, necessary, full of the promise of military triumph.

Many of these details I didn't know then; I would learn about them later, much later, when information was finally released to dogged journalists.

Humans have only ever been at the mercy of one another, although that didn't occur to me then, as I alighted in Hanford and smelled the fresh-cut wood and delighted in the new sights.

What I thought instead was, *Home*. Emotional, thrumming, I asked Beth to hold my place in line, and then I wandered away between two buildings to where I could be alone for a few moments and catch my breath. I stepped from the shadow of the edifice and there, a quarter mile away, was the Columbia River and beyond, the bluffs.

I considered all that had happened to me along the comparatively tiny Okanogan River: The visions, the night-walks, the altercation with Mother. To think of all of that as just droplets in a tributary, discharging into something vaster and far more powerful, was a relief. Now my life would leave its narrow pathway and merge with a larger purpose.

The big river pulsed with a current I couldn't see.

"I'm here," I murmured. "Finally."

The wind picked up, ruffling the sand and the river's surface. The water nodded.

TERMINATION WINDS

Milly.

Milly, Wake up.

I was awake. Wasn't I? There was dust in my hair and grit in my mouth.

Watery light flooded the stars. The wind slammed into my chest.

Wake up this instant.

Snap out of it.

I wiped the heavy sand from my eyes, straining to remember where I was. I sat cross-legged in an open field in nothing but my briefs and cotton nightgown. To the north squatted short, narrow buildings like coffins awaiting burial, quiet and dark in the dusty twilight. I'd walked here from those buildings. But for what? Even from a great distance I sensed the long, unflagging serpent of the Columbia slithering through the canyon. It called to me: *Come, Mildred Groves.*

I will, I called back. *Soon.*

I wasn't alone. I'd seen a rattlesnake. Eyes were on me everywhere here. My power raised their curiosity. My thoughts drifted in and out, hazy and winking like the starlight overhead. How good the night air felt, even with the stinging wind, even with the sharpness of the sand knifing my bare skin.

There was a coyote, watching me from the grass. There was nothing sneaky or predatory about his demeanor. He watched me with disinterest.

Hello, I said, but the sound was muffled, my mouth filled with grit.

You're sleepwalking.
Milly, I'll pinch you if I have to.

At some point I was pulled along, toward the buildings. A force yanked on my arm, refusing to let go. I followed, half-thinking it was the wind that dragged me, but no, the wind was pushing me the other way. My bare feet left long hesitant trails in the sand. I kept looking over my shoulder at the coyote, who shrank in size as I moved away from him. I was so tired. I closed my eyes and allowed whatever force it was to guide me into bed.

There are animals out here, Milly. We could
be eaten alive.
Will you remember this tomorrow?

I awoke at dawn on my cot, the mattress covered with sand. For a moment I blinked, confused, at the triangle of the pitched roof, the blank brown walls, the windowless, long room. There was a loose humming, the lungs of two dozen sleeping women issuing breath in multicolored strings of sound from their simple, narrow cots. The sound gathered into a magnificent ball of noise, its soft yarn spinning overhead. I could reach out and touch it, this gentle, moving thing. I turned my head and saw Beth asleep on the cot next to me, miraculously beautiful just as she was in her waking life. A thick joy poured into me. *I'm at Hanford!* For another hour I lay happily in bed, while around me the noise changed and the smells shifted—body odor, lavender scent, Dew deodorant, Listerine—as women rose from the cots one by one to ready for work. Some of these women had already been here for a few weeks, assisting in the building of the units, but others, like myself, were here for the early days of production. We had no idea of the outcome, just that it would win the war. We were as dedicated to it—even in its unknowability—as we were to our loved ones. A loud bell sounded from somewhere on the campus, waking the groggiest of the lot. Beth yawned and sat up in alarm, her eyes seeking me out urgently.

"Last night was crazy," she said.

I didn't like that word. I remembered, keenly, my waking dream, feeling deepened by it, but when Beth pressed me, I feigned ignorance.

"What are you talking about?" I said.

"You were sleepwalking. You weren't in your bed and I went outside and found you a good half-mile or more away, sitting on the ground with sand in your mouth. The wind was brutal but you grinned like it was a picnic. Do you remember this?"

Beth looked tired. I apologized to her for the trouble. She must have been the distant voice that I'd heard, the force that dragged me back to the barracks. Why hadn't I seen her? It occurred to me that she might have powers of invisibility. I giggled lightly to myself. *Magic Beth! Magic Milly!*

"Is this normal? The sleepwalking?"

I admitted that it was. "Sometimes I wake up in different rooms, or in the yard. A few times I've waded into the Okanogan River. Usually I remember a little of it, but it's always strange, like it's part of a different world."

An alternate kingdom, I thought, delighted.

"This place is dangerous," she said, and her tone sobered me. "You shouldn't be out there alone. There are rattlesnakes. Coyotes. You could be killed, for God's sake." She paused here, collecting herself, and I sensed that she was thinking of her sister, Annie. "And the men . . . if they saw you dressed like that . . ."

"I'll be fine. It's just the newness of everything."

I spoke with a more serious tone now, but the truth was, I was happy. I didn't want to tell Beth, but the reverie told me that I was finally home.

This was where I belonged, where I would exist to my very fullest. The heat of it coursed through me. I was more alive than I had been in years.

I reached over and clasped her hand, shaking it gently until she smiled hesitantly at me.

"Don't worry, please," I told her. "I'm overjoyed I'm here."

Beth relaxed. "Well, you certainly *look* happy. Well-rested, even. I wish I felt the same. I'm nervous. I hate starting a new job."

I loved her even more for admitting her vulnerability.

"Here's to the newness," I said.

We embraced, sitting on my cot in our nightgowns.

And then we hurried, dressing in our simple work clothes, primping our hair, making our way to the mess hall for breakfast. We needed to report for our assignments by 8:00 a.m.

BIG DOG

The job they'd given me was in Unit B. I was proud to hand the sheet of paper to the woman at the payroll window, *Mildred Lovell Groves, Secretary for Dr. Phillip Hall, Unit B. Green Cattle Car from Barracks at 7:45 a.m.*

"Well la-de-da," the woman said. Payroll was carved into a small brick building, staffed by two women, one of whom leaned slightly out the window as she spoke to me. "This job's cream of the crop. You come very highly recommended by Mr. Pierce in Omak."

She wrote my name and employee number on a card and then handed it to me.

"This is your punch card. Don't lose it. There's a time stamp machine in Unit B, right at the entrance, and you need to be sure to stamp in and out every day and evening, okay?"

"Sounds terrifically easy," I said brightly.

"Yeah, well, you'd be surprised by how many knuckleheads boggle it up."

I reassured the woman I wasn't a knucklehead.

"A knucklehead never thinks he's a knucklehead," she said irritably.

Her sour attitude didn't matter to me. I was beaming. I was proud to be a secretary. I was sure they'd assign me as a typist or a stenographer, but now it seemed I had some real clout. I peered at the name Phillip Hall; it had a poetic ring to it. I told this to the woman, wondering if she liked Frost or Yeats.

"Poetry?" she said. "I don't have time for poetry. None of us do. The only thing I want when I'm done working is a hot water bottle and an aspirin."

A colleague seated at the opposite window teased her. "Nonsense, Dot. You like beer and dancing more than any of us."

"True." Dot sighed. "I do love beer."

"Beer is delicious," I said, and the women exchanged a glance as if they could tell I'd never swallowed even a thimbleful.

"Or so I've heard," I added more timidly.

"You'll get your chance," the woman who was not Dot said. "Enjoy Unit B, sweetheart."

"Easy to go khaki whacky there," Dot said, laughing.

I wasn't sure what *khaki whacky* meant, but I smiled at them, energized by the attention.

Then Dot looked to the man waiting behind me and called, "Next!" and he split from the line and stepped up to Dot's window.

I left the building's wooden deck and walked toward the bus stop. There was Beth, crossing the dry earth with Kathy and the other girls in nursing uniforms. They were heading to the clinic together, I guessed, their arms linked at the elbow. I frowned seeing them so immediately friendly like that, and then I chided myself for being silly. Beth would always have other friends. She wasn't like me. She was popular, beloved. Maybe it made me a more popular person, too, just knowing her. The nurses rounded a corner of one of the dozens of buildings and disappeared into the recesses of the camp.

I threaded my way through the rows and rows of barracks, hunting down the Unit B bus stop, which I'd been instructed was in the southeast corner of the camp. Hundreds of my colleagues made their way to their own jobs, and we bumped and jostled against one another politely.

It was marvelous, I thought, how this seven-hundred-acre town sprang up overnight and I was now a part of it. It was a renewal being here, a gift.

After a bit of wandering and asking around, I found the cattle car stop and stood in line behind the hulking form of a man that I soon recognized was Gordon Nyer. I went very quiet and hoped he would—and wouldn't—turn around and see me.

He turned.

He saw me.

"Mildred Groves from Omak," he said, and I was, despite myself, touched by his accuracy.

"Hello, Gordon," I told him. "You're assigned to Unit B?"

"The big dog," he said. "I requested it specifically. I always get what I want."

"I'm a secretary," I said, and he shrugged as though to say, *What else would you be?*

"Where's your pretty friend?"

"Beth?"

"The mean one. Pretty and mean both, that girl."

"Yes, Beth," I said. "She's not mean. She's wonderful. She's protective."

Gordon took a step back, eyeing me head to foot. His eyes raked over me, from the old shoes that pinched my feet to my brown stockings and skirt. He reached forward and plucked a long strand of auburn hair from off the chest of my gray blouse. Not my own, I recognized, but Beth's. His eyes lingered on my breasts and neck.

"You're a big girl, in a lot of ways. How old are you? Twenty or more?" Here, I nodded. "You can handle yourself."

"I do."

"Well, then," he said. "Beth needn't be so mean."

In front of him, a short, wiry man with crooked teeth punched Gordon on the arm.

"Hey, Gordo," he said. "Introduce me to your friend, why don't ya?"

"This gentlewoman," Gordon said proudly, as if I were a cow for sale, "is named Mildred Groves. She hails from Omak."

"Omak? Well, I'll be darned! I'm from Tonasket!"

"You don't say," I said cheerfully. "We're practically neighbors."

"The name's Franklin Toms, but everyone calls me Tom Cat. It's so great to meet a local girl," he said. "I miss my mom and sisters already. Is that shameful to say?"

"I wouldn't know," I said. "I don't miss mine in the slightest."

Gordon laughed loudly at this. "Shameful, indeed, Tom Cat. Your sentimentality betrays you. As for you," he said to me, "it's cute when a girl's independent."

It fascinated me, the way Gordon spoke, so poetic and vulgar both, like a drunk scholar. *Falstaff*, I thought. It would be easy to listen to a man like this every day, as easy as it was to look at his face. I admired his stridency. I wanted to bake it, to eat it like a large meat loaf so that it would enter my bloodstream and become my own. But I sensed already, beneath his easygoing manner, a cruelty that could crush Tom Cat and me in an instant, and, hesitantly, wrongly, I admired that, too.

Gordon half-turned away from me then and I saw again how very much his face—especially in profile—looked like Richard Quine's. He wasn't the sort I could ever make a husband—I was too plain, too dull—but I was suddenly both happy and unnerved at the thought of being his intimate.

A line of cattle cars pulled up on the dirt road, kicking up a dry cloud of dust. Several of us put our hands over our eyes and coughed. The wind sent the dust swirling, so that it stabbed and stung. We pushed into the vehicles, eager to escape the bad air. I didn't understand why they called these simple buses cattle cars, why they would choose to insult us in this way, but when I mentioned this to my companions, they laughed and told me it was meant only as a friendly joke. Still, as we boarded, I thought about the cattle cars I'd heard about in Germany, the ones ferrying the damned to concentration camps and gas chambers.

It made me grateful to be where I was—safe, appreciated, surrounded by new colleagues. I chose a seat directly behind Gordon. I assumed Tom Cat would sit with Gordon, but he scooted in with me, instead. I was flattered. We continued our conversation, with Gordon now and again pivoting in his seat to interject his many opinions.

Tom Cat had already been working at Hanford for a few weeks now, and I had a dozen questions for him, but he was homesick, he only wanted to talk about Okanogan and Grant Counties: the drought, the majesty of Grand Coulee Dam, the tension between the tribes and local government.

"I was at the Ceremony of Tears," Tom Cat said, "when the rising water for the dam drowned Kettle Falls. The Indian chiefs moved all of the ancestral graves to higher ground. It was very touching."

Tom Cat asked me if I'd read *Coyote Stories* by Mourning Dove, an Okanagan woman. He said it was his favorite book.

"I've heard of it," I told him. I remembered reading something about her dying in the Eastern State Hospital at Medical Lake, but it was a sad detail, and I didn't bring it up.

"Ceremony of Tears," Gordon interrupted. "Good grief. Indians are always crying about something. There's a band of Wanapum complaining about the site here, too. Sacred fishing grounds and such. Say if they can't get their salmon, they can't live. They don't give two shits about our war. Well, they should. We're trying to save humankind."

His strong opinions reminded me of Mother. I wondered for a moment if she would like him and then thought, *No, she hates any man who is too opinionated*, and that was probably why she married my father. If she were here, she would argue with Gordon just for the fun of it, even if she was likely to agree with him.

I glanced at Gordon nervously and he smiled in return. But when I blinked, his face blurred, then transmuted. The handsome squareness of his jaw narrowed. His heavy brow sharpened. It was the face of the silver-eyed coyote from my sleepwalking the night before, sly and too friendly. In the background, I heard Tom Cat arguing for the Wanapum's rights, but I couldn't follow his sentences. The bus released its brakes and began to accelerate. I put a hand over my stomach, feeling suddenly like I'd had too much breakfast.

Tom Cat quieted for a moment and then asked, "Mildred, are you unwell?"

"Oh, no," I told him, "I'm just excited."

But I didn't look up as I spoke. I feared I would find Gordon's good eye staring back at me, an uninvited penetration.

YOUR NEW GIRL

The cattle car, people-choked, sand-choked, reeking of sage and flesh, moved through light so intense that my head ached. There was a whole line of buses like ours snaking the five miles to Unit B. If only the noise would quiet so that I could feel alone with the landscape, the ivory hills, the burnished sand, the blue sky with its bone-pale lacy edge. I brought my hands up under my hair, the strands bursting with static, and then pressed my palms hard over my ears. Now the voices dulled, there was only the sound of the engine and of my own inner washings. There was no shade here away from the tidy angles of the camp, and despite how early it was in the day, the dryness of the open plain enkindled my lungs with a heat both cleansing and suffocating. I remembered sprinting with my sister through a field of alfalfa just outside of Omak, the grasshoppers beating themselves senseless against our shins as we loped, shrieking with glee.

We drew closer to Unit B, and I could see the gorge where the river ran, but not the river itself. I wished I could go there, remove my stockings and shoes, dip my sore feet in the chilly water. There it was again, a stab of lust for Susan Peters's shoes.

The line of buses paused one at a time at a gate a mile or so away from the unit. You could tell who was new on the bus and who was not: New recruits fell silent, reading the enormous signs on the fence line, while everyone else continued their conversations, the signs as mundane as any other quotidian display:

HANFORD SITE. RESTRICTED GOVERNMENT AREA. KEEP OUT.
PROTECTION FOR ALL. DON'T TALK. SILENCE MEANS SECURITY.
TELL NOBODY. NOT EVEN HER. CARELESS TALK COSTS LIVES.
RESTRICTED ACCESS. GOVERNMENT VEHICLES ONLY.

We didn't have to wait long. The guard waved all of our cattle cars through swiftly, and soon, amidst the flat nothingness of the desert, we pulled up alongside the other vehicles. Their front windows all faced Unit B in a neat semicircle, as though arranged for worship.

A few minutes passed. The heat in the cattle car grew onerous. Finally the driver gave a shout of farewell and drew the door open. We filed down the stairs and out onto the arid grassland. The dust settled enough for us to see the concrete fortress of Unit B, bigger and taller than a cathedral, its walls thick and gray like the face of a dam. From the center rose a long, dusky smokestack, and below it flapped the United States flag, whose vivid crispness brought much-needed spirit to the color-drained earth and concrete. The men near me must have felt similarly; some of them took off their hats and held them over their hearts. A whistle blew. The doorway of Unit B scraped open, and three official-looking men emerged onto the walkway. The first of them was dressed in military uniform, the second of them in a handsome three-piece suit, and the last in a crisp white lab coat.

"Good morning, Patriots," the taller of them—the military man—shouted. "For the many of you who are new here, welcome to Unit B. Your work here, your loyalty, and your discretion will help us win the war."

Tom Cat leaned in and whispered, "That's General Smith. And behind him, Mr. Redding, the DuPont engineer, and there's Mr. Farmer, the Italian scientist. They say that's not his real name."

"Do they welcome us every morning?"

"It's rare to see Smith and Farmer. They're very busy people. But someone greets us every day with the same message. They're very firm about it, so you know it must be true."

The official men gave a brief wave, then withdrew back into the building. The large steel door crashed shut behind them.

Our coworkers lined up at a much smaller side door some yards away.

"We clock in over here," Tom Cat said, motioning to the crowd, and Gordon started to move in that direction, but I stood rooted in place, staring at the massive blocky-shouldered edifice. Its firmness and coldness reminded me of something.

"Isn't she a beauty?" Tom Cat said, returning to my side.

Mother. It reminds me of Mother.

I let out a breath. "It's enormous."

"Women love big things," Gordon joked, waiting for us just a few feet away. "That's why they love me."

Tom Cat didn't laugh, and I liked him for it.

"Construction is almost finished here," Tom Cat said, "and then there won't be so many workers. I'm hoping they'll move me to the valve pit room or the clinic, something indoors. I don't like working outside. The wind is too much."

"It's not bad right now," I said.

Tom Cat gestured at the road leading back to camp. "Look."

I couldn't see anything, just a faint taupe smoke where the bluffs used to be.

"It's hazy," I said.

"That's sand," Tom Cat said, "heading this way. It'll be here shortly. It gets everywhere, in your ears and hair, your eyelashes. In between your teeth." He regarded the line of people working their way steadily into the building. "Hopefully we'll get you inside before it hits."

I eyed the spreading haze and then the line of workers before us.

The line moved quickly. Everything worked with a marvelous efficiency here, all polished gears and gadgets.

"We'll be there soon enough," Gordon said.

"Doesn't help me at all," Tom Cat said, sighing. "I'll be working on the river pumps with no shelter."

To me, Gordon said, "Women are pampered, getting to work indoors all of the time."

"Gordon, you don't even know," Tom Cat said. "You're being sent to the control room. You've got it easy."

I felt sorry for Tom Cat. He sounded miserable.

"Maybe they'll reassign you," I said.

"It's a little bit of wind, Tom," Gordon said. "You can handle it. This is baby stuff compared to what the better men are doing overseas."

I patted Tom Cat's arm. He shot his eyes up at me, his mien softened. I dropped my hand and blushed.

A little voice in my head spoke as clear as a bell, *It's him. Your future husband.*

"Mildred," he said, "after you."

I was inside, just as the first grains of sand began to slide across the walkway. Joining that great workforce, the flimsy weight of my girlhood dropped behind me on the ground like a discarded shawl.

I was handed a time card and given instructions for clocking in; I loved the time stamp adhered to the wall with its solid handle, how firmly it imprinted the time card and made my first working day official. I asked Tom Cat and Gordon if I could stamp their cards, too, and they allowed it, Gordon even saying, "Ain't she adorable, Tom?" The clean cards came away marked with ink: September 16, 1944, 07:56. New hires were directed to a table on the side of the narrow hallway and there I spoke to a man with a clipboard. He told me to report to the physicist's office. He looked very familiar to me.

"Didn't I just meet you in Omak?" I said. "At the US Employment Office? It's nice to see you again."

The man puckered his lips, considering this. "Farthest north I've been is Wenatchee."

He was teasing me, I thought. He was identical to the man in the Omak recruiting office. He even wore the same dark brown tie.

"You handled my paperwork," I insisted. "I'm sure it was you. Don't you remember me? Mildred Groves? You asked me about husband-hunting?"

A few men in line heard this and snickered. One of them called out, mockingly, "Marry her! A little chunky but she'll do!" More laughter followed.

I was glad that Gordon and Tom Cat had already disappeared ahead of me into the giant concrete corridors.

The man stubbornly shook his head. "Wasn't me, lady. I've been stationed here since we started building eleven months ago." Then with a wink, he added, "But regarding the husband thing, I wish you all the luck in the world."

"That's exactly what you said in Omak," I said excitedly, "wishing me all the world's luck. It's you, I just know it. And you have the same face." I drew my hand over my face and did my best worm's expression, puckering my lips and bulging my eyes.

The man grew irritated. "Look, doll," he said. "We've got three hundred people waiting in line. You asked if it was me and I told you it wasn't. Give it a rest, will ya?"

He came forward into the light as he spoke, angry now, and I realized with some embarrassment that he really wasn't the man from Omak; he wasn't the same man at all. They looked similar in the shadows and they certainly had the same taste in ties and the same bald, round heads, but in the light, one was a worm and one was a snake. I apologized, stuttering. The snake repeated where I was to go and sent me away with an annoyed wave.

I didn't go far: "Turn right, go straight, follow the hallway to the door that reads 'Physicist,' and then sit in the room and don't touch anything." I recited the instructions to myself as I walked, and I was tempted to do the opposite of everything I was told, only because I was free now for the first time in my life, and if I'd wanted to I could rebel against all of it. But I chose to be obedient. Just daydreaming of rebelling was an exhausting rebellion of its own.

I found the office and went inside and sat down in one of the two chairs, facing the physicist's large wooden desk. On the wall behind it there was a large picture window looking directly into Unit B's control room. The picture window was hilarious to me, one room looking into another, with no real windows anywhere else to be found, zero natural light. I supposed it was so the physicist could keep tabs on the workers at all times. The rows of meticulous shining knobs and dials thrilled me. I imagined running my hands along those clockwork faces, putting my ear up to them and taking comfort in their tiny soothing heartbeats. A lone man puttered about the control room as I watched, bending at the waist now and again to peer at a set of numbers or a line of ticker tape. Eventually he must have sensed my eyes on him, and he turned, saw me, and waved in a friendly manner. I smiled self-consciously and glanced away. Off to the side of the office was a small square desk, like that in an elementary school. My own, I supposed. It had a new black typewriter on it and I fought the urge to go and type a long, heartfelt letter to myself on its firm keys. *Dearest Mildred*, it would begin, *What a marvelous life you're leading. What a brave, stupendous young woman you've become . . .*

On the physicist's desk was a black iron fan and a ceramic container filled with identical Parker pens. I fingered a booklet of matches. *Strike at the seat of Trouble. Buy war bonds.* The desk was mostly free of papers except for a large open map of the facility and an unopened letter from someone—a woman, clearly—with exquisite handwriting. I returned the matches to their place near the container of pens. My hands itched, seeing the letter. It was a love letter, surely. I imagined the woman still lived in California or Paris or Belgium or some romantic place, and she was writing to tell him about the rain outside her apartment window and how its whisper sounded like his voice in her hair, and how soon she would return to his side, by plane or ship or something even more exotic—*a camel*—so that she could embrace him again and lock lips and hold him and be held. I raised up on my toes, not at all intending to read the letter but hoping to at least spy the woman's name, but someone entered the room then, and I fell back into my chair, swiftly, and then leaned down to toy with my shoe buckle, as a means of explaining, however weakly, why I had half-lifted from my chair in the first place.

The man who entered was neither short nor tall, thin nor fat, but smack in the middle, almost remarkable in how shapelessly average he was. For a moment he looked exactly like the sort of husband I envisioned for myself, everything about him cordial and ordinary, but then he moved into the room, adroitly, and the expression with which he regarded the room and myself was both perceptive and invasive. No, I would hate to be married to him; it would be an embarrassment to us both. He would loathe the way I ironed his shirts. I would go quiet beside him at dinner parties, terrified of saying the wrong thing.

He looked at me and then at the letter. He reached into the breast pocket of his shirt, lifting out a small key. Swiftly, with an annoyed frown, he took up the letter and locked it away in a desk drawer.

"But you didn't read it," I noted.

"None of your business," he said sharply. "You're the new girl?"

"Mildred Groves, yes. Are you Dr. Phillip Hall?"

"That's right," he said. "Dr. Hall, the physicist."

"I thought so," I said, jumping to my feet. "I'm pleased to meet you." I extended my hand and he shook it lightly. "I was Star Pupil at Omak Secretarial."

"Out of how many girls?"

"Five," I admitted.

"Not such a great feat then. I'm less interested in talent than I am in loyalty, secrecy, and safety. Are you a loyal sort of person, Miss Groves? Are you discreet? Are you aware of how your discretion will keep us safe here?"

I put my hand over my heart and swore on Mother's life that I was all of those things, but then I saw her screaming as she plummeted into the Okanogan River, and I frowned and added, "Or maybe I can swear on my own life, or yours, if you'll let me."

"I don't care about any of that," he said. "Just remember what I told you: loyalty, secrecy, safety. Remember those three things and we'll get along just fine."

"Loyalty," I said. "Secrecy. Safety."

"There's a pad of paper in your desk drawer. I'll ask that you retrieve it now. Also, a pen. You are not allowed to use the pens on my desk. Good. I like your speed. Now, Miss Groves. Please take dictation."

I was excited to get to work. When I next looked up, happily busy, swiftly writing in rhythm to Dr. Hall's musical voice as he spoke of cooling processes and productivity demands, Gordon Nyer stood at the large picture window, watching me with that wolfish look on his face. He held up his hand and waved and I, in turn, held up my hand, pausing in my writing.

Dr. Hall noticed, turned, saw Gordon standing there, and glared at Gordon until he moved away.

"What sort of person is that?" he asked. "A boyfriend of yours?"

I blotched pink across my chest and throat.

"I don't mean to embarrass you."

"That's Gordon Nyer," I said.

"He's a wildebeest."

"I don't have a love interest," I confided.

"About these things," Dr. Hall said, "please remember that discretion is best."

"Secrecy," I said.

"Exactly."

He opened his hand up for the pad of paper and I handed it over.

He looked over my notes, made a sound of approval in his throat, and handed them back.

"You have no problem dictating basic equations and chemical elements?"

Joy blasted through me. I had impressed him.

"My father was a science teacher," I said. "I was forced to do well in school, to read widely, to pay attention."

"Well, it seems I've finally received an adequate employee. You'll do Omak Secretarial proud, Miss Groves. Now where were we?"

I wanted to sing and dance, but I only allowed my toes to wiggle happily in their cramped shelter.

I'm here. A WAC at Hanford. I've done it.

It was the proudest moment of my life. I tried not to let it go to my head, but I swelled with glory, nonetheless.

ROUTINES AND DREAMS

We fell into a rhythm, Bethesda Green and I, waking together, breakfasting together, parting in the mornings but rejoining in the early evening with glad hellos, dining together, falling asleep next to each other in our matching cots. My days were fuller than they'd ever been, and I shared them with Beth the way a devoted preacher shares the Bible, joyfully, euphorically. If I annoyed her, I had no knowledge of it. She seemed as cheerful and receptive as I was.

Every evening after work we linked arms and traipsed to one of the eight big mess halls for supper, tripping over ourselves to summarize our days. Other girls followed us—Beth's friendships were many and deep—but she showed no one the attention and affection she accorded me.

We were served family style in the mess halls, from platters loaded with fresh baked bread, potatoes, baked or grilled meat, simple lettuce salads. The food was better than the food in Omak. At Hanford, there were no rations. For 67 cents a meal, they gave us whatever we wanted, heaping platters of it. They were desperate to keep us here, to stop the hemorrhaging turnover. I surprised myself by how much I ate. Mother hadn't cooked in years, and I hated cooking, finding it grueling to prep a meal, cook it, eat it, clean up after it, and then begin the whole process again only a few hours later. Here, I felt pampered. Sometimes Beth and I shrieked at each other just to be heard. There were thousands of people in the mess halls at any given moment, and even more waiting for seats. We choked down our food as quickly as possible and barely had time to finish our coffee before we were shooed away from our benches to make room for others.

"Isn't this a gas?" Beth liked to say, adoring the crowds and the noise in a way that I found contagious.

I agreed, smiling. The sight of all of those men guffawing and teasing one another both intimidated and impressed me. There were four times as many men at Hanford than there were women. For the last few years, Mother and Martha were my only acquaintances, interesting creatures in their own respects but not nearly as physical or impetuous as the men seemed. When there was a brawl, and there were many brawls, I found I couldn't tear myself away. I wanted to watch the men beat at one another until one of them surrendered or passed out. Beth was the opposite: She couldn't stand the violence. She said it was exactly what was wrong with the world.

"These boys," she'd say, rolling her eyes, but I felt that it was bigger than that, because these were full-grown men, and wasn't it impressive the way they sprang to action rather than simpering and stewing over their troubles like I did? I admired it all. *These are the men who will win this war*, I thought. I was proud of them for their passion. But I did, briefly, wonder about my father, his shakiness and timidity. Here, he might have been bullied. It was a good thing, I told myself, that he was never allowed into the army. He'd been barred because of his eczema, which embarrassed him deeply.

The men noticed us the moment we stepped too close. They raised their heads from their plates like mountain lions smelling a doe. When they turned and regarded me with their predatory grins, I awkwardly stumbled or hurried forward, reassuring myself that none of these men were as cruel as they seemed, surely they missed their mothers, their sisters, their wives. Some of them lived with their wives and children on the campus, and some were upstanding family men, I knew, Christian men who went to the campus church every Sunday. They were only fascinated by me, not hungry for me. And if a single one were hungry, so what? Couldn't it be that beneath that tough, hard demeanor there was a gentle, doting husband, just waiting to be cracked? The men responded to my nervousness like it was a bleeding wound. Their eyes trailed after me, certain I would be an easy target.

It was Beth, of course, who protected me, who scolded them when the teasing and flirting grew irksome.

"Leave us be," she told the men. "We're not in the slightest bit interested."

Because she was beautiful and strong and mean to them, the men respected her. They put up their large, work-torn hands in mock surrender and even apologized.

When she and I were alone, I told Beth about my job, about Dr. Hall and the sterile, hard beauty of Unit B, and she told me about the clinic, about the horrible accidents that happened almost daily at Hanford. She excitedly detailed the ugliest cases: a terrible burn from a mysterious chemical, broken ribs from a bad fall, a foot crushed in a rotating gear, a rattlesnake bite that led to a foot amputation. She tended to a man who had inhaled something poisonous; his entire throat was as black as charcoal, and when he spoke he issued not words but smoke.

"His wife will be notified," she said. "It's a terrible thing, if he survives. I don't think he'll ever speak properly again."

We were well into our third week of work. We sat at one of the mess hall's enormous tables, the length of a Viking ship. Kathy sat with us, which I tolerated but didn't enjoy, and two other girls from our barracks: Alma—daughter of a Hungarian man and a Mexican woman—who worked the earliest food-service shift, rising long before dawn to bake breads and muffins and cakes; and Susan, from Nevada, who worked in the laundry and smelled always of bleach and lye. Susan worked with a Chinese woman and a Jewish woman. "Melting pot of the world," she said irritably, but I liked that we heard so many different languages and saw so many different sorts of people. I'd never seen anything like it while living in Omak. I found Alma beautiful, with her coppery skin and her hair as black and shiny as a beetle's back. She was nicer to me than Kathy, but then, really, anyone was.

I asked Beth about the poor patient. "What did he inhale?"

She shook her head. "You know they don't tell us those things, Milly. It's all a big secret."

I thought of the three words that Dr. Hall made me repeat every morning. Loyalty. Secrecy. Safety. I told her that I was working on a new safety campaign with Dr. Hall and the general manager of the Hanford site, to minimize workplace accidents.

"Dr. Hall believes we can greatly improve conditions," I said. "His goal is to make it through an entire year without a single injury."

"Then I'll be out of a job," Beth laughed. "You must hear interesting details in your job, Milly. Has anyone told you what we're making?"

No one had told me much of anything, but I knew from Dr. Hall's dictation that it was a chemical element needed for the war effort. He called it the product. I almost told her this, but Dr. Hall's voice spoke to me over the sounds of the mess hall.

Loyalty. Secrecy. Safety.

I told her I really didn't know, and I wasn't even lying.

"Well, whatever it is," she said, "it'll be great at killing Hitler. It's maiming men already and we're not even operational yet."

It was then that I noticed Tom Cat, sitting on the opposite side of the table from us a few paces down. He waved at me timidly and I waved exuberantly back. Gordon Nyer was there, too. He returned my gesture with only a crude smile and wink.

"Don't encourage Gordon, Milly," Beth said to me crossly. "He's got a dirty mind."

"He's full of himself," I admitted, "but the man next to him is very nice."

Kathy laughed. "Good thing, because he's ugly as sin."

"He's very nice," I repeated, tensely.

"He looks like a turtle without his shell," Kathy said.

Beth pushed her plate away and stood. "I'm finished. I'm going to go meet the nice man you're berating, Kathy, and I'm going to go tell the other one to stop staring at us."

"Please, don't," I begged. "He'll get cross with me."

"Oh, he won't, Milly, I'll make sure he's only cross with *me*."

She set off toward them, and I paled and dropped my eyes to my dinner, staring sadly at my large bowl of canned peaches.

"You know why she likes you so much, don't you?" Kathy said, leaning forward onto her sharp elbows. "She's insecure, and it makes her feel much better about herself to be with someone like you."

Alma and Susan stiffened.

"Don't tease her, Kathy," Alma said.

"Think about it, Mildred," Kathy said, and I didn't want to think about it but there it was, an unwanted injection. Her voice was saccharine, thorn-laced. "Well, I'll see you all later."

She rose, leaving her tray with us, and blew us a mean little kiss good-bye.

When she was out of earshot, Susan leaned forward and said, "She's just jealous of Bethesda, Milly. Don't you listen to a word of it."

"*She's* the one," Alma said, but their voices were low and unconvincing, and I sensed how they seemed to enjoy Kathy's cruelty—entertaining if unjust—and I felt alone with the notion that it really did explain so much.

But I remind Beth of her sister, I thought. *Her sad, dead sister.*

I automatically searched for Beth and found her standing beside the shoulders of Gordon Nyer, looking down at his face, and to my dismay she wasn't reprimanding him at all but laughing with one hand at her throat.

This underscored Kathy's point. What was she doing, laughing with the man she disliked? I hurried over to Beth's side to see what was happening.

Gordon gave me a huge, friendly smile. "Mildred," he said. "A sight for sore eyes. Your friend was just telling me what a terrible brute I am."

When Beth turned and looked at me, I saw that, yes, she had been laughing, but it was not flirty laughter or kind laughter, it was triumphant laughter, the laughter of someone who understood her own power.

"I'm sorry if I haven't been a gentleman," Gordon said. "I told Beth here I would apologize to you. Despite what she might think, Gordon Nyer is a man of his word."

He whipped his long legs over the bench and slipped to the floor in one athletic movement, kneeling on the linoleum before me with his hands folded in prayer. His good eye stared at my face earnestly while the glass eye pointed at my torso.

"Please forgive me, Mildred," he said. "It's only that I like you, you see, and this makes me wrongly attentive."

For a moment I wondered if this was the man I'd marry, if this was the beginning of an abrupt and passionate wedding proposal, but then Tom Cat stepped forward and said to me, interrupting, "Hiya, Mildred," and I knew that I would wind up with someone more like Tom Cat than Gordon Nyer. This didn't upset me in the least, it was just a firm understanding, like realizing your home will never be a mansion on a hill but a quiet little farmhouse in the valley. I was fine with it, it felt comfortable to me, and I told Tom Cat hello in return.

Tom Cat moved toward me. "I'm sorry for Gordon's behavior, too. He has no manners."

Gordon rose to his feet and punched Tom Cat lightly on the shoulder. "I'm a man's man," he said, but then he bowed to me. I couldn't tell if the bow was sincere or mocking.

Another man stood up from his empty plate, his movements rough and loud and meant to grab attention. I recognized him from the Unit B cattle car, a short but powerful-looking man that I'd overheard another guy call "chrome-dome" because of his bald head.

"Get a load of this," Chrome-dome said, thumbing at Gordon. "These broads are turning our men into queers."

Gordon's theatrical expression of apology shifted. His face pulled in on itself as though the light in it had been shuttered. He pivoted slowly and addressed his heckler.

"I don't think I heard you correctly. Care to repeat that?"

Chrome-dome dismissed this comment with a smirk and said to Beth, "You rationed, sugar? I ain't seen a girl like you since San Francisco."

Beth soured, taking my arm. "Let's go, Milly. Nothing but morons today. I don't care if they kill themselves for our attention."

I let her guide me outside. Behind us we heard a bit of noise, some shouting and a scuffle, but Beth didn't turn around and I didn't, either, despite the urge to rush back and greedily witness the bludgeoning. Later we heard from Alma that Gordon and Chrome-dome fought, and that the fight was a good one: bloody, vicious, impossible to stop until finally Chrome-dome lay groaning, spitting out teeth, at Gordon's feet. I was sad I'd missed it.

Beth was combing my hair on the bed when Alma told us, and she paused for a moment before saying, "Gordon infuriates me. What is it with men? Why can't they let a silly thing go?"

"Hard to let it go," Kathy said, "being called a name like that."

I agreed with Kathy, it impressed me that Gordon could stand up for himself, although I would never publicly disagree with Beth so I said, instead, "Gordon's apology seemed sincere, at least."

Beth was silent on that matter. She combed my hair harder so that I winced.

Kathy said, "I heard Gordon is on probation for a week. If he gets in another fight before Friday, he'll be gone."

Beth's comb tore through my hair. "Good," she muttered, but I heard a small catch in her voice, a hesitation. "He's a troublemaker."

"He sure is cute," Kathy said.

"He looks an awful lot like Richard Quine," I agreed.

Kathy scrunched up her mean face. "Who is that?"

Beth laughed. "Milly obsesses about that Spokane-born actress, Susan Peters. Richard Quine is her husband."

"Richard is very handsome," I added. "And Susan Peters is wonderful, just wonderful, in *Random Harvest*. I saw it last year in Spokane and she was there for the showing. I almost met her. She was very pretty and so very nice. I'm saving up for the exact same pair of shoes I saw her wear. I've seen them in the Sears Roebuck catalog. They'll be much more comfortable than my own shoes, which really aren't my own shoes at all, but my mother's—"

"Mildred's in love with Gordon," Kathy sang.

It took me a moment to register her lyrics. It struck me in the skull like a mallet and its aftershock ran haywire through my bones.

"That's not true," I told her. My hands shook as badly as when I fought with Mother. I took a deep breath. "Take it back."

She sang it again, in a higher pitch this time, flapping her hands with girlish innocence. Her face was Martha's face, then Mother's face, then again, even worse, Kathy's. I kicked my chair back and approached her with my fists clenched, wanting badly to strike her.

"Milly," Beth said calmly behind me. "Milly, she's only teasing you." To Kathy she said, firmly, wrathfully, "Stop it right this instant, you hear?"

When Kathy sang it a third time, I flattened my palms over my ears and shut my eyes and shrieked at the top of my lungs. I'd never shrieked so loudly in my entire life. The size and power of the sound blistered me. I heard the footsteps of a dozen women racing into our corner of the barracks. Kathy backed away from me, hands up, saying, *Okay, okay, I'll stop!*

I was mid-shriek when I blacked out.

⁂

Mother and I stood at the river, arguing. *Take the bouquet, Mother*, I said, *Please take it, and I'll pick up the glass as best as I can*, and Mother cried, *Leave me alone, Mildred. You are my biggest disappointment. Even those flowers are pathetic.*

A portrait of my father and his glasses lay shattered on the rocks near the riverbank—my fault, of course, but why had she forced me to carry them, when we both knew how clumsy I was?

The burial was the week before, busy with people from Omak Presbyterian and my father's schoolroom, but today was supposed to be our own quiet celebration of him, just Mother, Martha, and me. This was Mother's idea: Bring his portrait to his favorite place on the Okanogan River, bury his glasses on the bank, say a few good words each about his impact on us. I was surprised—stirred, even—by Mother's desire for such a spiritual ceremony. Her imagination had always before struck me as limited and barren, a dispirited purgatory emptied of all affection, but this intention came from a lovely garden in her I hadn't known existed. She'd loved him, after all. I'd been content about all of this until three minutes before, when I'd tripped and cried out in horror as all of the breakable objects flew from my arms and crashed onto the stones.

When I looked up, Mother glared down at me. Her black hair and strong shoulders blocked out the sun.

I smelled her moss-laden disappointment, rich and deep, and the pain of the impact rang in my palms and wrists and knees.

Martha wasn't there yet, busy parking the car in the dirt lot half a mile away, but when she descended she'd pour her rancor into Mother's rancor and I'd drink the contents down, choking. The shards of glass winked grimly on the uneven terrain, scattered across stone and sand. I looked down at the flowers in my right hand, pretty purple echinacea, coneflowers that Mother called a sad excuse for daisies—didn't she remember they were Father's favorites?—and my fist gripped the stems so tensely that my knuckles whitened. Mother reprimanded me for letting her down, for ruining everything, for destroying even this small celebration of my father's life.

I half-listened, half-levitated. Her anger filled me with power and she couldn't even see it, how my feet floated a few inches above the river rock. In the sky, the gathering clouds were the same absent gray color as the stones. She turned away from me, disgusted. I recalled the faraway look in Father's eyes when Mother mocked him. When she finally left him alone, he would glance at me, smile, offer a sour joke.

I missed him.

It was not intentional when I did it, when I lifted the flowers overhead and then brought the blossoms down—*smack*—hard across the back of her skull, but the gesture was heavy with import. She reached up with a yell, clutching her head, teetering there on the patchy rocks that fell in a drunken stairwell toward the water's edge, and for a moment I clutched her shoulders and sensed how I cradled her very well-being in my hands, and how, if I pulled her to me, she could continue mostly uninterrupted in her tirade, and how we might still be able to laugh this mess off one day—*the time crazy Mildred ruined everything and hit Mother with flowers, ha-ha!*—and I held her steady for a full moment, considering, but it was so painfully obvious to me that nothing would change if I didn't let her fall, and *Push her, push her,* even the wind through the aspens whispered it, and I acquiesced, not with a violent shove, but with a gentle letting go.

Yes, that's what I did; I gentled her into the water. Gravity finished the job for me; she toppled down the bank. Tangled into a senseless knot of noise were the splashes, the hollers, the groans, the cracking open of bone, the struggling, and I scurried away from the river even as my sister, unlikely heroine, came sprinting over the lip of the shadowy hillside—her silhouette bleared by my own terror—and raced, shouting, down the slope, shooting past me into the shallows with more speed and grace than she'd ever before exhibited. Now I could only sit and watch as my sister and mother wrestled each other onto the shore. I lowered myself onto the rocks, hugging my legs, and made myself very small. I waited.

I didn't mean to hurt her, I babbled into my knees. They were good-smelling knees, dreamy with baking soda baths, and so smooth, like an innocent girl's. *I only wanted something to change.*

SKULLS

eth told me later: I fell to the ground, thrashing. She put her comb in my mouth to keep me from biting my tongue, but I thrashed and wept and stammered in what felt to her like a scarlet rage. Kathy shouted, *She's lost it, she's possessed,* and Beth screamed at her to shut up. Other women had poured into our barrack, summoned by my bloodcurdling shriek, and they stood over us, mesmerized, while Beth urged them away.

"She's seizing! Give her room."

When I returned to my senses, Beth had a cold compress to my head, one of her own blouses dipped in icy water, and my lips felt dry and cracked, my gums sore from gritting the comb.

"I didn't mean to," I managed, and Beth stroked my hair and hushed me.

"You need to sleep," she said. "You're spent."

"And Kathy?"

"I've sent her away. She won't bother you tonight." She waited a moment, then asked, gently, "Is this like the sleepwalking, Milly? Has this happened before?"

I was baby-weak, snuggled up against my friend. I shook my head and closed my eyes. *Nasty fits*, I remembered my classmates saying, but that was long ago. Beth leaned over me and pressed her lips to my forehead.

"Rest, sweet girl," she said.

I had a memory of Mother then, bringing me chicken broth in bed when I was a sick child. The rattle of the saucer on the plate, the salty meatiness of the soup; I tasted that good, warm liquid as it coated my sore throat. Mother sat with me on the bed while I sipped the broth, gently raising the saucer to my mouth. She, too, had stroked my hair and kissed my forehead, and then she'd departed with an affectionate look, urging me, as Beth did, to rest.

It was possible it had never happened, that I was imagining it wistfully or in reverse, that maybe I was the one who had brought broth to her, that I had been the one to nourish and succor. I was confused. Beth wrapped me up in blankets.

I was nearly asleep when I heard a voice say, "Is she all right now?"

"Kathy, I don't want you here. You trouble her."

"Is she sleeping?"

"Are you deaf? Please leave."

"If you knew what was good for her, you'd send her home."

If Beth communicated anything to Kathy then, it was silent: a look or a gesture or a push out the door. Starlight and comets streaked across the fabric of my eyelids; a warm summery darkness cushioned me. Other women shuffled in and I listened half-present to the sounds of undressing, the bodies sliding in between the sheets and pressing onto the cots. People whispered to one another, a gentle wild noise, wind through the aspens, and I fell asleep with the feeling that they weren't talking about me at all but of some other wretched soul.

※

Later—an hour? several hours?—the vision prodded me awake and urged me to rise. The same swampy, heady sensation fell over me, the one I always had during a vision, the sound of invisible wings in my ears. The weight of it took hold of me by the armpits and pulled me outdoors. I floated obediently east, through the dimmest shadows of the sleeping barracks.

I traveled the short distance to the western bank of the Columbia River, where the water whorled along the northeastern corner of the Hanford camp.

Over the river and through the woods, but there were no woods here, and my consciousness blinked in and out. I stumbled forward lazily, drunkenly.

The wings shuddered and the pressure around my chest released. A great blue heron materialized on the steppe—huge, nearly five feet tall—her thick throat like a rope, her shoulders hunched, her legs two pale orange stalks with high ankles like contorted knees. She stared at me ferociously with a round yellow eye and then squawked, trembling, and collapsed into another creature, a pocket mouse. The mouse raced forward and sniffed anxiously at my slippered feet. Then it stretched, accordion-like, squeaking and hissing, now a rattlesnake, firm and sleek in brown and ivory scales.

Aufhocker, my German grandmother would have said. *Shape-shifter.*

The snake rattled its tail but I felt no fear: My visions made me impenetrable. Perhaps sensing my disinterest, the heron returned to her natural form. She preened for me, and I longed to show off my own powers. I ignored the creature and glanced around me, instead, waiting for the stage curtain to draw open and reveal the future.

The wind, knotted in her dark shawl of glittering stars, crouched with her strong thighs all around us. A few yards away lay the disembodied head of a mule deer buck. His purple tongue hung from his mouth, the heavy antlers and neck mottled with blood. Killed by coyotes, no doubt, or perhaps by a lone mountain lion. When I turned, there was the heron, grooming her feathers with the whetted orange spear of her beak.

I hunkered on a precipice overlooking the Columbia. The water coursed indifferently toward the ocean, gripped in its basin by the rocky fist of cliffs on the eastern side.

The heron's black plumes stirred in the wind. I turned to her, waiting.

Her beak remained closed, but she spoke to me as loud as a branch breaking.

Watch the river.

I watched.

The water drained away, so slowly at first I wondered if I was imagining it, but then, yes, certainly, the water was leaving for good, as though the basin were no more than a long serpentine bathtub from which an invisible hand had pulled the plug. The shoulders of rocks appeared like dark scabs, thousands of them, and I fought the urge to run down the side of the basin and dance across them.

The heron lifted her speckled throat and the long feathers on her neck jutted like thorns. Then she cowered and in a deft movement lifted away from the hill's summit, beating her large wings ponderously, swooping toward the desolate river basin.

I beetled down the hillside after her, recalling how, when I was a girl, I would plunge down the bouldered embankment into the aching cold of the Okanogan River.

Don't think of Mother, don't even let yourself, stop now—

On the rocky beach the heron waited for me. She pointed her beak toward the belly of the riverbed. I ambled atop the black rocks, skipping from one to another, but they shifted beneath my feet. I slipped again and again, trying to gain purchase and failing. I wasn't annoyed. It was a game, no more, a fun game to play atop the rocks, and when I tripped into the small puddles of water—all that remained of the Columbia—I laughed and splashed. I put my hand against a round stone and was surprised to find it wet, not with water but with something soft and fleshy; algae, I assumed, moss. I drew the substance away like it were the top of a mushroom and it came off in my palm easily, with a little pop.

The smell was both terrible and good, a burning, like over-roasted meat. I turned the thing over in my hand and stared for a moment, disbelieving, before dropping it at my feet.

It was the skin of a child's face.

The black stone was no stone but a skull, grinning at me fiendishly.

I examined the other stones, the ones I'd danced across so clumsily and merrily, and they, too, were skulls, and beneath them, trapped in the mud of the riverbed, were the bodies. People of all ages, small children, others stooped and aged. A high-pitched whining started up in my left ear, the tinnitus I suffered during a vision or if I grew too exhausted. I found a woman with her breasts blackened and burned, pockets of flesh half-melted. Around her some of the skulls' mouths screamed; others were pinned tight, addressing their end calmly as though struck dumb by its arrival.

"Who are they?" I cried. "What's happened to them?"

The wind whipped at me, scolding me, and some of the skulls crumbled into dust beneath her words.

When I turned, there was the heron, picking awkwardly at the bones with her nightmarish toes. She lifted her head and gazed at me with the gold death-coin of her eye.

Eventually we must become who we are.

The heron's face became a coyote's, her bright beak a dull brown snout, and the canine face snarled and barked, but the long-necked body remained, a horrific creature winged and feral, a dog-faced bird of hell. My vision blurred. I thought, agonized, *Maybe it's almost over, maybe the dream is ending now,* but then the coyote's features sharpened and receded and the heron's face reemerged, the black plumes and the death eye and the killing beak. Her voice like a dagger in my ear,

There is more than one kind of predator.

The entire breadth of the river was covered in dead bodies. Thousands. Tens of thousands. Another child lay at my feet, cooked and cooled into an onyx stone.

"So many children," I said, and the wind whipped at me so that my eyes stung and teared. "How could anyone let this happen?"

The heron stalked over the empty bed, hunting.

They are the doomed. They will perish at the hands of the product.

I shook my head in disgust.

Better them than you.

"There must be something we can do?"

Only the wind answered, throwing sand into my eyes.

When I blinked and wiped the blindness away, the heron was gone.

A voice then, sharp, angry. My eyes ached, my body. I was up to my neck in the Columbia, its water, in a thunderclap, returned all at once to the basin. Near me floated the rotting buck's head, stinking horribly of death, gazing through me with its hollowed eyes. The river took hold of it and washed it swiftly south. It would soon curl west toward the ocean.

A man stood on the shoreline, waving his hands. "Hey, lady," he shouted. "What are you, crazy?"

My gingham nightgown swirled around me in the water. The wind howled at the man on the shore, telling him to leave us alone.

"Christ," he hollered. "Hang on!"

The current pressed against me with a menacing force. I paddled just enough to stay afloat. Beneath me swam thousands of ghosts-to-be. If I swam too vigorously I would stir them awake. Hungry for life, they would grab my ankles, my wrists, and pull me down.

The current tugged on me, whining. *Enough. Come with me, Mildred.*

I was not suicidal, not as far as I knew, but it occurred to me how wonderful it would be to stop thinking, to stop worrying. My muscles involuntarily relaxed.

There was a splash then, the man plunging into the water.

"Fight the current," he shouted, and then he swam hard toward me, big, looping strokes, a much stronger swimmer than I was.

His arm wrapped around my waist.

He pulled me back to shore, cursing.

"Be still. You'll kill us both!"

He dragged me from the water and released me to the ground. Panting, kneeling over, he said he'd been walking along the campsite road, heading to an early shift at one of the mess halls, when he heard me calling out from the river.

"Calling out?" I said. Water ran out of my nose, my eyes.

I tried to remember doing such a thing but could not.

He asked me again what the hell was wrong with me. "You gave me a goddamn scare, lady." Then, more gently, "You okay? You wasn't drowning?"

My nightgown, huge, wet, weighed a hundred pounds. I shivered uncontrollably.

"Sleepwalking," I said.

The man threw back his head and laughed.

"You're kidding! In your bare feet? I can't wait to tell my wife about this. She won't believe it."

He pointed to my ankles and I shrank with humiliation, acknowledging I was barefoot, in my nightgown, the fabric clinging to my breasts and the plumpness of my waist and legs, revealing far too much of myself. I folded my arms over my chest.

I glimpsed the soles of my feet. They were bleeding and blistered as though they'd been burned.

THE BELL, THE LARK

If what Kathy said was true, that Beth was friends with me only for selfish, vain reasons, Beth's behavior over the next few weeks suggested otherwise.

She doted on me, embracing me whenever we'd been apart for longer than an hour, exclaiming over my general wonderfulness whenever she introduced me to anyone new. She described me as the only honest person she'd ever met (aside from her sister, of course), the only pure and decent soul. I blushed when she spoke this way—Mother would have laughed in Beth's lovely face, and my sister would have given a dozen examples to the contrary—but it felt miraculous that someone saw me in this way and chose to present me as such to the other good people of Hanford.

Privately, she worried about me.

"This sleepwalking," she said one evening as we sat together in the barracks, each on our own cot, facing each other with our knees almost touching, waiting our turn for supper. "You could have died, Milly."

I demurred. I tried to explain it to her, but how do you explain such invigoration, such power?

"We have to make it stop," Beth said.

I didn't like hearing this. She thought what was right about me was what was broken. "It's like a gift," I said. "When I was a girl, things like this happened all the time. I woke up in the morning with such awareness. I see these amazing things, things waiting for us." I had a habit of picking at my chin as I spoke, and I did this now, but Beth reached forward and stilled my hand. "I thought I lost that part of myself, Beth. The only part of myself that felt magical. But now it's back."

The future chooses me. Warns me.

"Milly," Beth said, the light-brown agates of her eyes flashing with doubt. "People can't predict the future."

"But I can," I said.

Beth tucked a loose strand of my hair behind my ear. "Please don't talk about this to anyone else, okay, Milly? Now. Let's change the subject. I'm famished."

She didn't believe me. I was used to such disbelief; I knew when to stop talking. I used to wonder if eloquence would help me convince someone else, but I was beyond that now. Such attempts were useless.

Still, I'd never shared a friendship like ours. I held out hope that if anyone were to one day believe me and support me, it would be Beth.

But that night, after eating, after we combed our hair and put on our nightgowns and drew back the covers, she presented me with a gift.

It was a pretty silver bell. She tied it to a green ribbon.

"What's this for?"

"Just let me do this, Milly. It's because I worry for you."

I allowed her to knot it around my ankle. She instructed me to wear it nightly, and I agreed because I loved her. I ignored the feeling it gave me, of being a studied animal, trapped. Some nights later, when I stood mid-slumber and slipped from the room, the clear sound of the bell woke her, and she came after me and put me back to bed. This happened again and again. One night she slept through it, but the sound of the bell penetrated my dream, and I awoke outside of the barracks, surprised to find myself walking with my hands raised clear up over my head, as though I were sinking into deep water. I gathered my senses quickly and hurried back to the barracks, aware of my bare feet and throat. I tried to remember if I'd had any vision like the one I'd had of the dead bodies in the Columbia, but there was nothing, only the feel of the sagebrush and sand scratching at my feet and ankles, the persistent alarm of the bell, the smell of the dry air. I didn't tell Beth about this; she would have grown angry with herself for not rescuing me sooner, and I cared about her too much to serve her even the smallest portion of despair.

I tried not to feel resentment about the bell. I tried not to loathe the way it quieted my dreams. I didn't mind the danger. Danger was the necessary ingredient, I sensed, for the vivid visions that ensued. While waking in the middle of the ponderous Columbia had been a shock, certainly, it was far more frightening for the man who had saved me than it was for me. I had tried to explain this to Beth the day after I'd been rescued, but she'd only wrung her hands anxiously.

"You could have drowned, Milly," she said. "No, we can't have this. We need a solution. I can't have you drowning, too."

I heard the worry in her voice and I was confused. "Are you talking about Annie? Didn't she die in the hospital?"

"It was a dry drowning," Beth said, and as she spoke Annie materialized behind her, a mournful spirit, both desiccated and dank. The ghost coughed and a brackish steam rose from her lungs. "She choked in Puget Sound. I saw her flailing, drowning, and I dove in after her. I dragged her out of the water and she coughed, sneezed, but seemed fine. She played all day and we went home sunburnt and happy. Later that evening, she was very tired. She said her chest hurt a little. We assumed it was a cold. By the third day, she was unconscious. We got her to the hospital but it was too late."

I considered this. Annie turned once, slowly, behind her sister, showing me her damp nightgown and dripping fingers and shining dry braid, and after a full rotation she splashed into a puddle on the floor.

Maybe there were droplets of the Columbia in my lungs now, dormant, dangerous. When I shook my head, I could hear the water sloshing.

"I'm so sorry," I told Beth.

The puddle of Annie drew in on itself until there was nothing left but evaporated grief.

Beth's lips twitched into a furtive smile, an attempt to ease my own discomfort.

I was moved by Beth's great tragedies. She carried herself with such confidence, and I wondered if it was because she had lost so much, and knew exactly, unlike many of us, how much a person can bear.

"She was sensitive like you, Milly, wide-eyed and eager," Beth said. "Nothing slipped by her. She clung to every detail, just the way you do."

Annie was the major heartbreak of Beth's life. Having experienced it diminished the impact of her husband's death.

"Grief can be such a redundant thing," Beth said. "When Glen passed, I just thought, well, here it is, all over again, just as I expected. It was both terrible and familiar."

This, I believed, was why the bell limited me so. It trilled its own troubled history. Beth's husband had given the bell to her as a wedding present, and it was a pretty item, gleaming with a delicate, heart-shaped handle, engraved in cursive with the words MR. AND MRS. GLEN JOHN GREEN. Below was their wedding date, May 5, 1942. It shone with the silver aura of loss.

It irritated me in sleep, too, the ribbon chafing my skin, the bulbous metal knocking against my anklebone when I shifted or turned over. But she was Beth and I was Mildred, and I adored her. I would have done anything she requested. It at least allowed her to sleep better, which she sorely needed; her anxiety over my well-being had made her light sleeping even more delicate.

After a week or so, I convinced myself that the bell wasn't that big of a deal. I got used to the growing, foggy, stifled sensation in my head, as though there were swirling spirits stopped up there, wailing to be loosed. The long, dreamless nights of sleep had made me calmer if duller around the edges; I told myself this was a good thing. Meanwhile the other women in our barracks (Kathy, of course, was one of them) took to calling me Bessie. If I wasn't with Beth, they mooed at me in the hall-ways, whether I was wearing the bell or not.

To distract myself, I focused on work. Daily I bussed to and from Unit B, ferried along with Tom Cat, Gordon, and a hundred other men. I was one of the few girls who worked at that particular station, and usually the men regarded me like a much younger sister. If I was in ear-shot of a bawdy joke or if someone spoke too loudly about their dates or their visits to a brothel in Richland, they glanced at me, elbowing one another, expecting to see me flustered, embarrassed, but I only glared back at them stonily, patient for what they might say next. A few of them considered themselves upstanding Christian men, and women were to be treated with deference, innocent beauties before marriage, dutiful matrons following. These men were almost the worst of the lot, pedan-tic to a fault. I hated it when they shushed everyone, warning about my sensitive nature, when really I tended to lean in to overhear details about sex and corporeality, details that left me ripe and curious if not exactly lusty. None of the men were in love with me, but they tolerated me, and called me "Decent Milly." The nickname was used behind my back at first but then directly to my face, and I took it as a compliment even though I was fairly certain it wasn't meant that way.

On the cattle car, Tom Cat or Gordon usually sat with me or nearby so that we could talk. Gordon liked to tell me about his past and his work, and Tom Cat liked to chat about home, or about his mother, or about the poor conditions of his job outdoors. I spoke with them easily enough, and the time passed quickly. I liked it best, however, when I was left alone, when I could just look out the window at the bright beige world. Every now and again we'd see the wild horses racing for the river, kicking up plumes of dry earth that streamed like long cream veils behind them. Rattlesnake Mountain, fat and smug, hunkered above the curving frown of the river basin, and the rare tree cast a woeful shadow that only a mouse or gopher could use for shade. The wind was almost always there, too, just as harsh and honest as ever. I didn't let her bother me when I left the cattle car. I hurried inside where I could punch my time card, holding my scarf over my mouth and nose, shielding my eyes with my other palm. The wind terrorized many of the others. I once saw a man cry because of the way she spit sand in his eyes. I sorrowed for his weakness. Gordon couldn't stand it; he pushed the poor fellow forward, shouting at him to stop acting like a girl, and the man replied tensely that it was difficult for him, as he had to work outdoors in the wind while Gordon worked inside with the Unit B pile. The man complained that the wind sounded like a sack of bees in his head.

"I'll go mad from it," he said. "I just know it."

It was not an impossibility—people can go mad from subtler things than the winds of Hanford Reach—but Gordon hated this admission and said that the man was an embarrassment to us all.

"We're here for the country," Gordon scolded. "Stop acting like a queer. Why, even Mildred here has more nerve than you."

Later, when we stood in line for the cattle car to return us to the barracks, I whispered to the man, "It's okay, you know, to hate the wind. She's powerful and not always kind."

He gave me a grateful look, then raked his glance across the open grass and sand, from Rattlesnake Mountain on one side to White Bluffs on the other. "I've asked for a change. We'll see if they move me."

"I hope they transfer you," I told him. "Good luck."

Tom Cat came forward then and said, "I requested a move a few weeks back. Took some work on my part, but they said I could switch to a dining room position next week. But if you'd prefer the job, I'll give it to you. I'm not one for washing dishes."

The man blanched with joy, and he and Tom Cat spoke about the particulars while I smiled at them approvingly. They shook hands on it, agreeing to visit the payroll window together later that day.

We boarded the cattle car a few minutes later. I was hungry and tired. As we settled into our seats, I told Tom Cat what a kind thing it was he'd done.

He reached over and squeezed my hand. His touch startled me but not in a painful way.

"I don't want to wash dishes," he said again. Then, more quietly, "I wouldn't get to see you as much."

I laughed. I didn't mean to, but his comment surprised me, the sentimentality of it, the bashfulness.

He turned crimson; I'd embarrassed him. I put a hand on his arm and hurried to explain, "I'm just not used to someone wanting to see me."

But as I spoke my vision blackened. A spiderlike pain crawled behind my eyes, familiar, crushing. I pressed my palms to my temples.

"Mildred?" His voice sounded distant, water-logged.

Then the pain and the blackness dispersed. I released my head. I looked up at Tom Cat and watched, expectantly, calmly, *I know these nightmares too well*, as his face began to melt, the flesh dripping down his coat and onto the toes of his boots.

The skin of his throat and chest followed, peeling away with his clothes. Only a skeleton remained, sitting in a glop of fabric and organs and viscera.

"Oh, Tom Cat."

In his rib cage flopped a yellow-breasted western meadowlark. It nursed a broken wing. It cocked its head, peering up at me with one black eye, and then it threw itself wildly against the bones, desperate for escape.

There was nothing to do but wait until the vision ended, but I was trapped in it, my emotions stirred, too lucid.

"You poor thing," I said to the bird.

The jaw of the skeleton moved up and down. "You all right, Mildred? You've gone pale."

One easy blink and just like that, he was Tom Cat again, flesh intact, meadowlark concealed, his shoes clean and polished. The bus rumbled toward our destination and the men around us, unaware of their dim futures, spoke and chuckled undisturbed.

I would never learn why one vision would send me into seizure while another behaved like no more than a tap on the shoulder. Maybe it was a matter of fighting them or letting them be; maybe it was the time, or the stage of my emotions. Or it was random, as chaotic and furtive as anything else in our lives.

I released my breath like a spear. My hands cramped and ached, I stretched my fingers out wide to relax them; even my mind rattled with meaning and metaphor. At least I was upright, able to speak, if shaken.

"Do you need some air?" Tom Cat asked me. He leaned over me to crack the window. The breeze helped, I drew the fresh air into my lungs.

"I thought I saw something," I told him. My voice sounded foreign to me, accented and unsure. I liked Tom Cat. I wondered if I should warn him. "A vision."

The meadowlark. An illness? A memory? Tom Cat's fragility?

Tom Cat's smile wavered. "Visions? Like déjà vu or something? What'd you see?"

I hesitated, considering.

"I saw what a wonderful husband you'll make one day," I lied. "Because you're gentle. Like a bird."

Tom Cat gave me a funny look. *Mad Mildred*, I remembered. But then he said, "Was there a nest? Was I a father?"

I nodded, but I couldn't bring myself to smile. "Your children will adore you."

He beamed, then touched me on the arm and said, "That means a lot to me." He lingered in the moment, seemed ready to say something else. I was glad for the grounding sound of wheels on cement. It occurred to me that he took the vision as no more than a flight of romantic fancy.

"It's what I see for myself, too," he said.

It's not pretty what will happen to you.

I tried to feel like I'd done him a great favor, giving him something to picture that was good and wholesome, but I was what Martha had always called me, a liar and a coward, although really she only called me this when I told the truth.

People only believed me when I lied.

Dr. Hall was on the phone when I entered, speaking in slow, measured tones as though trying not to lose his temper.

He snapped his fingers under my nose and then made a scribbling motion in the air, and I rushed to take notes.

"You're saying to up productivity levels," he said into the phone, "but there are regulations in place."

There was a moment's pause.

"Well, you're the general, so please tell me what I can do." Another pause. "You're right, of course, especially if you want to destroy Hitler by summer. But I agree with DuPont: There are potential dangers to the environment. Upping production increases the risks." A pause. I wrote down every word for him, as instructed. "Yes, exactly. Three times the power, three times the output. I know what DuPont says. The engineers are smart enough people, I'm sure, but if you're going to listen to anyone, it should be the scientists. You need to think about injury. Accidents. We hope the wind and the river will dilute the toxins, but the full extent of the damage might not manifest itself immediately. DuPont's more worried about their equipment and reputation, but we're worried about much more than that." Another pause. "Why don't you speak with Farmer? He'll have an even better sense of this unit's abilities and dangers."

Dr. Hall looked at me ferociously for a moment as the voice on the other end of the line squawked in his ear.

My pen paused over my notes in a manner I thought was very professional. I always felt very professional and important in Dr. Hall's office. He was one of the few people at Hanford who knew all of Unit B's secrets. That I was his clerk gave me a confidence that I carried with me beyond the gray office walls.

"I don't know about that," he said. "It's more Farmer's baby than DuPont's."

His voice was pained, as if he were releasing a beloved child to her biological father.

"There's no other way around it. The data is solid. We either continue at our current pace and allow for steady dilution into the Columbia and the air, or we up production and create more waste. You can't have both, sir." Dr. Hall looked up at me and rolled his eyes. I smiled faintly in response. Then he sat back, sighed, and said, "Yes, the end game is important. Stopping Hitler is paramount. Have you any word of how close he is to completing a project of his own?" Another moment's pause. "Very troublesome. I don't like to think what would happen if he succeeds first." Dr. Hall frowned at me, or, rather, through me, as though staring across the multifold horizons to the mountains of Germany. I didn't like this race against Hitler: The hairs stood up on the back of my neck. *Hitler has his own Unit B*, I thought, and my heart throbbed with the danger. "I understand, the benefits outweigh the risk. This is a scantily populated region, and that's one of the reasons you chose it. But do keep in mind the thousands of workers we have here."

The voice on the other end of the line hooted loudly in agreement, then murmured something I couldn't hear. Dr. Hall nodded.

"I suppose I can support that. Do consult with Farmer. We are, I hope you know, curious to see all that the project is capable of. I don't mean to suggest otherwise."

Dr. Hall signaled me to put aside the pen. I did so obediently and sat primly with my legs crossed and my hands folded on my lap.

"Yes, thank you, General. Yes, sir. I'll expect to speak with Farmer myself. It will be a pleasure. He's a great man. A hero of mine. Of course. Take care, sir."

He hung up the phone, shaking his head.

"The engineers are too precious about their machinery, and the militaristic mind cares only for dominance. It's our job, as scientists, to make sure this is all done intelligently and ethically. What they're after is power. And this unit, I tell you, has more power in it than the whole length of the Columbia."

I thought of the river's undeterred strength, how she pummeled her way to the ocean, how she had nearly overtaken me and driven me south and then west.

"That's very strong then, Dr. Hall," I said. "Can I get you some coffee?"

"Yes, Miss Groves, please."

I rose and started for the door but he said my name again, questioningly.

"Yes, sir?"

"How much of this all do you understand, Miss Groves?"

I turned toward him and rested my hands on the back of my chair. "Well, not very much, sir. Just that what we are doing here is very important. It's our best shot at stopping Germany."

"That's right."

"And we might have to make sacrifices to do so," I added.

"Yes. Sacrifices. That might be the best word for it. More waste released into the river, into the air, which gives me pause. But you know this wind, Miss Groves. It will dilute the air quickly. We're hoping it won't cause too much damage."

He smiled at me, and while I very much respected Dr. Hall, was proud, indeed, to work for him, the smile reminded me of the skulls I'd seen in the Columbia riverbed.

"Is it true," I began hesitantly, "that Hitler has his own project? A project similar to this one?"

Angles of worry punctured Dr. Hall's plain, intelligent face. "It's why we're rushing. It's why we began this all in the first place. Einstein sent Roosevelt a letter, you see. He was very worried. We all are."

"Hitler has killed many children in Europe, hasn't he?"

"Yes. Hundreds of thousands. Dead and dying still."

"And women?"

"Women, men, the very aged, the innocent. He has no respect for life. He must be stopped, Miss Groves."

"I had a dream," I said, and as I spoke I felt I was speaking not in my own voice but in the voice of a more confident Other. "A dream about the children and women and elderly, all burnt to a crisp. They were in the Columbia riverbed, hundreds of thousands of them, choking it with charcoaled bones."

Dr. Hall's graying eyebrows raised. "A nightmare."

"A vision," I said.

"A sign of a troubled past," Dr. Hall said quickly. "I must admit, I've been having similar dreams, of being bombed here in the Northwest. But our dreams, I'm sorry to say, mean nothing. You've heard of Freud, I presume?"

"No," I said.

"Good. He's a quack." Dr. Hall ruffled some of the pages on his orderly desk and then said, more kindly, "You're an interesting sort of person, Miss Groves, but we mustn't flatter ourselves that our dreams mean anything more than an anxious mind."

"Oh no, sir," I said. "I don't. Of course not." Then, the very next moment, despite myself or because of it: "But it will come true."

I closed my eyes and the rattlesnake appeared on the black screen of my eyelids. The snake rose up, hissing, and shook its corn husk tail.

"All of those bodies," I said in a clipped, firm voice, the voice I used with my mother when I needed to move her from the toilet or the tub. "Bodies upon bodies, skulls upon skulls. More than you can possibly imagine. The children. The women and the infirm."

For a moment it felt as though he heard me, as though he really listened to me, and I held my breath.

"Yes," he said, and his words broke the spell. "That's what will happen if Hitler wins."

I swallowed, hard, realizing how this could very well be true: Hitler would win, and even more innocents would perish wretched, sinister deaths at his hand.

But then a voice in my head, the voice of the heron, said resolutely, *No.*

"He won't win," I said, but there was no cheerfulness in my tone.

Dr. Hall smiled. "That's the spirit. I have no doubt you're right. Keep in mind, we're trying to save people, not hurt them."

I paused, then said, "The people I saw weren't from here. They were foreigners and—".

"We're saving the whole world, Miss Groves, yes, that's true."

He would disregard my every word, I realized. I grew light with the familiar ghoulishness of rejection.

"I'll get your coffee," I said, turning for the door.

In the hallway to the break room I slowed. A crowd of men gathered there, pointing at the ground and laughing.

"Mildred," one of them said. "Come see this. A bird flew in through the shipment door."

I came forward, sensing what I would see before I saw it: the bird hopping on the ground, its wing sagging plaintively behind it. The bird tried to rise, tried to rise, failed.

It was the yellow-breasted meadowlark I'd seen in Tom Cat's rib cage.

"Pretty little thing," someone said. "What kind of bird is that?"

"A western meadowlark," I said. "They sing beautifully."

"The bird knows her birds," someone joked.

"My dad," I said hollowly. "He loved the outdoors."

"Someone put it out of its misery, please," someone said. "It's pathetic."

A man came forward, raising his large black boot. The shadow fell cruelly over the bird and it stilled, perhaps sensing the doom at hand. The boot dropped and stomped and some of the men cheered. Only one of them turned away, holding a hand to his mouth as though he might be sick. I met his eye and frowned. It was the man who had dragged me from the river. He recognized me but didn't say hello.

I started to walk away when one of the men called me back.

"Clean this up for us, would you, doll? We gotta get back to work."

I went to collect the mop from the janitor's closet and filled a bucket of soapy water. I tried to clean up the meadowlark without looking at it, but the gore was inescapable.

When I finally returned empty-handed to Dr. Hall's office, he asked me *what in Sam Hill* I'd done with his coffee.

I returned to the hallway. It gleamed now, the gruesome mortality wiped clean. I tried to forget about the meadowlark, about Tom Cat. But there was a small granule of excitement planted inside of me, and it glowed in my gut like a jewel.

It hadn't happened to me quite like this before, a vision so immediately manifesting itself in this way, as if I hadn't merely envisioned the meadowlark but given birth to her. I was troubled by the fate of the meadowlark, of course, and what this might mean for Tom Cat, for myself, but I was also galvanized.

I didn't want to grow vain about my power, but I thrummed with it.

THE GREEN NIGHTGOWN

When I finished my typing, I dusted the shelves of Dr. Hall's office and straightened his desk and my own small table. Now and again I glanced through the viewing window into the control room. Three men worked there, sitting dutifully before the labyrinth of control panels, checking their watches, preparing to hit a button or turn a dial at just the precise moment. I wasn't friendly with any of the men, but I picked out my favorites from afar. The best of them was a man with a large brow and a bashful demeanor. When he wasn't working, he read paperback books. He was nearly as big as Gordon but you could tell he wished to take up less space, and I liked that about him.

Gordon worked in the unit core and the valve pit room. He told me that he usually wore a bodysuit and heavy gloves and boots, and when he handled the "metal," as they called it, he wore a respiratory mask that made him look like a mad insect. It's true that when I finally saw the men in their gear, passing them in the hallway as I delivered mail or searched for fresh typewriter ink, they no longer seemed human. They were lonely ghost-like creatures with the terrifying magnified faces of dragonflies. I could only guess what would happen to them if they didn't dress in such constricting garb. There was imminent danger in what was referred to as the product. I wondered what the product looked like. In my dreams it was a green glowing orb with golden eyes and sharp teeth. It spun and hummed, waiting. I mentioned the product to no one, not even to Beth. I wanted to tell her more than anyone else, but I took what Dr. Hall said to me very seriously: Secrecy was paramount.

A few more men entered the control room now, saddling up to their stations in large wooden chairs. These boys were young, fresh from high school. Their smooth-shaven faces reminded me of the Omak boys who rarely spoke to me in school. Most of those boys had been sent overseas, and I wondered what was wrong with these young men in Unit B, that they weren't drafted. Myopia, weakness, femininity. I liked the idea that these were gentler beings, that they might make kind husbands and doting fathers, even if they didn't look like Richard Quine. Surely these boys would be kinder than the ones back home.

Those silly boys, I thought, standing there in the physicist's office, ignoring the terrible pain in my feet, my mother's shoes too tight and pinching. Those Omak boys called me spinster, even back then. They didn't realize, of course, that I would become a great lady one day, married to a good, kind man from Hanford.

When we return to Omak with our darling first child, I'll be sure to be kind to all of those immature boys, to show them how I don't take things too badly.

I refused to be like my mother or like Martha, who believed too deeply in the strong grudge.

I was one of the few women in the building, and a woman of any sort, even a woman as plain and shy as I was, caught their attention. They waved at me if they caught me gazing, and I responded with a lifted hand and a warm smile. But they didn't come to speak to me, not in the office and not in line to clock in, and I wondered if this was because of Gordon, who stood beside me like a sentry, his big chest as rigid and intimidating as a Clydesdale's. He put me on edge. He criticized what I wore and teased me relentlessly. He sometimes poked his finger into my waist and laughed, saying I was as soft as a sugared doughnut. Once Tom Cat noticed my discomfort and asked Gordon to lay off, Gordon responded by calling Tom Cat a meddling twit. He punched my defender in the shoulder, causing Tom Cat to take a few steps backward and embarrass me with his pained expression.

I told Beth about how uncomfortable Gordon made me, and she formed a sort of fortress around me whenever he approached.

Around Beth, Gordon behaved differently. He was quiet and observational, and if he did utter something crude, he shrank beneath her disapproving gaze and apologized quickly. He was an untamed sheepdog who benefited from a more disciplined owner, and I never managed to take up the whip with him. All I could do was ignore him. But I felt safe with Beth and Tom Cat nearby, and I tried to never go anywhere that Gordon might be without one or both of them at hand. Tom Cat, it became clear, had feelings for me, and I imagined that maybe I had feelings for him, too. How would I know? What did having feelings even mean? I tried to think of myself as falling in love. I knew Tom Cat would be a hard worker and a kind man to live with for the rest of my days, but the bloodied meadowlark returned to me, flashing its panicked yellow breast, beating its good wing against the glass bars of Tom Cat's rib cage. Maybe that, in itself, was what love felt like.

One evening during dinner I grew queasy. Beth and the others wanted to go to the beer hall, and I told them to go ahead without me. I wanted nothing more than to have a bicarbonate of soda and lie down until the tension in my stomach waned. Beth offered to walk me back to the barracks but I refused; I worried I might get sick en route and it terrified me to have a witness. I hurried off into the dusty wind of the gloaming.

This was my favorite time of day here, when the circle of the sun dropped behind the mountains, spikes of light tailing behind it, washing Rattlesnake Mountain and White Bluffs in a garland of pastels, daylily and periwinkle and gladiolus. The wind was eager but not so much that I couldn't enjoy the view. The air smelled cleanly of rime and sage. Christmas was only a week away. I pulled my old sweater and coat closer around me and ambled along the frost-stitched earth. The mess halls emptied and the beer halls filled up, one building for the whites and another for the coloreds. The thought of beer disgusted me. My stomach churned and I slowed, willing myself not to get sick on the frozen sagebrush. As I moved, my muscles loosened: I began to feel better. The fresh night air was the best tonic.

Along the perimeter of the women's barracks, a group of men were finishing up their work for the day. Tall poles shot into the air as high as ponderosa pines.

"What's all this?" I asked.

A man wearing cowhide gloves spooled a length of barbed wire. He continued his work but answered me in a friendly-enough tone. "We've had some events here. This is for your protection. We dug the holes before the ground froze too much. Now it's just a matter of getting these wires stretched. Should be fairly quick now."

I'd seen them out here digging in the last few days, but I'd assumed it was for more latrines, more barracks. There were so many of us.

"Events? Like what?"

I marveled at the height and breadth of the fence, of the ferocity of its barbs.

The man shook his head. "I'd rather not say. It's upsetting."

"Murder?" I asked.

All of the men laughed now, shaking their heads.

"Nothing like that," the man said. "The girl who was hurt is fine enough now. They've spoken to the guy about it. He's sorry and all."

"But what—"

A sharp whistle came from behind me and I turned to see Gordon there with his handsome wolfish face. He wore only a buttoned-up shirt and no coat, but he seemed perfectly comfortable despite the stinging chill.

"Trying to keep us out, are you?" he joked to the men, and they laughed and joked in return that they were doing their best.

"If a man wants a woman badly enough," one of them said, and then trailed off with a chuckle.

"She shouldn't be walking out here alone at night," another man said to Gordon, thumbing at me.

"I know. Her friend sent me to fetch her home."

"Beth?" I said, incredulous.

He winked an affirmation.

It surprised and frustrated me that Beth would do such a thing. It was not like her to entrust someone else with my safety.

"I'm fine," I said. "I don't need anyone's help."

"Nonsense," Gordon said. "All women are dames in distress."

It bothered me how handsome he was, how sharp-jawed and strong. His lips curled upward, cruel and inviting. For a moment I was Susan Peters, standing before my life's love. I wanted to throw my arms around him and admit to him, yes, I was always in distress, *I need someone, anyone, really, to take care of me*, but then his face turned to the side and there was the coyote in his aquiline profile, and I turned away, half-jogging for my barrack.

On all sides the night sky deepened and thickened, souped with stars. To the east the cliffs of White Bluff rose like knives from the dirt. The women's barracks, rickety, makeshift, sat lonely in the dim light like so many discarded matchboxes, mostly emptied except for girls like me, the unfortunate ones who didn't feel well, the timid ones with shaky nerves. Far away I heard the music of the beer halls. Their throbbing sound magnified my loneliness.

Gordon fell into step beside me, menacing in his silence.

When I reached the door of the barrack I turned to him and offered my hand. "Thanks, I guess," I said.

"You guess?" He ignored my hand and pushed past me through the door.

"You're not allowed here," I said.

A girl, lounging on her cot with a book, screeched. She was in her bathrobe and curlers. She jumped to her feet, scolding me. "You can't bring your boyfriends here."

"He's not a boyfriend," I said.

"Cool your jets, doll," Gordon said to her, and he began poking around the room.

The girl watched us sullenly for a moment before leaving the building entirely, either for the neighboring barrack, where she could complain about us to the women there, or for the cold toilets a quarter mile away.

"You need to go," I told Gordon when she'd gone.

"You girls keep this place so neat. No wonder we hire you to make our beds."

"You're grown men now," I said. "You should make them yourselves."

"I'd pay you a tenner to fluff my pillow now and again," Gordon said, and laughed loudly at his own joke.

I loathed the sight of his teeth, yellow from too much coffee and hard and dull as river rock.

"Bethesda's?" He pointed to the cot next to my own.

Beth had placed a photo of herself with her dead husband on the small dresser beside the bed. The photo captured all of her beauty, her wavy hair and long neck and generous, happy eyes. The dead husband was featureless beside her, already turned into a shapeless ghost by her very vitality.

Gordon picked up the photo and studied it for a moment before laying it facedown on the little dresser. "He seems like a twit," he said.

"You need to leave. You'll get me in trouble."

He opened up a drawer in Beth's dresser and smirked, fishing around with his enormous hands.

"Stop that," I said.

I stood beside him and pushed at him, trying to move him away.

He captured a shining rayon garment. He brought it up to his face, sniffing it deeply. I recognized it as her green bias-cut nightgown, a flattering shape I'd been so envious of when she'd worn it to bed on our first night here.

"This will do," he said, grinning, and then he bid me good night.

"Bring that back!" I shouted after him, but he waved his hand dismissively over his shoulder.

Overwhelmed with my powerlessness, I called after him, pathetically, "Good riddance!"

I readied for bed, finished by tying the bell onto my ankle, uncertain of whether or not I should tell Beth what he'd done. The woman with the book returned. She looked at me spitefully but I didn't care. I was just happy to be in bed, warm and aching beneath the blankets. Sleep folded me inside and out, there, then not.

I awoke later to Beth undressing and putting on her flannel nightgown. The returning crowd had snapped on all of the lights.

"Go back to sleep, Milly," she said to me. "We didn't mean to wake you."

I squinted at her, my eyes adjusting. Other bodies rustled nearby, settling into their cots. The room smelled of perfume and beer.

Beth scurried into bed, shivering, and pulled the blankets up to her chin.

"How was your night?" she whispered.

"I slept," I said.

"Your stomach?"

"Better now."

"Too many doughnuts for breakfast," she giggled, and I smiled.

Someone flicked off the lights again and the room flattened.

"I'm glad you're back," I told her.

She reached her hand out across the gap between our beds and I did the same. We squeezed each other's fingers, mine toasty warm and hers like a bouquet of slender icicles. I willed my warmth into her body. I hated to think of her being cold.

"Sweet Milly," she sighed sleepily. "Are you wearing the bell?"

"Kind Beth," I said. "Yes, I am."

I didn't mention the pilfered nightgown. I was ashamed I hadn't been able to stop him.

And I didn't want her to think that Gordon and I had been alone in the barracks, that there was something happening between us. Or maybe I didn't want her to laugh at me. *Mildred as Gordon's lover! How ridiculous!*

The secrecy kept me safe from her disapproval. I was a selfish, horrible person, just like Mother and Martha always said I was.

"I love you," she murmured, and I told her the same.

I released her hand then and turned onto my side, the bell on my ankle jingling faintly.

SAVE ME FROM THESE CRETINS

I took the bus to Richland on Sunday, our only day off, missing the church service but wanting to phone Mother. I told the operator, "Okanogan 8-1521, please," and I put in my pennies and waited while she patched me over. The phone rang for a long time, a surprise to me knowing how nosy all of the neighbors were on the party line, but everyone was at church, I supposed; Mother usually stayed home for one reason or another. Finally the phone lifted and I heard Mother's labored breathing. I wanted to say hello but I didn't. I just listened to her and closed my eyes, and for a moment I was back in Omak, next to her bed, reading *Heidi* to her, her favorite book, in a rare peaceful moment of togetherness.

"If this is Angel's boy," she retorted, "I'll let you know you're in hot water for marrying that Indian. You broke your poor mom's heart. She won't speak with you."

"Mother," I said. There was a moment's silence. I put my palm against the wood of the phone booth and my skin came away sticky with the unknown.

"Mother, darling. It's me, Mildred."

"I know who it is, Ferret Brain. Don't condescend me."

I squinted into the bright light of the road, the new, pretty buildings constructed by the government, the families in their finery hurrying along the sidewalk to worship. I thought it would be nice to leave the barracks and come here one day, to live in a real town by myself in a little house all my own. Husband first. Then house. Then children. Things I'd been told to desire my whole life. A mother yanked on her son's hand not far from where I stood in the phone booth, her tone tense and disapproving. The poor child. I'd be so much more gentle with that little boy. I'd buy him an ice cream cone from the drugstore; I'd let him choose whatever toy he wanted.

"Rupert married Matilda Jim, if you haven't heard. And of course you haven't, having flown the coop."

"I thought he might," I said. "Where are they settled now? I'd like to mail them a letter, if I can."

"What business is it of yours? This isn't your home anymore. None of it concerns you."

I made a small throaty sound of acknowledgment. Then, brightening, "Mother, I suppose you've received the checks?"

"I don't handle the money. Martha does, and that dull lump of her husband. He plods in and out of here like a dying animal. I can't stand the sight of him."

"He adores you, Mother. He's a good man. Try to be kind."

"I couldn't go to church with them today because of my gout. It hurts something awful, Mildred."

I was comforted by the direct way she addressed me. I said to her, lovingly, "I would rub your feet for you if I was there, Mother."

"Dr. Sheppard agrees with me that I've worsened since you left. He says how very sad it is my children don't support me in my weakened condition."

"Mother, I've sent you nine checks so far, much more money than we've had in a long time. Please check with Martha to make sure they've arrived safely. There are nine total and a tenth should arrive—"

"Angel Shea," Mother shrieked, "I know you're listening, you rat. I can hear that damn dog of yours in the background. Hang up this instant! I don't listen to your conversations with that redskin-lover of yours."

"Mother," I said. "I don't think——"

A soft click sounded, clearly Mrs. Shea hanging up on the party line.

"Mrs. Shea may be a good bridge partner, but she's a terrible friend," Mother said. "She told me I should forgive you as God would like me to. What a moron. God doesn't give a flying pancake about forgiveness. He's a vengeance man. He likes a firm swat on the rear."

A line formed at the phone booth, and I turned my back to it so that I wouldn't see all of those expectant faces.

"Mother, it's good to hear your voice. You sound well."

"What is it you're doing there, anyway, Mildred?" she said then, and I was startled by the question. It encouraged me that she might care about my work. I paused a moment, gathering up my excitement. I wanted to make her very proud.

"It's secretive, Mother. I work for one of the top scientists here. He's a physicist."

"A scientist? Are they making a chemical inhalant? Like the showers at Auschwitz? No reporters will write about Hanford here. I check the papers every day and there's nothing."

"No, no, they wouldn't, it's not allowed."

Journalists, I'd learned from Dr. Hall, were strictly forbidden to research or report on the Hanford site.

"So how do I know you're there? And not off gallivanting in an Egyptian harem?"

"The checks I send you come from the government, so that means——"

"You can't even tell your own mother what you're doing. You don't even know. You've always been full of nonsense, Mildred. Your father thought you held such promise. 'She's a reader,' he'd say. 'She loves words and stories. She's wonderful at math. She'll be as educated as they come.'

But I knew, we all knew, that you were living in a fantasy land. And even now, even now, you have no idea—"

"It's a weapon, Mother. Something that will help us win the war. I think you'll be very proud of me. We're making something they all refer to as the product—" and I stopped here, horrified with myself.

Secrecy. Safety. Loyalty.

"I can't talk about this, Mother, I can't. I've said too much already."

"A weapon," Mother said. "Big whoop."

Behind the gauzy veil of her labored breathing came the familiar creak of Mother's front door opening, and I remembered how the bright winter light shone through the front windows and onto the enamel-topped table, a table Mother adored and showed off proudly to her bridge partners. I recalled weeping at that table as a girl, Mother standing over me and scolding me for embarrassing her in front of her friends. I couldn't remember what I'd done, but it had something to do with talking too much.

Mother's tone changed now to one of entreaty.

"Quit that silly work, Mildred. It's time to come home. Save me from these cretins. Martha is a mean brute. She isn't careful like you. Her children are loud and awful. She's broken three dishes since you left and one of them was on purpose."

I heard voices rising behind her, Martha's shrill peal, and Walter's thin, watery request for his wife to remain calm. The phone was wrestled with, pulled this way and that, and I suffered through the shuffling sounds with much nervousness.

Martha triumphed. Her shrill voice came on the line. She launched into me, shouting horrible words I'd never heard her say before. Spent, she finished by saying, "I hate you. You've ruined my life," and surrendered the phone to Walter.

Someone knocked on the glass door of the phone booth. The first service of the day must have been over, people were gathering in a line outside of the accordion door. I ignored them, hunching over the phone protectively. I hurriedly added more pennies.

Walter said, simply, "Hullo, Mildred. How are you?"

"I'm fine, Walter," I said, but I was so rattled that my hands shook. "And you?"

"Martha is worried for you. That's all she means."

"Oh, it's all right," I lied. "It's good for her to vent."

"She thinks you'll get hurt or hurt someone else or wind up dead down there." He laughed uncomfortably. "She's smoking on the front stair with your mom now. She'll come around."

"Have you been getting the checks, Walter?"

"Yes," he said. "Thank you. It's a great deal of money you're making. More than I am. We're all grateful." An awkward laugh. "Maybe I should get a job there."

Walter was a planer man at the local sawmill, but the pay was dismal and now and again Martha worked in the school cafeteria to make ends meet. In one of her bad moods, Martha had once told me that Walter was too clumsy with the planing equipment, and that the foreman always joked that one day soon Walter would saw off the tips of his fingers. I had hoped she was wrong and that the story was simply one of her usual moments of derision and nothing more, but one day he came home late from work with the tops of two fingers bandaged: he'd cut the top third of them off, joint and fingernails and all.

Walter continued, "Your mother bit Martha the other day, and the stitches were expensive, and we're lucky Martha didn't haul off and smack her like she wanted to, but—"

"You're kidding," I said. "How awful."

"Right on the hand. Because Martha was trying to feed her an arrowroot cookie and—"

"Mother is capable of feeding herself. Don't listen to those requests of hers."

"But the hand is healing nicely, the bruising has almost faded although I'll tell you I nearly dropped dead at the sight of the blood—"

I was out of pennies.

"Walter," I said urgently, wanting to impart some advice, to contribute in whatever helpful way that I could. "Please tell Martha not to let Mother take over her whole life."

"I'm not sure I should tell her that, Mildred, although I'm sure you mean well. She feels very much that you—"

The phone went dead. I felt dizzy in the small box, closed in as though I was standing in my own coffin. The man rapped on the glass again, not rudely, but I frowned at him anyway. I was so anxious. The muscles in my face cramped and trembled.

I pushed through the annoyed crowd, some of them muttering at me under their breath, and picked my way to the bus station. A woman waited there, too, with her handbag dangling from her wrist. When she saw me she winked conspiratorially and asked me what I thought we were making up there at Hanford.

Not you, too, I thought. *Why do people ask so many questions? They ask and ask and then don't listen to the answers.* I regretted saying so much to Mother. I worried I couldn't trust myself.

"Loose lips sink ships," I said.

The woman grimaced, probably disappointed in my lack of good humor.

"You know what I heard?"

I feigned disinterest. "It doesn't matter."

"I heard they're making toilet paper. Sounds silly, sure, but I think it might be true. We're helping the war effort by making good-quality toilet paper for the troops."

I looked at her to see if she was joking.

She was not.

"Don't make that face at me," she pouted. "I'm no fool. I heard it from a good source. Think about how a solid roll of toilet paper could boost a man's morale. Well, I'm half-convinced."

"I work in a physicist's office at Unit B. It's not toilet paper. I promise you, it's not that."

The woman looked away from me, toward the approaching tan and crimson cattle car. Behind the bus were frozen brown waves of fallow earth, and curving through the brown was the Columbia, broad and gray, the color of Mother's cataracts.

"But it could be," she muttered, "for all we know."

DON'T WORRY YOUR PRETTY LITTLE HEAD

O ne evening I returned home from work with a file under my arm, some manuscripts I needed to copyedit for Dr. Hall. As I passed by the payroll window I was happy to see Beth's shining profile. She was speaking to our house mother off to the side of the avenue. Each barrack was assigned a house mother, a woman in charge of the dozens of residents. Our own was a jovial if silly woman. She snored away when I sleepwalked, and when she received word of a resident's misbehavior, she waved her hand in the air and said in bad French, "Chacun à son goût." In my opinion, she was the laziest and drollest of the house mothers, good for a laugh but not for any real comfort or advice, and most of us regarded her the way we would a generous if inebriated aunt. Her name was Sue Berry but Kathy called her "Beef Stew Berry" because of the way she slurped her soup in the mess hall.

I walked up to the women cheerfully, glad to have finished another long day, looking forward to supper and maybe even a beer.

"Yes, we're close friends," Beth was saying. "I care about her, is why I'm telling you. I just wanted to let you know."

Mrs. Berry gave Beth her usual useless, dismissive platitude, "Don't worry, dear, all will be well."

Then Mrs. Berry saw me standing there.

"Well!" she said. "Speak of the devil! Hello, Miss Groves."

"What's going on?" I asked hesitantly.

"I was just telling Mrs. Berry about your sleepwalking," Beth said. "So she won't hear it from someone else. And, frankly, I thought she might be able to help. In case there's another incident."

I tried to smile. I told myself to be flattered by the attention. Beth meant well. Nonetheless, a vicious part of me snarled and thrashed.

Never talk about me behind my back.

"Ready for dinner?" Beth asked me, offering her arm.

Shifting the file into my free hand, I took the offered limb with false pleasure. I pictured biting into her neck, that sweet, peach woman flesh, and I ground my molars together with such ferocity that my ears ached.

✷

Our barracks were next to the barracks of the black women. We ate together in the mess hall, but they had separate sleeping arrangements and a separate dance hall. Beth worked with two of the women at the clinic. They did the fouler tasks there, cleaning up after men who had soiled themselves or changing out the urine bags, mopping the blood from the floors and wiping up vomit in the bathrooms. Beth said they were decent at their jobs but that she once overheard them complaining about the working conditions. One said her brother was a highly skilled welder but was forced to push a mop around in Unit B, and when Beth relayed this to me, I knew exactly who she meant, a man named Stanley Johnson. They muttered, too, about how they were banned from the Richland restaurants and all of the major entertainment; on holidays, they were allowed only card tournaments in their dance hall. One of the women called Hanford the Mississippi of the North. I thought of this when I went to watch the baseball games where the men played together, black and white. I wondered if people were grateful for that at least or if they would have rather formed teams of their own.

For me it was exciting, all of the differences at Hanford. Some work-

ers spoke Chinese, some spoke Spanish. There were beautiful variations
in skin tones and facial features. I slowed down and listened excitedly
when I passed people speaking in foreign languages. I was, in a way, seeing the whole world. I delighted at the idea of bringing my sister here.
We knew many Okanagan Indians in Omak, but the rest of us were
lily white. Martha would be terrified here; she would cower and whine.
I imagined telling her, *There, there, Martha, I'm used to this. I'm now a very
cultured person. There's nothing to be afraid of. None of these people will hurt you. I
know, because I'm here every day.* She would have no choice but to submit to
my wisdom.

Gordon said, "I don't trust a Negro." He said he had his reasons
for it, that he'd worked with a few in Nebraska and had once been hood-
winked. He couldn't say how exactly and I doubted the veracity of his
story: He was gloating about empty hatred the way some men did. He
loomed over us at lunch now, sitting next to Beth and me possessively.
He called us "his girls." Beth tolerated him, but she retorted once that
he didn't own us; we weren't *his* anything. He always softened his tone
when she scolded him, lowering his eyes and glancing at her timidly
through his long lashes. He was so swift with his apologies that she
accused him of being insincere.

"I don't know why you insist on bothering us," she told him. "Milly
and I just want to eat our biscuits in peace."

Gordon grinned. "And how I enjoy watching you eat!"

She turned to me. "He's as receptive as a bedpan."

But I noticed she fought with him less and less, issuing complaints
and then shrugging off his responses and simply ignoring him rather
than pushing him away.

"I wonder if he isn't in love with you, Milly," she said one evening.
"He just won't leave us alone."

"That's not true," I said. "I'm not good enough for him."

Beth's eyes shot up to me. She'd been scrubbing a stain from her
nursing uniform as we spoke. Our barracks smelled of baking soda and
vinegar. "What did you just say?"

"I'm not worthy of him."

"You don't really believe that, do you, Milly?" She watched me for a long moment, and I grew awkward under her piercing stare. "That's absurd. You couldn't be more wrong. You have more beauty in your little finger than he's got in his entire body."

I started to say something and she stopped me.

"Don't give me that 'He-looks-like-Richard-Quine' business, Milly. In the right light, he looks like a constipated moose."

I laughed.

"We should tell him to buzz off," she said. "Once and for all."

When we saw him next, however, Beth was distracted. After a long night at the clinic, covering for a sick nurse, Beth was allowed to go to work later than usual, and so, following a cheerful breakfast, she accompanied me to the bus stop. As we arrived, there was a scuffle. A short, burly man whom I recognized from the Unit B control room—Clarence was his name—hauled off and shoved a black man in the chest. This was the Stanley from Unit B, the welder-turned-janitor whose sister worked with Beth.

"What are you doing that for?" Beth said.

"He called me a fool," Clarence cried. "I won't let no spook call me a fool."

Gordon appeared behind us. Stanley rose to his full height: He was big, slightly shorter than Gordon but broader. He straightened his shoulders and gave Clarence a hard look.

A group of men, Gordon included, stepped toward Clarence, but Beth, before I could stop her, hurried forward, put her arm on Gordon's, and whispered something in his ear.

"He called me liver lips," Stanley said. "'Move back, Liver Lips,' he said."

"Stating the obvious," spat Clarence.

Gordon had taken Beth's arm and was leading her over to where I stood. Clarence watched this spitefully.

"What'd she say to you, Gordo? She's no coon lover, is she?"

Gordon raised his eyes to Beth's as he settled her next to me.

"Don't matter," Clarence said. "We'll teach him, anyhow."

The men pressed in around Stanley, who put up his hands and said, "Now, listen here."

"Okay, okay," Gordon said loudly, breaking into the circle of men. "Let's knock this off." He looked at Stanley. "That means you, too, Stan."

Stanley lowered his hands but his fingers remained clenched into tight fists.

Clarence frowned. "Whose side are you on, Gordo?"

"We're fighting for the same side, aren't we?" Gordon scrutinized the other men. The armpits of his work shirt were stamped with damp circles but the river water of his voice was big and steady.

Silence dropped over the group like a disorienting fog. There was a muffled discussion, a few low voices.

"At least he ain't a Jap," someone offered, more loudly.

"Goddamn Japs," another said. "Good thing they've been put in the camps."

"It's time to get to work," Gordon said. "We've got a job to do. All of us."

Clarence kicked at a stone and it skipped noisily across the frozen ground. "What the hell are we even making here? I'd like someone to tell us *that* at least."

"That's enough from you," Gordon said, and the other men, even Stanley, nodded around him.

A piercing squeal sounded in my right ear, high and desperate like a pig at the slaughter.

"Secrecy and security," I said loudly, and a few people in the crowd glanced at me, surprised.

I half-walked, half-floated toward Stanley.

My tongue narrowed into the rattlesnake's tongue, forked and black. The world shook slightly at its edges and a bright pain licked at my brow.

My hands parted from my wrists and hovered near Stanley's face.

His eyes swelled shut. His throat empurpled. His front tooth fell out.
Welts exploded like blue flames on his flesh; lacerations ripped open.
My disconnected palms fell on his shoulders and he flinched. A raft
slid into the water of my thoughts. The stream of images parted around
it, giving space for me to warn him, slowly and clearly,

"They'll very nearly kill you, later tonight, after supper."

He tried to pull away from me but I couldn't let go of his shoulders. I needed him to listen. The rattlesnake tongue clicked and hissed.

Beth took hold of my arm, shaking it at first gently and then more
wildly.

"Milly," she said. "Milly, let go of him."

"She's gone mad," Stanley said. "Get her off me."

"Listen to me," I told him desperately, "I'm trying to save you. Don't
go out tonight, stay put—"

Once, as a girl, I'd complained to Mother, *No one believes me. I'm only
trying to help them.*

Mother had chided me. *No one wants your doom and gloom. Why don't you
say something nice for a change? You make it so easy for people to hate you.*

Stanley's battered ghost-to-come gaped at me as though I were diseased. Blood poured down his jaw but no one else saw it. Between us
hung the thin fabric of the vision, as sheer as it was assured.

"They'll beat you half to death."

Stanley backed away from me.

"Don't be scared of me," my snake tongue hissed. "Be scared of
them."

Gordon and the other men watched me, their expressions curious,
uncomfortable. If they sensed the truth of my words, they didn't admit
to it. Between us Stanley bled and swelled.

Beth put her arm around me, peeling me away from the group. She
led me in the direction of the encampment. The shroud of my vision
lifted. When I looked over my shoulder, Stanley's face was returned to
its present state, unmarred, unharmed. Regardless, the rough fists of the
future waited for him.

"Mildred," Beth said, and the lack of my nickname worried me: I was no longer an adorable pet. "I'm taking you to the clinic."

How could I explain it to her, without sounding mad?

It's not what's the matter with me, it's exactly what's right.

"They'll hurt him, Beth," I told her. "It's the truth."

"If you don't stop, they'll make you leave Hanford," she said. "You can't act like this here." Then, following an exasperated pause, "It's like you want it to happen, Milly. It's like you were planting an idea in their heads."

It felt like a finger had reached into my gut and struck a hard chord there; I vibrated with unease and annoyance. I wasn't sure if I could trust Beth. I looked at her for a long moment, pleadingly. The rattlesnake in my mouth loosened, relaxed. My tongue became again a neutral organ.

"I'll stop," I told her, even though I wouldn't stop, didn't want to. "I'll do whatever you say."

She hurried me along as if she hadn't heard me, but when we reached the clinic she held the door open for me and said, "I only want what's best for you," and I was relieved to hear the affection in her tone.

Sometimes the only way to get on someone's good side again is to agree with everything they ask of you.

"I want that for you, too," I said, but saying it made me realize that I didn't know what *best for you* meant, and I didn't think Beth knew, either.

✿

We were in the clinic for over an hour. The clean coolness of the room, the stillness of the air, shushed my inner workings, at first to a murmur and then to a simple hum in my mind. The room smelled of camphor. I closed my eyes and slept a little, lying on the gray sheets of a thin and creaking cot. Beth left me alone for a time, managing to track down Tom Cat just as he caught the cattle car to Unit B. She sent with him a note to Dr. Hall, saying I was ill.

"He was very worried for you," Beth said when she returned.

"Dr. Hall?" I said, surprised.

"Tom Cat, silly."

Beth squeezed my hand. I rose onto one elbow and then the other to smooth my cotton percale day dress and then resettled myself on the stiff cot.

"Don't you need to work, Beth?"

"Soon. Not before I speak to Dr. Harrington, Milly."

I was relieved to hear her call me Milly again.

"You're better than a sister," I told her. I said it purposefully, trying to reestablish myself in her mind as a refurbished Annie.

I thought of Martha, too, recalling how cruelly she had sneered at me when I'd broken my wrist—*You deserve it, you deaf idiot*—having fallen from a tree that she'd warned me not to climb.

"I'm a friend," she said. "And I love you, Milly. I hate to see you in pain."

"I'm not in pain," I told her.

"We're all in pain," Beth said dismissively.

I assured her I was not, but my insistence seemed to bother her. She half-turned away from me. I admired the sensuality of her profile, the long line of her nose, her smooth forehead, the sweep of her eyelashes, her pretty, downturned mouth, her charming ear with its elegant pointed tip, the strength and sculpted beauty of her shoulder in its brown cable cardigan. I thought of her green nightgown, now in Gordon's possession. What would she say if I told her about the theft? I relished withholding a secret from her.

The doctor entered and Beth greeted the older man eagerly. Beside her, he appeared short and wrinkled and cantankerous, with the aspect of a gargoyle.

"Dr. Harrington, this is my friend, Mildred Groves," she said. "She works for Dr. Hall."

"You don't say," Dr. Harrington said. "I hear he's an intelligent man."

"He is," I rushed to say. "The smartest person I've ever met."

Beth ignored this small talk. "Mildred is very tense. I worry for her nerves."

"Women are like this, you know," he replied lightly. "It shouldn't cause too much alarm."

Beth looked at me quickly and then back at the doctor. "She had a very upsetting interaction with some friends. She's wound up. And not just today," she said. "She's had other episodes. Sleepwalking, for example."

"Sleepwalking, yes, I see." Dr. Harrington withdrew a pen and a small tablet of paper from his breast pocket and scribbled down what Beth said into it. *Or is it what Beth says*, I wondered. Perhaps he was writing *Remember to set out the laundry tonight* or *Buy butter at the grocer.* Maybe he wrote, *Woman with amazing powers arrives at Hanford and transforms all of our lives.*

"Yes, but not *normal* sleepwalking, Dr. Harrington. She wanders outside, to the riverbank. She nearly drowned in the Columbia. And she thinks she sees things, she starts talking crazy—"

Dr. Harrington smiled gently and patted her arm. "Now, now, Mrs. Green, let's remain calm for our friend's sake, please."

Beth glowered for a moment, considering this, but then bit her lip and nodded. She was curvy and perfect in her day dress and sweater, and when Dr. Harrington touched her arm, his fingertips lingered against the flesh of her wrist.

"Now, Miss Groves," he said to me, kindly, "how are you enjoying your work here at Hanford?"

"It's going very well, thank you," I said.

"And where is your family? How are things back at home?"

"They're in Omak," I said. "Happy as pigs in mud."

"And are they very proud of you?"

I began to say yes but then I corrected myself.

"As much as they possibly can be. I send them the largest portion of my check every month. It's more money than they've ever had."

"She ran away," Beth interrupted. "She left her mother and her sister, both. They've given her a very hard time. After her father died, she was her mother's lone caretaker. The poor child. To know only mortality and death . . ."

"I had a wonderful conversation with Mother recently," I said, which was really only a partial lie, because it really was a good conversation, as far as conversations with Mother went, "and she asked me to come home for the holidays."

I didn't add that she wanted my return to be permanent.

"And you would like this?" Dr. Harrington pressed.

"I can't go," I said. "I'll be here working," I went on, measuring my tone to sound quite sane, "and I like it that way. I don't want to go home. I love it here. It's a marvelous place, wouldn't you agree, Dr. Harrington?"

The doctor looked at me crossly and then shook his head, indicating that he was not the one on trial. "Tell me, Miss Groves, how do you like the strong winds we have here?"

"I have no trouble with the wind," I said. "She and I get along just fine."

"Lots of good men and women have left because of the winds. They can make a person feel trapped. But you don't feel this way?"

I shook my head, no.

"And how are you tolerating the rudimentary lodgings?"

"I find them quaint and comfortable," I said.

"The long work hours? Are those taxing for you?"

"Caring for Mother was far more taxing, Dr. Harrington. You would understand if you met her."

"And have you felt any discontent at all since arriving? Any wish to leave?"

"The opposite."

I want to stay here forever.

Beth took up my hand and laced her fingers through my own.

"Maybe some valerian would help her, Doctor? Something to calm her nerves?"

"I'm perfectly calm," I said.

"I think valerian would do nicely," he said. "This is a classic case, of course, of hysteria brought on by strain."

"But I'm not strained," I said. "The opposite, really. I'm freer than I've ever been."

"Sometimes," Dr. Harrington said smoothly, "we trick ourselves into believing we're well, but that's when cracks appear in our behavior."

I considered this silently. It unnerved me, to be told this, as if I didn't know myself in the slightest. At any moment I could reveal myself as my own enemy. Three years ago, after I'd pushed Mother into the river, I'd catch myself staring obsessively at my hands, worried about what they might do to others or to myself. I sat on them whenever I could, certain that if I let down my guard they would shoot up and wrap around my own throat.

"In 'The Princess and the Pea,'" I said suddenly, "the girl just needs the pea removed."

Beth laughed at this, uncomfortably. "She has an astounding mind, doesn't she?"

The doctor, however, seemed to understand me perfectly. "It's a charming analogy. We just need to find the pea," he said, smiling, "and pluck it out."

I liked this idea very much. It satisfied me, that the problem could be that simple.

The doctor continued. "I must inform you that anyone not of sound mind will leave Hanford on the instant, Miss Groves. I'm afraid I will need to report any signs of mania—"

"My mind is as sound as a gong, sir," I insisted. *Sounder,* I wanted to add, *bigger, louder, brassier.* "I've been overtired is all."

I was at risk of being sent home. I threw an irritated look at Beth. She, too, was stunned. She mouthed the word, "Sorry," at me. I understood that she wanted to help me, not to get rid of me, but I was angry, nonetheless. I swallowed my irritation. I needed to remain calm until we left the clinic.

"She hasn't done anything worth reporting," Beth said in her professional nurse's tone. "I would tell you, Dr. Harrington, if I thought otherwise. She's strained, as you said, and she has these intense dreams. I thought if anyone could help her, it would be you."

I noted the flattery and its intent, but Dr. Harrington only nodded and continued bitterly, "Women patients and their moods. I see dozens of you a year. It's been the biggest headache of girls joining the workplace, this extreme sensitivity. All that 'Rosie the Riveter' toughness is lost on the average girl. Meanwhile the good men are off dying in battle, all while you fuss and complain here on the home front."

He continued his harangue until Beth carefully interrupted him and asked again for some sort of helpful prescription.

"Of course," he said. He gave me a stern look. "Miss Groves, if I see you back here, I'm afraid it will be for the last time. For obvious reasons, we can only have the sanest minds working here. That's how important this work is for the war effort."

"You won't see me here again," I promised. "Not even for a common cold."

He smiled and patted my knee.

My work here was only beginning. I belonged here. The whole of me belonged here, including my visions, especially my visions. I gave him my sanest, kindest, most convincing smile.

I left with a bottle of valerian and a diagnosis of common female hysteria brought on by sleeplessness and rattled nerves. The sun blazed but the air was cold and dry like the inside of an icebox. Beth waved with some concern from the clinic's haphazardly constructed porch. She looked like a perfect little doll settled within a crude toy village. I waved good-bye to her and smiled brightly to reassure her, belying my frustration.

I'm right as rain. Don't worry your pretty little head.

JUMP

The vision collected me from where I slept on the cot, hooking into my shoulders with her harpy's talons and dragging me first across the room of gently snoring women, pushing against the barracks door, and then over the chipped gravel sand of the desert so that the skin on the tops of my toes tore and bled. The vision had been gathering strength for some time. I didn't fight her. I was relieved she was here. She'd plucked out the eyes of the guards so that they couldn't see me. They laughed and joked together over a flask of beer, unaware that their eyes had been replaced with chewed-up mulberries. Their sight was useless now; otherwise they would have cried out, pulled me free of the harpy's hooks, returned me to the barracks, and scolded me in tones of incredulity. But mulberry eyes, sweet and dumb, see nothing. The vision croaked and opened up her wings and we flew the short distance to the bluff overlooking the river.

Snow fell in fragments of fine white thread. The vision flapped her wings and my line of sight sharpened. I was released onto the icy earth, a glittering reflection of the firmament. Out of the wintry shadows slowly floated the heron, clever shape-shifter, the yellow circle of her eye staring at me from the side of her tapered face.

The wind was less angry tonight; she played gently with my hair and knocked lightly at the bell on my ankle. The heron came forward and stabbed at my leg, bloodying it, catching the ribbon in her beak. The ribbon came loose; the bell fell away. I was relieved to be free of it, but I warned the heron that Beth would be very angry with her.

The heron gazed at me flatly. *As if she matters at all.*

The wind stilled, agreeing. Above us gleamed the white avenue of the Milky Way, carving a path through the heavens from nothing to nothing. It reminded me of Mother's old white head scarf, tied loosely around her hair. I saw her face then; the stars were her age spots, the lined cliffs of White Bluffs her throat. The Columbia was the black blood coursing from her body, an unending menstruation.

It was primordial and breathtaking.

The heron flapped her wings where she stood, gathering my attention. Her beak pointed east, toward the water.

A woman emerged from the river, shoulders dripping, picking her way up the steep side of the bluff. A baby was wrapped to the front of her chest. She neared a vertical rock wall and rather than find her way around it, she stepped directly onto it, her spine now parallel to the river. I cried out, certain that she and the baby would fall backward, but her feet adhered like a spider's to the stones. She glided up the wall, face to the sky, backside to the water, and then crested a ledge and edged toward me, perpendicular again, her face unreadable in its exhaustion.

The skin sloughed away from the soles of her feet in pale leaves. I scrambled along the ridge and begged for her to sit down on the uneven outcropping, and she did so, gratefully, with a pained moan. Her clothes hung in shreds around her body, as though torn apart by a storm of knives.

"What's happened to us?" she asked, confused, in a language that was not my own but that I could understand perfectly through the vision's soft filter.

I began to say, "I don't know," but the heron squawked and I fell silent.

I heard the heron's calm voice in my head then, and I repeated, "It was the boy made by men."

The words I could give her, even if I didn't understand their meaning.

The baby nursed at the woman's bare breast. Mother thought nursing women were foolish and abnormal, but I leaned in, finding such nuzzling babes darling, symbols of protection and hope. But his face, to my horror, was stabbed through with shards of glass, and he bled profusely from his eyes and nose.

I looked up at the mother in alarm.

"I was on a bus," the woman recalled, loosening the wrap a little to give the baby more room, "and a man offered us his seat. I accepted it, sat down. There was a loud sound. A queer smell. The next thing I knew, I was outside. The bus was ruined, on fire. I looked down at my son, and he smiled up at me. He couldn't feel the broken glass in his face."

He'll die tonight, said the heron.

"But he can't," I protested.

The heron plunged on her tall legs away from me. Something near her moved in the grass and in one deathly swift moment she speared it. An animal screamed.

"He's sucking the poison out of me," the mother said, "so that I can survive."

The heron, behind her, lifted a large rabbit from the grass, bloodied, stunned, and tossed back her head to draw the body farther into her maw.

"Your poor child." I offered to hold the baby for the mother and she shook her head.

These last few hours between mother and child would be excruciating, precious.

The rattlesnake appeared from his den in the earth, slithering toward us across the frozen sponge of ground. He wound up the woman's ankle and onto her thigh. He put his fangs onto her free breast and began to suckle there, too. The woman nursed and wept.

Now only the feet of the rabbit protruded from the heron's beak. Her yellow eye found me.

Here come the other hibakusha.

Scores of people lurched from the icy waves, some of them eerily calm, stunned dumb, others screaming or begging for help. Open wounds leaked blood and pus. The coursing lines of bodies created a gruesome canvas, entire torsos and spines flayed open. The heron's voice, deep and ugly and female, continued,

There will be little help for them.

"But why?" I was angry. "Surely there are doctors, hospitals."

Supplies will run out. Most of the doctors and nurses will be killed or maimed. The hospitals will be obliterated.

A man with emptied eye sockets approached us, his eyeballs having melted down his cheekbones, drizzling now from his chin. He wore a uniform that was oddly pristine given the ruin of his face.

"I can't see," he told me.

These are the lucky ones, the heron said. *The ones who will live.*

"But look at them. Look at their faces."

There are others who seem unscathed but will drop dead within hours.

The man with no eyes pawed at me for a moment. I tried to give him an apology, to tell him, *I have no way to help you*, but he continued to scrabble at me until I stood and shoved him forcefully away. He made a sobbing noise in his throat and then turned his back to me. He returned to the river, waded into its cold belly, and then sank until I could only see the top slope of his head. Maybe the water soothed him like the Lethe, inspiring relief and forgetfulness, however temporary.

"This is a cursed place," I told the heron.

I was used to frank visions of death, gaping mouths and blank eyes and regret like a sharp rock in the throat. But this was different. This was monstrous, incalculable. For the first time in my life I hated my clairvoyance. I remembered the book of Greek tales my father had given to me, the one about Cassandra, the gifted prophet no one believed, the cursed woman who called the house of Atreidae "the shambles for men's butchery, the dripping floor." She was grateful for death; there was no blessing in seeing the damned. I wanted the bejeweled hand of the sky to lower and wipe all of us away. This—the butchery, the dripping floor—was what kingdoms of men did to one another. We were no more than instruments of hatred.

"Make it stop," I said. "I've seen enough."

We showed you the dead, and now we show you the living, the heron replied crossly.

"Please let me go home," I said.

The heron barked at me and then ascended. I was struck by the fetid wind of her. What a gorgeous creature she was, enormous with her serpentine neck, her voluminous gray feathers, the jackknife beak like a primitive stabbing tool.

Follow, she said, looping toward the river.

The wounded and despairing had returned there, too, melting into the water. They lifted their faces and the sky grew heavy with the weight of a thousand pairs of eyes.

The great blue heron wanted me to cross the river. I held up my hands to her. *How?* Her long neck seemed to stretch in annoyance, and she turned back for me. I waited. In the heron, *harpy, chariot,* was the power of my vision refusing to be pinned down. As those wingbeats approached, the sound hurt me; the pressure nearly split my head open. My ears rang and rang.

I closed my eyes. The darkness dropped; the landscape flattened. I was lifted, again. When I opened my eyes the water of the river flowed beneath me, dark and glittering like squid ink, and in it the victims thrashed. From this height it was like they were children, playing in the water. They had all been children once. Some were children now. I hung from the talons of the heron like a broken doll.

The talons let go. I fell onto the gravel of the far bank. While I dusted myself off, making sure I had no broken limbs, the great blue heron waded in the water to hunt. She bayoneted a mountain whitefish. She tossed her head back and choked it down with repulsive jerks. When she was finished, she regarded me sidelong with her cold yellow eye and then flew up the hillside.

I followed her, hiking up a steep trail. I slipped on the ice and banged my knees, cursing my bedroom slippers. My ankle was already scabbing over from where the heron had pierced the skin.

Near the summit of the trail, she waited for me. As I neared she began to tremble and writhe, feathers becoming fur, wings and talons becoming limbs and tail, bird becoming dog. *Aufhocker,* I heard my grandmother say. *They will attack you by the larynx.* Then she was a he, the coyote, glaring at me. He coughed up a bird bone and pricked up his ears, noticing me.

He pressed forward to snuffle one of my slippers.

"Just show me what you need to so I can leave."

The coyote licked softly at my bloodied ankle and then turned, leading me up the hill.

We summited a bluff and I was surprised to find it covered in soft, white sand, as though we'd traveled to an ocean beach. I panted, gripping my hips and bending at the waist to catch my breath. Below was the canyon where the *hibakusha* swam.

Look down, the heron's voice said.

"I am," I said. "I see them all. They're looking at us, aren't they?"

Straight down.

My gaze pulled back from the river. Below me was the sharp pediment, darkly shadowed beneath the white cliffs, bare but for rock and a basalt cornice.

This is where you must go when it all becomes too much.

I went down on my palms and bruised knees, peering over the brutal edge. On the rocks below lay my own body, an exploded treasure chest of rubies and garnets, gems and bones, liquid, solid. Mildred, spilled and shattered.

I shouted into the basin, at the ruin of myself: MILDRED, HELLO.

The ruin began to shimmer and shake and draw itself back together, building a New Me. I watched excitedly. The New Me was beautiful, tall, stately, even, but with a sloped back, like that of an old woman.

When I raised my eyes to the Columbia, the miserable throng of the *hibakusha* was gone. They all rushed with the water toward the future, preparing for their gloomy exhibition.

Beside me, the heron again. She lifted her beak into the air and shrieked mournfully. The sound spooked me. In it, I heard my younger self, my seven-year-old self, shrieking. *Grandmother wakes up, pets me, tells me to go back to sleep.*

The next minute I was caught up in the claws of the heron again, hurtling over the river. I felt a keen sense of fear that I would be dropped into the water. How fragile, really, were my dreams? In the brush of the bank I saw a four-legged animal slipping away over the lip of the ridge, his tail between his legs. The coyote, I recognized, but it seemed too timid to be the animal I'd known. I felt myself split in two at the sight of it, a woman of confidence, a woman of uncertainty. To be both, I worried, meant I was nothing. Too much balance erased identity.

The wind kept me company, whistling in my ears as the vision hurtled me west, over the river and bluff and then down and through the manned gate, the barbed-wire fence. The men stared at nothing with their mulberry eyes.

We moved away from them. We rounded the corner of the line of barracks, quiet and still like the chambers of the dead.

Whatever birdlike creature held me—heron, harpy, demon—now dropped me, roughly, to the earth.

I entered the barracks limping. Something was clearly wrong with my foot. The middle toe was numb, beyond aching, protruding from my body like a dead thing. I hurried clumsily inside, threw out my damaged slippers, and took off my icy clothes. From the small suitcase that served as a makeshift closet beneath my bed, I chose a fresh flannel nightie. I struggled into it, my limbs like lead pipes. I burrowed into my sheets but I couldn't warm up properly, so I rose again to put on my coat. Then I climbed back into bed and thought about fireplaces, warm bricks, hot soup, anything that could warm me from the inside out.

"Milly," came Beth's stern voice from the cot beside me. "I'm so mad at you I could scream."

"I was only—"

"How dare you take off that bell? I've been lying here worried sick for the last two hours. I tried to find you, following your footprints in the frost, but then they just vanished—"

"I went to the bathroom," I whispered. The lie was pathetic, my voice thin and childish. I was exhausted from all I had seen, and I only wanted to sleep, so grateful to be back in the bunk, so cold.

"I could scream," she said again, and I felt burned by the steam of her anger. "You could freeze to death out there."

"I'm not in my right mind when I sleepwalk. I didn't mean for the bell to fall off."

"What am I going to do with you, Milly?"

I didn't like her fed-up tone.

"Quiet down over there," Kathy demanded from a few cots down. "I was dreaming about Van Johnson—*before* his car accident. We were eating a chocolate cake. You've ruined it."

"Go back to sleep," Beth said.

Other girls stirred, too. Beth pressed a palm to her forehead, then stepped out of her cot. The next moment she ordered me to scoot over. I obeyed and she slid in beside me, cursing when my chilly feet grazed her bare shin. My toe, warming, ached horribly. It had been chewed apart by the cold, broken somehow, but Beth's arms went around me and the pain became less important.

"You know they'll send you away, right? You have to stop."

I drew away from her in the bed. A war exploded in me.

How dare you tell me *what to do. How dare you try to limit me.*

But there was also, *I love you please don't leave me alone you're all I have I love you I'll stop I promise I'll stop*—

"I mean it, girls," Kathy said in her cruel, offended tone. "Not another peep."

Beth's eyes glowed black in the dark. Their expression was open and affectionate and not at all hateful. She was supplicating. I could tell from the sentimental downturn of her mouth that she saw her little Annie in my face: She wanted to save me from drowning. I tried to fold my features into the features of her sister, to fit inside them perfectly like a protective shell. I worried one day that she would see me only as Milly, and this would make me no more than another of her ailing flock, a patient to care for at the hospital but to forget the moment work was done.

She reached for my hand and squeezed it and the kindness of this gesture moved me. *Oh, Beth.* How normal she was, and how predictable. I was not. I kept secrets from her. I pitied her. I was filled with power, a power made all the more glorious by my presence here in this place of secrets. It was a terrible power, and I saw only terrible things, but it was power, nonetheless. I gave her a brief nod, indicating that I understood, that I would do anything she asked of me, and she closed her eyes for a long moment, and when she reopened them, she was almost smiling. In this way, we were cleansed.

Then I whispered into Beth's ear that I didn't much like Kathy.

She laughed and whispered back to me, "No one does."

Kathy heard us laughing and said, "Pipe down, you chickens!"

Beth and I sniggered and I felt my body warm and relax, the pain in my ankle a snug irritant, the pain in my toe a deep, relaxing throb.

We fell asleep in each other's arms, Beth and I. Even with the strange sensation in my foot, even with all of the horrors of my vision, it was the best night of sleep of my life.

MERRY AND BRIGHT

The holidays were thrilling at Hanford. I was relieved to not be in Omak. I phoned Mother to inform her that I wouldn't be returning home. I couldn't afford to take even one day off. My presence was essential for the war effort, I told her, and even a few hours away slowed down productivity too much. She feigned indifference.

"So I don't have to listen to your little ferret squeaks across the dinner table," she said. "You've saved me some peace. I should be thanking you, but I won't, since you don't appreciate it, anyway."

But I sensed from a fullness in her tone that she was feeling sentimental; she missed me, too. She told me that Martha was a wretched cook; she dreaded eating a turkey that tasted like it had been soaked in bathwater. She also hated the way Martha folded the napkins, "Like the goddamned Chinamen she folds them, so intricate I can't pry them apart," and that the children never washed their hands properly and left grease marks on the davenport. Still, she paused quite a lot as she complained, as though trying to control her stronger emotions, and I took this as a sign of her love for me.

"Do you wish I was with you, Mother?" I asked her, half-smiling.

"Nope," she said. "Have I told you about my cankers?"

We spoke of her cankers for several minutes, and by the end of our conversation we were both in decent spirits.

"I'll send a very large check this month, Mother," I told her. "Almost my entire Christmas bonus. We all get one. For our excellent service, the government says."

"A bonus won't buy my love, though, you poor ferret face," Mother said.

I told her to quit teasing me. I was a responsible adult now, and I deserved better.

"I don't tease, dear, I tell it like it is. I'm the most honest sort of person. The Lord broke the honesty mold when he made me."

She said it as though to hurt me, but I knew she was in a good mood if she was flattering herself.

"Now, if you were honest like I am, young lady, you would tell your old sick mother what it is you're doing at Hanford. Or haven't you a clue?"

I laughed nervously. I hated when she pried like this. I wanted to prove to her that the work I was doing was real and powerful, but I knew better than to disclose anything important.

"Mother, you know I can't. Mum's the word."

"You haven't a loyal bone in your body, Mildred. If you had, you never would have left me the way you did. I think they don't tell you anything there because they don't respect you. I think—"

"No one knows anything, Mother," I said, and the shrillness in my voice hurt my own ears. "No one knows what we're doing."

"I could phone them and tell them, you know," she said then. "There are numbers a person can call. I could tell them what you told me the last time."

"I didn't tell you anything," I said, but my stomach roiled. I struggled to remember our conversation. *She would do it. I know she would.*

"About the weapon. The product. That's more than I've heard

anywhere else." A sucking sound, the sound she made when worrying a licorice wheel with her tongue. "That would send you back home, wouldn't it?"

I closed my eyes and put my right palm against the cold windowpane, steeling myself with the sensation of cold. I pictured releasing Mother into the river, the immediate sense of joy and horror I'd felt at the letting go of her, of witnessing her topple away from me into the rock-stippled waters. When I opened my eyes, there was the glass phone booth, the cheerful, decorated storefronts of downtown Richland, the hazy streetlamps glowing kindly behind the smoke of my blue breath.

"Mother, don't do it, please. If you have any love for me at all."

"If I had any love for you, I'd bring you home," she said. I heard her speak to someone else, holding the mouthpiece away from her, "Now stop it. Wait your turn."

It was my sister, scrabbling to speak with me. Mother muttered that she was a meddlesome magpie, but she handed the phone over.

"I'm not surprised you're staying in Hanford," Martha said, "deserter that you are. Now what's this about a bonus?"

I told her, and she listened reasonably.

"Well, I do hope you mean it that you'll send the whole thing. The three girls are in need of good winter boots. They've been losing toe-nails all season because their boots are all a year old. And Timothy, surely you remember Timothy—"

"Martha, please, don't be dramatic. I've only been gone a few months."

"He's the boy, my oldest, the one with freckles and brown hair and jaundiced eyes. Not that you care which one he is, seeing how you quit being his aunt. Anyway, he wants to play baseball come spring and the price of the gear is nothing to sneeze at—"

"Of course, Martha, I'll send the check soon."

"And we'd like a gift for each of them this year, maybe two, even, and while I can't promise we won't be angry with you still, I can certainly say that we will stop telling your nieces and poor Tim that their aunt is as good as dead."

"You surely haven't—"

"And one more thing: Please don't go and make Walter feel so unmanned. We hate it when you rub your money in his face."

I waited a moment, expecting Walter to rush to my defense, but there was only a long silence.

I'll send whatever you want. Just so long as no one makes a phone call, just so long as I can stay put.

"So, dear," my sister said, and I was warmed by the sudden generosity of her tone, "what do you want for Christmas?"

How wonderful it would be to receive a package in the mail! I rushed forward, stupidly, to say, "I've been eyeing this pair of shoes in the Roebuck catalog that are a ringer for Susan Peters's shoes, do you remember, the ones we saw her wear in Spokane? Remember when I said, 'Why, those shoes would make any gal look pretty!' I thought I'd take a little money from the bonus and—"

Martha clucked her tongue. "As selfish as ever," she said. "I'm not surprised. And all for a silly starstruck pair of shoes."

I stuttered for a response, chiding myself for my boldness. She was right, I knew. I was selfish. I'd up and left them—just like that, without warning—and they'd had no choice but to accept the fate I'd forced on them. I cheered myself by thinking they missed me, that their annoyance with me was no more than misplaced grief. For a moment the sight of Martha loping down the embankment flashed in my mind: her panicked eyes and widened nostrils, her loose hair, her thick arms and strong thighs pumping in her good Sunday dress. She had blown right by me as though I'd been invisible. In that moment, my presence hung in a peaceful limbo between the act and the reckoning. I was not yet seen, or judged. I was still, for one bare ephemeral moment, a good person.

I would send them all of the money. I would listen to their complaints. They could have done anything to me, sent me away to a state hospital, put me in a woman's prison, but they hadn't, they'd simply trapped me in my childhood home. My mother threatened to report me but she wouldn't. Right? She couldn't. They were trying their best to forgive me.

Still, the conversation disquieted me.

"It was just a silly wish," I told her. "I'll send you all of the money. I will."

She took the receiver away from her mouth and said, just loudly enough so that I could hear, "Mother, you're right, she'll never grow up."

There was a long silence. I stayed upbeat.

"Merry Christmas," I said, but no one replied.

The line was dead.

NIGHT OF DEMONS

Christmas arrived with its spidery web of frost draped across the flatland, the colorless mountains garlanded with bands of fresh snow. As I waited for the cattle car at the encampment, my toes and heels froze into hard wooden knobs. They thawed later at my little desk in Dr. Hall's office, wet and throbbing in Mother's pinching shoes. My frostbitten toe alternately tingled and burned. I didn't mind the sensations. It was how my mind felt when I was in the middle of a profound vision.

Unit B was warm and loud and comforting. The roar of the Columbia's waters through the motor-driven pumps soothed me. I relaxed into it the way I imagined a baby relaxes into the commotion of her mother's womb. We worked tremendous hours then, twelve per day, hurriedly increasing output of the product. From what I learned in the meetings Dr. Hall hosted with Colonel Matthias, Mr. Farmer, and the various DuPont managers, production was proceeding smoothly. Dr. Hall marveled over the flawlessness of it.

"Sure, there was that little hiccup in the beginning. But after that, we've sailed along beautifully. Hardly a hitch! It almost makes me nervous. This unit is the first of its kind, Miss Groves. It's miraculous how flawless it all is."

I beamed with pride when I heard this, as if I, myself, had helped design the unit, with its awe-inspiring symmetry, its tubes and gears and pumps and blocks, its tense precision and monstrosity. *I've contributed to its greatness.* But when I blinked, an image flashed on the black leather of my eyelids: the dark harpy feathers, the baleful eyes of the heron, the nursing mother with her baby of shattered glass.

What are we making here? What dark force encourages its perfection?

I guarded my thoughts. I nursed them quietly. I was too grateful for the work, for my status, to put my job at risk. I hated myself for my selfishness, but there it was.

On Christmas morning, Dr. Hall asked me if I'd like a tour of the facility. My typewriter was tipped over onto its backside, my hands stained with ink. I was applying Nutype cleaner onto the ribbon and gummed-up keys.

"This very moment?" I said.

I showed him my inky fingers.

"I have an hour before the colonel stops in. Would you like to know more about the unit?"

I was surprised to even be asked. I mentioned that I thought it wasn't allowed.

"I can't show you all of it, of course, but I'm itching to share some of its workings with you. After all, it's Christmas Day! Consider it a gift. You've done well here, you deserve it. Wash up and then I'll share some of the unit's secrets."

I smiled and agreed, humbled by the request. It delighted me that he thought I was instrumental to Unit B's success.

I hurried to the restroom. I had to pee, and, unsurprisingly, the stall was empty. I locked the door behind me, pulled up my skirt, unfastened my girdle. I'd been holding it in all morning, my bladder as taut as a rubber ball. I released the pressure, taking a long moment, listening to my own pointed stream and to the faint rushing of the water through the core room. I'd peeked into that room before and was awed with the symmetry and height of the graphite pile. It stood taller and wider than a movie screen, towering four stories high, a manufactured marvel made more astonishing by the two thousand aluminum process tubes that punctuated its face. They held slugs of the substance Dr. Hall referred to as "metal." They were key, he'd noted, in creating the product. I thought maybe the water from the river was there to cleanse the product, but at this suggestion, Dr. Hall had shaken his head.

"No, Miss Groves," he'd said. "It's there to cool it."

"Cool what?" I'd asked him.

"The reaction."

"What reaction?"

"Our entire location was chosen because of that big river out there. Our very success depends on the water of the Columbia."

In this way I received informational puzzle pieces about Hanford's product, but I never figured out how to fit them properly together to answer my questions. I wasn't upset by this. I worried that if I learned too much, I wouldn't be able to keep my mouth shut, especially with Mother. I didn't trust myself where Mother was concerned; I never would. Now that she'd threatened to report me, I barely spoke during our phone calls, despite being hammered by her questions.

But I knew more than most. The visions kept no secrets from me.

An awesome weapon. A weapon that kills indiscriminately. A weapon that generates so much heat, it melts eyeballs from their sockets.

I shook myself. *Stop it. Stop flattering yourself. You're not some sort of prophet.*

I pulled off a square of toilet paper from the roll. Just as I went to flush, I heard the door open and then close. There was a small rap on the side of the stall where I sat, not quite a knock but close enough for me to assume someone's impatience.

"Hello?" I said. "This stall's occupied. I'm almost finished."

There was a shuffling noise, as though someone had a dog on a leash, and then, after a moment, a heavy object slammed into the stall door.

The sound upset me. "Wait just one minute," I said. "I'll be out soon."

It wasn't rare for other women to come to Unit B, even if I was one of the only permanent female staff. There was a laundress who came a few times a week, and there was a maid who dusted the offices and dials in the evenings. There were a handful of other women who delivered or retrieved packages and messages. There was even a female physicist, a recent hire that filled me with a tremendous curiosity. I had yet to meet her, but the rumor was that Unit B's restroom was there only because of Mr. Farmer's respect for her. Simply put, women came and went at Hanford. I heard from someone at Human Resources that we were less likely to leave than the men, and this didn't surprise me: We were built for endurance. We tolerated poor treatment, haphazard accommodations, and tedious weather with little complaint. Tolerance of abuse was threaded into our bones. Men believed they were too good for certain treatment, but we'd been told for generations that we were not.

All this is to say: I would have welcomed a woman's presence in the restroom, even if she had seemed impatient and violent and impolite, pounding on the stall and refusing to speak to me. But I didn't hear the click of a woman's pumps on the floor, and I didn't smell a woman's perfume, and what I heard and smelled instead—the *tip-tap* of claws, the wet pine scent of animal fur—alerted me to a different creature entirely.

It snuffled against the baseboards.

I flushed the toilet and refastened myself, smoothing down my skirt, careful not to get ink on the fabric. I had yet to wash my hands.

"Who are you?" I said again.

A long brown snout pushed under the narrow slat of the stall door.

It was the coyote. I found it strange that I was caught up in a vision so suddenly, without warning. There was no ringing in my ears, no ponderous beating of wings, no dizzy spells or headaches. But I saw the coyote's eyes then, yellow, as round and strong as planets. The heron's eyes.

The canine drew back his lips in a snarl and then retreated.

A loud knock rattled the big door to the restroom. "Anyone in there?" a voice called.

"Occupied," I said.

"Janitor here, ma'am. Take your time. I'll wait."

I opened the stall door and washed my hands. The animal brushed by my legs and slipped into the stall behind me.

"You," I whispered harshly. "Come out of there."

His big fluffy tail beat the floor.

"Ma'am?" the voice in the hallway said. "You say something in there?"

"Just a second," I called.

I opened the door. Stanley stood there. I hadn't seen him up close since my vision of his beating. We both winced, taking stock of each other. I could guess what he thought of me now, after all that I'd predicted for him. I'd never been thanked for sharing a vision, only reviled. Stanley's pained expression, his physical recoiling, was familiar to me. He hated me, maybe even more than he hated his attackers. He blamed the messenger. I thought of the meadowlark, the feeling that I'd somehow made it happen. I was more at fault than I realized.

The assault had been severe. Stanley was greatly changed. They had caved in one of his cheekbones. Part of his left ear was gone. I remembered what his sister had said about him being a talented welder. I had a ridiculous thought that maybe he could weld the ear back onto his head.

"Hello, Stanley," I said.

"Hello, Miss Groves." His voice was strained. "You all finished in there?"

"Yes," I said. "But I——" I wanted to say, *I need to warn you*, but I feared what he would say to me if I repeated such a thing to him. Instead, I blurted out, "There's a coyote."

"A coyote?" Stanley looked at me puzzled for a moment and then grinned, meanly, showing his broken teeth. "You think I'm a fool, Miss Groves."

"He's there," I said. "In the stall. Just—be careful."

His smile thinned. He stepped around me and put his palm on the heavy wooden door, pressing it open. He peered into the room for a moment and then I heard him gasp.

I told you, I wanted to say, but didn't.

"Good grief." Stanley turned around and looked at me with visible irritation. "What's the matter with you women? Can't you clean up after yourselves?"

He muttered something under his breath and turned back toward the supply closet, leaving his mop and bucket in the hallway.

Nonplussed, I pushed open the door. The stall was unrecognizable, the floor and toilet covered in blood.

"Where are you?"

I found the coyote skulking beside the toilet, nosing a small object on the floor. I crouched down to get a better look. It was a creature, curling into itself like a large mealworm. The thing had eyes on its stomach and a featureless face. The limbs were half-formed, the brain visible from a cleft skull. It was small like a newborn goat but had no fur. A small purple heart beat furtively, unevenly, beneath a thin layer of translucent pink skin. Whatever it was, it would soon be dead.

"What is it?"

The coyote rested his yellow eyes on me. The voice of the heron, then,

A thing born on the night of demons. A lamb, but not a lamb.

"Put it out of its misery."

From a litter of monsters.

"You shouldn't be here," I said. "Why did you bring this here?"

The coyote scooped up the creature in his mouth, the ball of demented goo that it was, and then slipped slyly from the stall.

I followed him into the hallway, crying, "Shoo, shoo!"

The canine dove like a falcon into the hallway, skidding around the corner just as Stanley returned from the supply closet. He shook his head as he walked, disapproving of me. He held a bottle of bleach in one gloved hand, ammonia in the other.

"It wasn't my fault," I told him. "It's not my blood."

"Whatever you say, Miss Groves." He had a resolved look on his face. Neither of our opinions would be taken seriously if he spoke to a supervisor. I could sense he didn't want to cause trouble for himself.

"I have to get back to Dr. Hall," I said.

"We both have work to do."

Stanley grimaced, entering the restroom. The door swung closed and I was alone. A few scant droplets of blood led from the restroom down the hallway where Coyote had run with his demon. I didn't follow them. I returned to Dr. Hall.

I told Dr. Hall I was ready for the tour, remaining on my feet as I said so. I assumed he would guide me to the door and then to the core room, but instead he urged me, eagerly, to sit.

I waited patiently in the chair while he finished his work.

"Almost done with this, Miss Groves. Just had to tweak a few things from the original."

I peeked at the sheet of paper in front of him. It was filled with neat, straight rectangles and squares. He wrote tiny, inscrutable words inside all of them. In the top corner I read, *Unit B, based on Chicago Pile-1 by E. Fermi, ne. Mr. Farmer.*

With a grunt of satisfaction, Dr. Hall twirled the sheet of paper so that it faced me. Leaning over so that I could smell the coffee and mint on his breath, he said, "Let's begin in the entry hall, shall we? From there we'll see the charging area, the discharge elevators, and the inner room. Beyond that is the labyrinth."

"Labyrinth?"

"Yes, it's a corridor that buckles to and fro and blocks the dangerous effects of radiation." He stopped himself here, perhaps noting my quizzical expression. "You must not, of course, mention any of this to anyone."

"Of course not. I never would." I said this firmly, but I badly wanted to know what caused the radiation. *Heat,* I thought. *From the product? Testing it or creating it or . . . ?*

He continued, "We'll finish with the control room, which you can see right through the windows here. I can't go in depth about what it all is, but it will be nice for you to know a little bit more about our castle here."

Labyrinth. Castle. I was the princess, searching for her knight. It was a romantic dream. And somewhere, I thought, somewhere deep within, a monster. A newborn demon.

And then as Dr. Hall droned on, I realized he didn't mean to show me any of it, not in person. He only meant to tell me about it.

He was describing the purpose of the discharge elevators when I interrupted him. "Is this the whole tour? Looking at this piece of paper?"

He smiled at me condescendingly. "Miss Groves, it would not be prudent for us to interrupt the progress being made today. It would also be unsafe."

"Just to look at it?"

"In some instances, you would be dead within moments."

I thought about the cases Beth had seen at the clinic, chemical burns, injured lungs, a man's eyesight damaged by mysterious vapors. In each of these occurrences, Beth said, the men had not been following proto-col. Most of the workers here visited a changing house before they came to work, donning equipment meant to protect them from whatever it was they were assigned to handle. Even the men in the control room had started wearing white all-body suits and shiny hard hats. I was beginning to feel naked in my work dress and stockings and tight shoes.

But the safest place is always the center of the storm.

"There is one place I can show you," Dr. Hall said. "Follow me, Miss Groves."

He led me down the entry hallway where the men had stomped the meadowlark to death. The walls were clean, emptied of anything but the drab olive paint that was used for all army facilities at the time, but when I blinked the blood flashed there, the guts and innards and feath-ers smashed into a gelatinous pudding. I followed Dr. Hall around the corner to the large doorway where a beacon whirled, flashing red. Beneath it was the incomprehensible lit-up sign,

MONITORING—REQUIRED

SPLINE REMOVAL

START UP

CRANE OPERATING

"Have you seen the pile yet, Miss Groves?"

"Oh, yes, before it went critical, as you put it. I was awestruck."

"It's massive, isn't it? Larger and taller than most homes."

"My house in Omak could fit in its foyer, sir."

"This morning we heard excellent news. This product you've heard
so much about? We've executed our first successful slugs of it today. And
you know what this means, of course. The war will soon be over, Miss
Groves."

I gasped. "What wonderful news!"

Despite my fears of the product, or maybe even because of them, I
swelled with pride. I had gone from caretaker of Mother to caretaker
of the world. I was a happy little cog in the machinery of Unit B, small
but necessary. Without my singular effort, the product wouldn't exist.
We all had a vital part to play here, and shame on those who felt otherwise.

The product! I pictured it as a brown poisonous sludge, then as a disas-
trous ray of light, and then as a dark, cloaked hero with knives for
hands. The Germans would cower in terror. My mind swarmed and in
it waved the limbs of the ruined people I'd seen in the river.

"The product is born," Dr. Hall said, smiling. "The merriest Christmas gift of all, Miss Groves."

"It must be very powerful," I said.

"Over here, to the right," he said, and opened a door into a small
room. There were a few white suits hanging there, and a suitcase marked
with red stencils, TOURNIQUET AND SAFETY KIT.

He opened a door on the other side of the room and went through it.

"Wow," I shouted when we passed into the cavernous valve pit room.
It was noisy. My shout hardly registered. We stood on a bridge of metal

overlooking a waterfall of stairs and gangplanks. The valves were like humongous steering wheels designed for an armada of giants.

"This is where we process water lines and water analyses," Dr. Hall called back to me over the noise.

I admired the view, putting my hands on the railing. It wasn't a full tour, but it was still new to me, austere and beautiful. At my side, Dr. Hall reached over to pat my arm in a contented manner, and I accepted it the way a lover might, with a tingling at the base of my spine.

But there was the coyote, lurking behind one of the valves. I looked in a panic at Dr. Hall, but he hadn't seen him. The physicist walked in the other direction, toward a worker standing at a basin with a clipboard in his hand, and he began speaking to the man good-naturedly.

There was no sight of the lamb. I assumed it was dead now, nudged into a corner somewhere within the reactor.

The coyote padded over to me, tongue hanging out of his mouth. Those yellow, wheeling eyes.

There is a way to destroy all of this.

"Leave me alone," I said. "I'm working. You'll get me in trouble."

It would take one mere, small error to cause a fire. It would set back the project for years. I can tell you what to do—

I listened irritably, hearing the instructions without committal.

—jam slugs, drop them here but not here, combine these metals, you'll find them here, start a SCRAM by messing with the panel-lit gauges.

"What we're doing here is good," I argued. "We'll win the war."

The animal growled and nipped at my ankles. It tickled more than it hurt, but I kicked him angrily away.

Then came a shout.

It was Dr. Hall.

"Get that animal out of here!"

The man in the suit came forward, frowning in his hard hat, clapping his hands at the coyote.

"Out," he said. "Get out!"

They see him. It's not just me.

Coyote put his tail between his legs and ran for the door. It opened right as he reached it, pushed ajar by another worker, and he flew through it. Dr. Hall and the man sprinted after him and I followed, pumping my legs.

Coyote struck a northern path along the hallway, dodged right, flew past Dr. Hall's office, and came to the entry door where we clocked in and out. He skidded to a halt there, trapped, and turned to us, arching his back and snarling.

"Get him out of here," Dr. Hall said again.

The men hesitated, nervous about approaching a wild dog.

"There's a rifle in my office," Dr. Hall said, and one of the workers turned to fetch it.

The yellow eyes bored into me.

Let us out.

Dr. Hall watched the dog in terror; he likely feared the product's contamination more than he feared being bitten. I hurried forward and reached over the coyote's trembling body to open the dense steel door. The wind yowled coldly at me, scrabbling at my skirt. The animal raced into the whiteout and I let the door slam shut behind him.

When I turned, Dr. Hall was watching me strangely. "Thank you, Miss Groves."

"You weren't afraid of that mangy mutt?" one of the workers said.

Another worker returned with the rifle. This made me laugh.

You can't kill an aufhocker, my grandmother once told me. *You can scare them away, but they'll always return.*

"Where'd it go?" the man with the rifle demanded.

Dr. Hall accepted the firearm from him. "Miss Groves saved the day," he said.

I asked about the remainder of the tour.

"We've seen quite enough for today." Then, after a moment, "How did that animal get in here? Can you two please check the other doors, make sure they aren't ajar?"

A couple of men nodded, hurrying away. Dr. Hall ordered the rest of us back to work.

I thought of the lamb, the hunk of breathing meat that the coyote had shown me, a fetus ruined by some unknowable force. We reentered the office, and I went over to my little desk but then stopped and turned.

I asked him, with more worry in my voice than I intended, "How dangerous is the product? How at risk are we of being harmed?"

Startled, Dr. Hall looked up at me. His expression slid from surprise to annoyance to condescension.

"Of course you've heard me speak about the safety regulations here," he said. "You realize the efforts we've taken."

"But we're ignoring those regulations—"

"Because we've been ordered to, Miss Groves, and because we have a bigger battle at hand. The truth is, we don't yet know what will happen."

"Farm animals," I said. *The night of demons.* "Produce. The organs of any person eating the food. We're poisoning the very soil."

Dr. Hall, to my surprise, laughed. "Are you a scientist, Miss Groves? You have quite the brain for it." He wiped at his eyes beneath the frames of his glasses. "Look, Mildred, if I may be candid in this moment, I do enjoy working with you. You're not a dummy. You do what I say the second I say it and you don't complain. You ask questions that I find annoying but that are also interesting to me, scientifically. Your line of questioning right now is one that my colleagues and I are considering. Please trust that we aim only to win the war, not to harm ourselves. That's not to say, of course, there aren't dangers in this business, it's just to say the benefits greatly outweigh the risks. So please don't worry about these matters. Do what you do best: Duck your head, do your work, be respectful. You'll go far for a woman, I think, as long as you can remain steady."

"Remain steady," I said, and I really did want to, but as I turned back to my desk, I stepped awkwardly onto my frostbitten toe, and a thunderbolt of pain rocketed from my feet to my jaw. I winced and nearly cried out, but as quickly as the pain hit me, it passed.

Dr. Hall didn't notice. Instead, he gestured at my messy desk. "You forgot about your typewriter."

"I'll clean it up straightaway," I said.

I sat in the stiff wooden chair and finished applying the cleaner, and then I righted the typewriter and went to wash my hands again in the lavatory. As I walked a disturbing tune whistled through my head,

LOYAL MILDRED GROVES

LOYAL MILDRED GROVES

A LAMB WITH NO LIMBS

AND A LAMB WITH NO NOSE.

I was relieved to find the bathroom spotless and clean. Stanley had been very thorough. I wondered where the lamb-that-was-not-a-lamb was now. Being digested? The *aufhocker* would eat anything.

When I went back to the office, Dr. Hall stood at the big picture window, admiring the precision and orderliness of the control room. Two men busied themselves with the examination of buttons and dials. It was a world that made imminent sense, a man-made triumph that could be controlled and calculated and understood.

This, I realized, was why I put so much hope in Hanford.

What if I let the coyote in, I thought, watching Dr. Hall's back in his tan, worsted wool jacket. *Just like I let in the meadowlark?*

See, breathe, come to life.

My own world could never be explained.

WEDDING DRESS

The holidays came and went, and those of us who stayed at Hanford, the vast majority, as it turned out, worked long, twelve-hour shifts but were then treated to exciting events by the commissary, boxing matches and variety shows and even a circus troupe. On New Year's Eve they fattened us with endless flowing beer and heaping plates of food, ham and biscuits and gravy. I ate so much that the top button of my skirt popped off, and I had to hurry back to the barracks and repair it before the dancing began. When I returned, I danced with Tom Cat. I tried flirting, but I wasn't very good at it, and neither was he. He seemed distant and sad. He was, unlike me, homesick. He said he wasn't feeling well and when he left early I decided to leave, too.

That evening I dreamed I was in a chapel, standing next to Tom Cat in a dark wedding dress; it dripped with a wet, heavy liquid. Tom Cat briefly put his hands on my hips and they came away stained with blood. He lifted his palms to show me and beamed proudly. *It's wonderful to have our child right here*, he said, and the audience watching us broke into applause. I looked for our child but there was only a dark spider on the floor, circling a pool of blood near my feet. In the front pew sat

Gordon, and next to him, radiantly beautiful, was Beth. She dabbed at her misty eyes and mouthed, *Lover's leap.*

I woke remembering that red was the color of love. *It wasn't necessarily a nightmare,* I told myself, although the unease of it dug into my bones, swelling my joints. It seemed inevitable to me now that Tom Cat and I would be married. *Think of it as a good thing. This is what upstanding young women do, marry, have children, domesticate. I've been told so my whole life.* He would be as good a husband as any.

Later that day, when I saw him at the mess hall, we shook hands in a jocose manner and my right hand came away wet. I turned it over. My palm was smeared with blood.

"Mildred," Tom Cat exclaimed. "You're hurt!"

His own hands were as clean as a newly washed sheet. He retrieved a wet rag from a waitress and used it to wipe the blood from my palm. There was a gash across the entire pad of my thumb, shallow but long.

"I must have cut it," I said. "I must have sliced it on something."

On my dream, I thought, and I shivered.

"Must have been my own bones," he said, and laughed, and I laughed, too, because there was something true to that, really. He pressed the rag to my palm and went with me to the clinic, where they wrapped my hand in gauze.

Beth walked by as one of her colleagues attended to my hand. She carried a pile of clean sheets.

"What happened?" she asked, pausing in the doorway of our examination room.

"We're not sure," Tom Cat said. "Mildred cut her hand. Not much deeper than a paper cut, but it bled some."

Beth gave me a hard look. I held my chin high. *I didn't do anything. I've been good.*

Beth softened. She looked at Tom Cat with gratitude. "I'm glad you're taking care of her."

"It's nothing," Tom Cat said. "I like being with her is all."

Beth smiled at him. I read it all in her face: She pictured a wedding, too. But what she pictured wasn't like the wedding in my dream. She envisioned an ivory dress, pastel cakes, a golden cross, a bouquet of dahlias. She couldn't know that the dress was red, blood red, and the blood would only touch me, it wouldn't affect Tom Cat in the faintest.

I remembered the spider on the floor, circling the pool of blood—how easy a creature it would be to destroy.

There were children at Hanford. Not a lot of them, but a few. Some of the men brought their families to live here, although most didn't stay for long. I enjoyed seeing the youngsters around the campus, decorating the mess halls and the small, makeshift school with their funny drawings of snowmen and Santa and Jesus. In their faces was the light of the season; you could smell the excitement haloing them, the aroma of sugar cookies and cinnamon.

I didn't buy myself the footwear I wanted. For the rest of the season I would wear Mother's pinching shoes and my old boots with the patched soles, and I was fine with it, having sent almost all of my money to Martha and Mother. For the most part I was comfortable enough, except for the frostbitten toe, which had gone numb and registered no sensation now other than a foreign dullness.

"You've damaged the nerve," Beth said.

I tried to tell her it wasn't my fault, but she rolled her eyes in response, a cold thing to do, and she urged me to take some responsibility for myself.

"He's asked about you, you know. The doctor. He wants to make sure you're mentally sound. I've told him you're as healthy as a plump pear."

I noted her insulting tone. She told this to me as though wanting me to argue with her. I didn't. I just smiled and thanked her.

She watched me for a moment and then said, sighing, "Of course you're just fine. And that's what I keep saying."

I *was* grateful to her, but I didn't like the suggestion that I was being watched.

"He checks in with Dr. Hall, too."

"What?" The notion panicked me. "He can't do that."

"He has to, Milly. There's so much at stake here, he says. He has to follow up with all potential head cases. If it weren't for Dr. Hall and me, you'd have been fired already."

This comforted me. It meant Dr. Hall had fought for me.

"Dr. Hall likes you," she confirmed. "He told the doctor that while you're certainly naive, you're quick to learn and as loyal as a mutt. He doesn't usually trust his secretaries, he said, but there's something different about you. He admires your candor and, oh, what did he call it . . . your *inquisitiveness*. But that's what makes them nervous. They're letting people go for asking too many questions."

"I can't lose this job, Beth," I said. "I can't go back to Omak."

"Of course you can't," Beth said, and whatever coldness she'd shown me evaporated. She hugged me, quickly, firmly. "But please take care of yourself, Milly. If there is any other strangeness, I'll feel very guilty for hiding it."

I assured her: I would be nothing more than Boring Old Milly, and the affectionate look she gave me almost convinced me that I could suppress my powers.

I'd had no sleepwalking incidents since the night of the *hibakusha*, and the valerian helped me relax in the evening. But every now and again I woke with a feeling that my feet were sore, or I'd have a scrape on my cheek or hands as though I'd been bouldering the basalt cliffs near the river, and I'd wonder if I was still meandering about, but clandestinely, somehow, unbeknownst even to me. I worried about what the heron said to me without my remembering. But then, maybe I was safer this way. I let it go. It was better for these secrets to unfurl in the darkness.

At work, Dr. Hall kept me busy. He didn't like it when I sat around fidgeting, so he piled my desk with papers. He had me shorthand all of his phone calls and interviews with his important men. When Mr. Farmer arrived, speaking heavily with his Italian accent, Dr. Hall urged me to curtsy. As calm and collected as Dr. Hall always was, I could tell that he was falling over himself to impress Mr. Farmer, and he didn't fail. When Mr. Farmer readied to leave after a day of intense discussions, the two men shook hands and, for a moment, Mr. Farmer refused to let go.

"I'm impressed with you, Phillip," he said to Dr. Hall. "Your head is in the right place. Try to see that your heart is there, too."

Dr. Hall's usually calm expression fluttered for a moment. He said, modestly, "What do you mean?"

"I mean that Albert and I want what's best for the people. All people. Not just the ones here, but worldwide. Yes, even our enemies. That's why this implement is so important. It's meant to stop violence, not create more of it. Do you see?"

He smiled encouragingly at Dr. Hall and Dr. Hall nodded.

"The general says we're making great gains there," Dr. Hall said. "If we don't hurry up, we won't even need the blasted thing." He laughed. "What a waste of effort and expense that would be!"

Mr. Farmer was silent for a long moment, looking at Dr. Hall curiously. The men had been holding on to each other's hands this entire time, in a friendly, confidential manner, but now Farmer let go.

"Maybe it's for the better," Mr. Farmer said, but there was a note of longing in his voice.

"I've been asked," Dr. Hall said, "to hurry along the production, whatever it takes, no matter the safety measures. This pushes more waste downriver."

"I suspect downriver won't suffer to the extent that the environment downwind will suffer," Mr. Farmer said. "Have you seen the steam rising from the smokestack? We thought the wind would diffuse it all— it's certainly persistent enough—but the vapor hangs on like a stubborn woman."

"We're doing what they tell us," Dr. Hall said. "We really have no choice."

The men were silent for a minute, standing together philosophically with their arms crossed.

"War is a terrible thing," Farmer said gravely.

"I'm guilty of wanting to see what will happen."

"We'll all be guilty, if this is handled poorly."

Mr. Farmer nodded kindly at Dr. Hall and then turned for the door. On his way out, he stopped before me and I nodded at him modestly.

"You seem like a sweet girl," Mr. Farmer said in his lilting Italian accent. He turned to Dr. Hall. "She's an able secretary, no?"

"Miss Groves is as discreet as a stone," Dr. Hall said.

"Secrecy and safety," I said. "So very paramount."

Mr. Farmer beamed at me. "A very good girl."

He congratulated Dr. Hall, as though he were my father, as though he had formed me out of clay from the riverbed.

"She doesn't disappoint," Dr. Hall said.

I lowered my eyes. "You're all very kind."

I was blushing, caught up in the heat of a flattering moment, but I wasn't feeling as bashful as I seemed. I struggled to swallow a roar of triumph.

What a frightening roar it would be.

It would tear the coats right off their backs.

LOVEBIRDS

For a long time, I was calm.

Other Hanford residents were not.

One day in early spring I waited for Tom Cat at the cattle car stop. Lately we'd taken to sitting together and mutually ignoring Gordon's blustery stories. A week earlier the driver had swerved, avoiding a deer that had lurched into the road from behind a scabby boulder. We were all jolted and I gave a surprised shout. Tom Cat grabbed my hand and squeezed my fingers tightly. "We're okay," he told me, and I bit my tongue to avoid telling him, *I know.* We held hands the rest of the way. *A good husband. Something every young woman needs.* I tried to banish my earlier premonitions of the meadowlark in his rib cage, of the red wedding gown.

I thought instead of our future visits to Omak, how we would endure Martha and Mother together, forming a team against them. We'd have a curly-haired daughter named Susan and a sweet-natured little boy we'd call Harold, after my father. My daydreams, I mused, were so much more pleasant than my visions. They made the sweat and weight of Tom Cat's hand tolerable. When we left the bus that day, Tom Cat gave me a warm smile and I went up on my tiptoes to kiss him quickly on the cheek. It wasn't like me to do such a thing, but I wanted to show my gratitude.

You and me against Mother and Martha. I didn't care that I was getting ahead of myself.

"Lay off it, lovebirds," Gordon had said, laughing cruelly—he saw us as two poorly told jokes.

Now it was March, and I waited for Tom Cat and the cattle car, standing awkwardly in my spring jacket and my mother's pinching shoes. I'd decided to order the new shoes in May, just in time for summer. How pretty they'd be on my feet! Tom Cat would approve, I was sure of it.

Gordon arrived. I wasn't very happy to see him. He always stood too close to me, and sometimes he guided me around by the arm in a commanding way that embarrassed me. He grinned when he saw me and complimented me on my lipstick. It was the same tube I'd purchased in Omak, the *whore's color,* as Mrs. Brown had described it. I always dotted it on sparingly, with my pinky finger, and even Beth had told me how pretty and adult it made me look.

"I'm waiting for Tom Cat," I told Gordon, half-hoping this would encourage him to leave me alone.

"Good ol' Tom. Poor kid. He's smitten with you, isn't he?"

"He's a friendly person."

"Modesty becomes you, Milly," Gordon said sarcastically, and then pointed. "Here he comes now. But who's the sad sack with him?"

I turned, smiling, and saw Tom Cat's stubby, strong figure moving toward us. He was slightly backlit by the morning sun. Beside him walked another man, ambling jumpily with a frightening grin, a show of broken teeth. My alarm grew as the two men approached.

Tom Cat put an arm around me, trying to steer me away, clearly believing this man to be dangerous, but I withdrew, overcome with curiosity. Crooked, bungling, the man moved like a broken pull toy.

It took me a moment to recognize him. It was Stanley Johnson. I hadn't seen him since he'd cleaned up the coyote's blood in Unit B. Almost immediately following, he'd accepted a transfer to an outdoor position at a new reactor being built a mile or so away. To get away from me, I'd presumed.

Now he stood before us barefoot, dressed only in his pajamas. His pants and person were bemired, as if he'd spent a week sleeping outdoors. His grin faded, seeing me.

"Well, if it isn't Miss Groves," he said.

I tried to say hello, but my voice caught in my throat.

"What's your beef, Stan?" Gordon asked.

"Never felt better," Stanley said. "I've been troubled by the wind, you see, but this morning, I just decided if you can't beat her, join her!"

He unbuttoned his pajama top and withdrew it from his shoulders. The sun magnified the scars, the brokenness of his face, his severed ear. I pitied him. The wind birched at his skin and he laughed like a little boy. I put my hand up to my eyes to shield them from the whipping sand. He sang and outstretched his arms and floated with the wind like it was a dancing partner. Gordon lumbered forward, cursing, and tried to stuff Stanley's arms back into his shirt.

"You're making a damn fool of yourself, Stan," he said. "You're in front of a lady. Cover up, for crissakes."

But Stanley shook Gordon away and began to strip off his pants. Tom Cat left my side and went to help Gordon.

"Leave me alone, you goddamn bullies," Stanley cried, and his shrill voice frightened me more than the shed pajamas.

I threaded through the jostling men and put my hand on Stanley's forearm. "Stan," I said. "I know about the wind, how cruel she can be. But don't let her take you over, she's only as powerful as you—"

"You're the worst of all of them," he said to me, yanking his arm away. "Stay away from me, witch."

Tom Cat hollered at him now, defending me, but I held Stanley's gaze. He knew what I was, even if the others didn't. It was strange to be so understood. I rightly terrified him.

"I only want to help you," I said, but he bucked and thrashed and yelled as if I'd branded him.

My heart sank. We'd broken him. Maybe I'd broken him most of all. The visions, the horrors that followed. He'd transferred from Unit B to shake free of me, of us, but he only slid further into the ruin I'd projected for him. He would be forced to leave Hanford.

Off to one side, Gordon spoke to one of Hanford's officers, who had emerged from a black and white Dodge. Tom Cat stood tensed between Stanley and me, asking Stanley to calm down. He wanted to defend me, but I wished he would go away so that I could talk to Stanley alone, so that I could convince him I meant no harm.

"This place will save you or kill you," I told Stanley.

"I don't have a choice," Stanley said, "unlike you."

I glanced at Tom Cat, and he shrugged at me, *What more can we do?*

I hoped they'd let Stanley go home to wherever he'd been before he came here, but most likely they'd send him somewhere else, jail, probably, a place where he'd undergo his final unraveling.

I considered his sister, the assistant nurse. Was she aware of Stanley's current state? Had she tried to help him? Or was she one of the hundreds who'd already left Hanford, sick of being tormented by the wind and worse?

The officer approached, Gordon at his side.

"Hey there, mister," the officer said. "Why don't you come with me?"

Stanley shook his head. "I could use a stiff drink." He was calmer now. He sensed it was almost over.

The officer laughed in a way that sounded forced. "We all could, huh?"

"He's had enough of this place," Gordon said spitefully. "Bye bye, birdie."

Stanley nodded as though Gordon had been kind.

"Yes," he said, straightening. "I'm all done."

He put his pajama shirt back on and walked away, limping, ill-dressed, head down into the wind. She fought him with every step. We watched him, shading our eyes. The officer walked beside him with one hand casually resting on his belt's revolver.

"Chicken liver," Gordon said.

He spat between our feet.

"Termination winds," Tom Cat said. "We're losing a lot of men this way. Working outside stirs up too many thoughts."

Tom Cat still worked outside, of course. He seemed steeled against it, and I both hoped and feared that his determination had to do with me.

"Losing a lot of chicken livers is what," Gordon said. "Why, even Mildred is tougher than *that* cotton picker. Good riddance, I say. He doesn't have the spine to work for this country. And after I helped him out. Those people don't appreciate a goddamn thing we do for them."

I glowered at him. "You helped him only to hurt him later."

"Like most women, Milly, you don't know a damn thing," Gordon said. "He got what was coming to him. I had nothing to do with it."

Tom Cat was silent. I tried to read his face but it was clouded, perturbed. I was tired of both men in that moment, Gordon and his hatefulness, Tom Cat and his reticence.

Gordon glared after the departing police car as if he wanted Stanley dead.

Repulsed, I turned away from him, now facing Tom Cat directly. Our eyes met and the cloud of doubt on his face parted. What I saw there, pure adoration, disquieted me. I glanced away, at the prairie grass, at the dull brown horizon, at the miserable humps of the mountains. There was nowhere to hide.

On the cattle car Tom Cat sat next to me, the silence between us filled with his gibbous affection. I didn't speak. I was worried about puncturing our muteness, about what would spring from his lips if I said the wrong thing.

We joggled along like that, not speaking, for a good few minutes, and then, gently, Tom Cat put his hand on mine, wrapping his fingers all the way around my palm so that his knuckles briefly grazed my inner thigh. A sensual, aching fire shot through me from groin to throat. The feeling was too intense.

"You're a good soul, Mildred," he whispered to me, and then he let go of my hand, with a passion that I nearly mistook for anger, and turned to gaze out the window.

DARK TWIN

On March 9, the day we fire-bombed Tokyo, I ran into my twin in the immense hallway of Unit B. The Other Me was dressed in a white lab coat; she carried herself with import. Her eyes were sharper and darker, her nose less round, and she was thinner, but she was otherwise my duplicate, same height, same searching brown gaze, same smooth brunette hair combed with care behind her ears. When she passed me she glanced at me hastily and then did a double take: She, too, noted the resemblance. I lifted my hand to her, smiling, and she lifted her hand, too, frowning, and our disparateness intensified our sameness, a scientist scowling at a fortune-teller, seekers, both. She walked quickly away from me as though to separate our twinning selfhoods and I held back from crying out, *But I'm you and you're me! Without one, there is no other!*

Only an hour later, I came upon her speaking with another scientist, a man I later learned was her husband, muttering how she was nothing more than a babysitter for Unit B's operators, accomplishing nothing more glorious than supervision as they dipped slugs into and out of molten flux, and that she was "murderously" bored. "Tell me when we can leave this godforsaken place," she hissed, and then looked up and saw me watching and tugged on the man's arm and hurried away. I liked that I made her uncomfortable.

I asked Dr. Hall about her and he confirmed that she was the physicist I'd heard about, Luella Woods. She was rumored to be one of Mr. Farmer's favorite pets, plucked from her work on his Unit B prototype in Chicago. From what I'd heard, she was brought here almost against her will, and she wasn't fond of the living conditions, especially the weather. She'd had a baby recently, a little girl watched dutifully by Luella's mother. Her husband was also a physicist. She lived in Richland and developed friendships with other WACs, but I wondered how distant she felt from all of us women, educated as she was, superior in intelligence and status.

I was proud of myself when I saw her, as though our shared looks had anything to do with her success. I was certain she was who I would have been if I'd been born into a wealthier family, which instantly gave you access to things like college degrees and dumb luck. I was almost disappointed when I heard she came here with her husband, because I felt this threw us into two vastly different social circles, and I'd never be able to properly meet her. She worked mostly at a different building under construction, a new unit across the Hanford campus, but she was with us the day Unit B went critical—and how strange I hadn't met her until a few months later, as if the men of Unit B disliked the idea of more than one woman in a room at any given time—and she was here again now to oversee, or "babysit," as she put it, the manufacturing of our mystery product.

The secrets. She knows them all, I thought with wonder.

A skulking avian presence in my gut chittered, *Don't be jealous, Milly. They know what this unit makes, but you've seen what it destroys.*

I asked Dr. Hall about Mrs. Woods's opinion on all of this. I assumed, being my more intelligent twin, that she would feel similarly ambivalent. But Dr. Hall told me that she had stated quite plainly her concern over how grave a situation we were in; she rooted wholeheartedly for us to win the arms race against Hitler, at any cost.

Maybe she was the stronger woman of the two of us. I was impressed with her confidence in the matter: destruction at any cost.

Dr. Hall told me what she'd said in a recent meeting: *No regrets. Anybody against our efforts here is a crybaby.*

He also confided that he wasn't entirely sure he agreed with her, but he admired her for her strength, especially as she was the only woman at Hanford.

I stared at him. "She's not the only woman."

Dr. Hall glanced up at me, sputtering. "Oh, you know what I mean, Miss Groves. The only *professional* woman."

I muttered that education and compassion did not necessarily go hand in hand.

"You should thank her," Dr. Hall scolded me. "Without her, there wouldn't be a woman's restroom in Unit B."

"So that's what education has brought us. A private toilet."

Dr. Hall laughed. "You know," he said, removing his glasses and peering at me, squinting, "you look an awful lot like her, in the right light."

Before, this might have delighted me, but now I fell silent, irritated. I didn't like what made us different, what made us the same.

SPEED UP

One morning in late April, I scooted my hard wooden chair closer to Dr. Hall, struggling to hear both his side of the phone conversation and the low, masculine voice issuing from the receiver. My pen moved swiftly over the paper. I liked to impress Dr. Hall with the speed and precision of my shorthand. I was, admittedly, showing off. He had once called my shorthand "a small miracle," and I longed for another compliment. Still, despite my every effort, I missed quite a lot of what the other party said.

"But if the war is almost over," Dr. Hall said tersely, and I felt a thrill run through me at this news, "then all of our work here will be for nothing."

The voice muttered in response. I wrote down a word, *speed*, and another, when I heard it, *dismiss*.

"We've already forgone certain safety measures," Dr. Hall said. "It could cause problems to relax even more."

I underlined the word *safety*. I couldn't help myself. I always underlined *safety* and *secrecy* and *loyalty* and *security* and any words related to those. It seemed to entertain Dr. Hall.

I heard the voice on the other end say, "Japs." I wrote it down. Common shorthand for Japanese was JPN but since he said JAPS, I just wrote JAP. Dr. Hall would recognize that abbreviation even quicker.

"And do you have targets already decided?"

The general replied with two words I couldn't quite make out.

"Yes, a difficult decision, surely," Dr. Hall said, but I heard the impatience in his tone.

He caught my eye and grimaced. He liked to tell me that the government officials meant well but were constantly interrupting scientific process with their red tape and bureaucratic bickering and paradoxical demand for immediate results.

"Is there a chance they'll surrender before we're ready?"

The general responded with a staticky, "Perhaps."

I'd heard the opposite: That the Japanese were ruthless, that they would never surrender, and I made a little noise in my throat from surprise.

"We're so close," Dr. Hall said.

The general spoke loudly then, so that I heard him word for word. "It's not up to us. The Germans will surrender any day now. Japs could follow in a few months. We've blockaded the entire island. They'll go broke and starve to death if they keep going." He waited and then said, less noisily, "I want this as much as anyone."

"Progress here has been commendable," Dr. Hall repeated. "Have you spoken to Farmer?"

The general spoke more softly now. I strained, practically falling into Dr. Hall's narrow lap in order to hear better, but it was no use.

"Yes, he would say that," Dr. Hall said. "But he's as curious as any of us."

They exchanged a few more words, nothing more than pleasantries, really, and then Dr. Hall hung up.

"Germany's about to surrender," he summarized, "and the Japanese are likely to follow. The military is pounding them with B-29s and naval blockades. Their economy is tanking. If I were the general, I would pause and let them regroup for a moment. We're so close here. It will be a great tragedy if we're not allowed to test all that we've accomplished here."

"But perhaps," I said helpfully, "you can still test it, just not in the war."

Dr. Hall scoffed. "Of course, we'll do that, too. But we'll never know the scale of its power until it's dropped on a militarized setting."

"But aren't you at all glad that the war is almost over?"

Dr. Hall took off his heavy glasses and rubbed at the bridge of his nose. He leaned away from me in his chair and swam his myopic eyes at me. I must have appeared grainy and blurry before him. I uncrossed and recrossed my legs. The heat was cranked in the little room. My inner thighs were slick with sweat.

"What will happen to you, Miss Groves, when the war is over?"

I hadn't thought about it. "I'd like to keep working here if I can," I said.

"You can't. When the war is over, you better believe we'll be over, too."

I closed my eyes. I saw myself hugging Beth good-bye, boarding the crowded bus back to Omak, reestablishing myself in the tense boredom of Mother's house. There would be no crowded mess halls, no dancing with friends, no smiling at strangers, no foreign languages, no feeling small in a big crowd. I would be exiled from the Columbia, from the clean sands of White Bluffs. My conversation with the wind and the wild creatures would be silenced. There would be no more magic, no more distinction.

I would be lonely.

I opened my eyes. Dr. Hall's thin lips curled upward. He knew me too well. He pushed his glasses back onto the edge of his nose. On the wall above him, a round clock ticked off the seconds of the day. Beneath the clock was the picture window, framing the control room of the beautiful invention of physics, the whole of it working marvelously, clattering and purring in its rhythmic, carefree manner.

"You see, Miss Groves, we belong here, you and I. Neither of us can leave. Our whole life is here. No one else loves us but this place. Don't you feel the same?"

For a knifelike moment, his gaze fell on me with absolute focus. I was an algorithm he had solved. This pleased me; it meant I was worthy of an intelligent man's attention and understanding. It was, of course, the first time he'd ever looked at me so directly, and for many, many months, it would be the last direct glance I would enjoy from him. There were far bigger concerns in his life than Mildred Groves from Omak, but for that one trim, flattering moment, I was an important subject.

"But what can we do?" I asked him.

"Ah, Miss Groves, an excellent question," he said. "We can work even harder."

He beckoned for me to take up my pen and paper.

I did as I was told.

It was no surprise to me when, just a few days later, Germany surrendered.

Beth wept with joy in the barracks and we embraced. Everyone raced outside to find the newspapers and read the headlines. That evening the mess halls were filled with happy drunks. The servers carried around endless trays of beer. Gordon came up to us and lifted Beth clear up off her feet, swinging her in a pretty circle. He tried to kiss her cheek and she frowned and ducked away from him.

"Milly, I'm furious," she whispered to me. "He's as bold as he is stupid."

But her eyes glimmered. She was happy. Everyone was. The happiness was almost contagious, but I remembered what Dr. Hall said. Despite my smile when we all sang the National Anthem, so loudly it seemed the roof would peel away from the mess hall's lofty frame, I trembled with an unsettled feeling, a rattling in my bones that hit a fever pitch when I sang the word *Free*.

TRINITY

My shoes arrived on a Thursday, sent via post to Dr. Hall's office at Unit B. When they arrived, he was away, saying he had to run an urgent errand, and I was alone in the office. Of course, it never felt like I was alone, given the giant window that observed the control room, and all those men out there working, cracking jokes when their supervisors weren't around, waving at me flirtatiously if I happened to lift my eyes from my work.

I used Dr. Hall's letter opener to cut the box open, and the smell of the shoes—oiled leather, rich and syrupy—ravished me. And how pretty they were! Like two adorable puppies, both of them a gorgeous calfskin brown, complete with chunky heels and brass buckled tongues that I could open and adjust for my comfort. I drew one of them up to my cheek and held it there—it was warm and alive against my cheekbone.

"You're a dream," I murmured. "You're more beautiful than I ever imagined."

Someone tapped on the control room window. A man stood there, holding his own shoe up to his face, his eyes closed in rapture. His coworker, standing nearby, hooted and laughed. I stuck my tongue out at them and then bent over my feet to try on my shoes.

I'd just finished tying them when Dr. Hall arrived. He paused at the doorway and said, "After you," and, to my surprise, a glamorous woman swept by him. Despite the heat, she wore a simple white scarf and a bronze silk gown, high-necked with a fitted waist. I hadn't seen real silk on anyone since before the war, and it was beautiful, the way it shone against her body like a copper river. She was tall and sinewy with long, wavy brown hair. As she moved into the room, I noticed that she dragged one leg slightly as she walked. She managed to do so with grace; I even wondered if it weren't an act, a subtle movement just to appear more unique and interesting.

"Miss Groves," said Dr. Hall, "this is Miss Dee. She's an actress."

I jumped to my feet and extended my hand. "Hazel Dee! I know precisely who you are! I saw you just a few weeks ago at the auditorium, doing *Euripides.* You were *wonderful.*"

She looked at my hand with incredulity and then her eyes dropped to my feet.

"Darling shoes," she told me, and I gushed that they had just arrived, and that they fit perfectly, so well, in fact, that I wanted to weep with joy, and I added that they were the same pair I'd once seen on Susan Peters.

"Susan Peters," Miss Dee said, one of her dramatic eyebrows lifting. "I know Susan Peters. She's from around here, isn't she?"

"Portland," I said. "But she was born in Spokane."

"Right. Spokane. Same as that other dope."

"Bing Crosby?"

"Hideous man," she said. She sat on the small sofa off to the side and rested her long arm languorously across it. "Susan's all right, though. She's a tough broad. An athlete and a hunter, did you know that? She hunts for all sorts of game with that beau of hers."

I was awestruck. First at someone insulting Bing Crosby and then at someone knowing Susan Peters personally. And Susan Peters a hunter! A bona fide Artemis from the Northwest! I adored her even more for this eccentricity. I wanted to pounce on Miss Dee and shake all of the gossip free of her.

"I want a cigarette, Phil," she said to Dr. Hall.

"I'm fresh out," he said. "I'll go find you one."

"Please do," she said, and I was glad when he left. I had Hazel Dee all to myself.

"I adore Susan Peters," I said. "She's a doll. I saw her once—"

"'I saw her once,'" Miss Dee interrupted loudly, dramatically, "'hop forty paces through the public street, and having lost her breath, she spoke, and panted, that she did make defect perfection, and, breathless, power breathe forth.'"

I applauded lightly. "That's just lovely. Are you a poet, too?"

She simpered. "It's Shakespeare, sweetheart. *Antony and Cleopatra.*"

"Shakespeare," I said stupidly. I'd never heard anyone quote Shakespeare that way. "How delightful."

She considered me scrupulously, her eyes laughing even as her mouth stayed firm. "Nothing's more delightful than you are, my darling." She closed her eyes, and I saw pain streak behind her eyelids, and then the pain fell from one of her perfect ears and swung in a parabola into my own head.

Not now, not here, not with her. Then, *Now. When I say so. Watch.*

The room disappeared from under me and my vision went black except for a small white light in the center of the darkness: a snow globe, shaken and confetti-stippled, and Hazel Dee within it, too, in a wheelchair, hunched over herself like a question mark. Dr. Hall pushed her through the white paper snow, whispering desperate plans to her hanging head.

The snow globe shattered and the sound of the glass rang in my ears. The room returned to me as it had been. Hazel Dee's eyes were still closed. I was relieved to have all of my faculties—I had not embarrassed myself, not this time.

"He's in love with you," I said.

Hazel Dee's eyes flew open in surprise, then narrowed at me. After studying my face, she relaxed, chuckling, and said, "Yes, dear, I know. The poor fool."

I sat down at my desk, recovering myself, but my head ached. I was nauseous. I put my face in my hands.

"You don't love him back," I said through my fingers. I didn't want to say it. I didn't want to upset her. But it was too late, the words coursing, set free by the ache in my head. My hands dropped to my lap. "You never will. You're using him, because of your illness. You hope he will help you, but he won't. He'll want to, he'll do everything he can, but no one can help you."

I wasn't looking at her, but I could feel her stare, the force of it. She was the sort of woman I would never be. No matter her future, I hoped she would never lose the memory of her power.

I thought, for a moment, that she might rise to her feet, approach me, smack me across the face. I waited for the normal reaction to my visions: a jigsaw puzzle of hatred, anger, denial that if it were rearranged would show itself to be no more than pure fear.

Her face, beautiful in its maturity and intellectuality, was as still as a pane of glass.

But after a long silence, she said, "But what choice do I have?"

I didn't respond. Choices were alternate passageways that descended in one way or another to the same dark crypt.

"A girl mustn't give up hope," she added, but her tone was grave, listless.

Dr. Hall returned then with a pack of cigarettes, and he immediately handed one to Miss Dee and lit it for her with gallant ministration.

"The mood's gloomy in here," he said. "I hope Miss Groves hasn't been boring you with her Hollywood crushes."

"Quite the opposite," Miss Dee said, and when I glanced at her to see how mean she looked, her expression was instead kind, sorrowful, as though she'd realized my own future and mourned the trouble we both faced. "In my opinion Miss Groves is your resident genius."

"She's fairly useful, isn't she?"

Dr. Hall squeezed my shoulder, an affectionate, paternal grip. I felt how grateful he was in that motion: He ached to impress Miss Dee.

"If you see Susan Peters again," I said to her, "please tell her hello from Mildred Groves."

"I'll tell her about your beautiful shoes."

She came forward and kissed my face, first one cheek and then the other, and then, turning to Dr. Hall and briefly placing her palm on his chest, she excused herself, saying that she was very tired. She would return to his home in Richland for a long nap. He offered to walk her to the cattle car and guided her into the hallway.

I tidied up the office, humming. I tried and failed to remember the words from *Antony and Cleopatra*. Brief phrases only: *Forty paces . . . defect perfection . . . power breathe forth.*

Luella Woods appeared in the doorway, peeking her head around the frame, showing only her strong throat and too-familiar face. I looked into the mirror of her. We reflected each other cleanly.

"Is she gone?" she asked me.

I nodded.

"Pathetic, isn't it?" She stepped fully into the room. I took note of her reasonable shoes. My own suddenly seemed lavish. "An actress with a physicist," she said. "Sounds like the plot to a bad play."

Luella Woods's laugh was low and swift, the laughter of someone who was too smart to be truly happy.

"I can see it in the marquee now," she said without much inflection. "*A Doomed Love*, starring Hazel Dee and Phillip Hall."

I stared at her flat-mouthed, wondering, *Does she see their future as I do?*

"What I'm saying," she said, "is we're here to work, not to fall in love or *think* that we've fallen in love. There's too much to accomplish."

I emptied Dr. Hall's ashtray and returned it with a clunk to his desk.

"I'm telling you this because you're practical like I am," she said, and I found the humorlessness of her tone oddly calming. "You concentrate so well when you're on the job. So do I. It's a waste of government money, these actresses and singers and musicians they bring here." I almost laughed here—I personally loved all of these events. "There's more important work to be done."

She was awkward, standing there in her lab coat and plain shoes. She was trying to talk in a friendly way but her words fell like bricks to the floor, heavy and hard. If she noticed how limp and one-sided the conversation was, she didn't let on. In this way, too, we mirrored each other.

"I see myself in you," I said, out of compassion, maybe, or discomfort.

"Exactly," she said. "We're like-minded. We know what needs to be done."

I see myself in you and I don't like it.

"Those shoes are not something I'd buy, though." She motioned to my feet. "They'd destroy my ankles. I'd trip and break my face."

"They're very comfortable. Much better than my last pair."

"Well, I've got to run. Lots to do. Lots to oversee." She gave me a little wave. "See you soon."

"Okay," I said, and waved, too. "Have a good day, Mrs. Woods."

Alone again, I struggled to remember what I was doing. I fingered the papers on Dr. Hall's desk, then decided to leave them be. I pushed his ashtray around until it looked properly aligned in the corner; I returned some pens to their container. What I liked about myself was my ability to fade away. Movies, stories, books, daydreams, shoes even. Luella Woods didn't understand such thinking, perhaps because it was the inverse of thought. I enjoyed the bright tapping sound my new shoes made as I paced the office. I told myself (lied) that I didn't care what she thought of me.

Dr. Hall returned a minute or so later and slumped over his papers, staring into them as though he couldn't comprehend the language printed on them. I didn't tell him about Luella Woods. He was thinking of Hazel Dee. The romance of it pained me low in my belly.

After a time he told me, "She's sick, you know."

"Oh? Hazel?" I feigned surprise.

"She'll be fine. I'm helping her."

"She'll rely on that help," I assured him.

"She's been here a few times, you know, to help with morale."

I thought of my Dark Twin, how incapable she was of enjoyment, how sad that made me for her. *I should take her to the movies,* I thought. I pictured her sitting there in the dim light, glowering with impatience, fingers percussing the armrest.

"We met the first night she performed," Dr. Hall continued, "and I'll admit, I'm quite taken with her."

"She's magnificent," I said.

His shoulders relaxed. As he did only in moments when he was deep in thought or very troubled, he took out the package of cigarettes. He withdrew one and lit it from the matchbook in his front pocket. Then, apologetically, he offered one to me but I shook my head; I hated the smell of cigarette smoke. It reminded me of Mother and Martha, of the moments when they stood together on the front stoop, conspiring against me.

"I don't like to smoke," he said, as if to nobody, "but now and again it calms me."

I waited. He wanted to speak, and I didn't want to interrupt him.

"You know, Miss Groves," he said, "I'm happy you met her. Sometimes I think she's not real. It helps that you've seen her, too, and that you also find her magnificent."

She will destroy your life.

"Magnificent," I said again, and he nodded dreamily, no doubt thinking of Hazel Dee in her bronze silk gown, but when I spoke I didn't see Hazel Dee, I saw Hanford, Unit B, herself. I thought of the pile with its hundreds of metal slugs, how they looked like furious, unblinking eyes glaring with malice through the thick concrete walls, through metal and steel, over the river, over the mountains, across the oceans, fastening their gaze to the terrible, indescribable lands beyond, places crawling with an endless supply of enemies.

Dr. Hall, it occurred to me, was in love with both Unit B and Hazel Dee, not one more than the other, but neither party would ever love him back.

KING AND QUEEN

Part of my job on the Safety and Security Committee was assisting with the plans for the big S&S Dance, where we would crown King Safety and Queen Security and acknowledge the departments with the best safety record. Unit B was a contender for the prize. A painted sign next to our time clock read, NO WORK-RELATED INJURIES FOR 268 DAYS. I traded out the tiny wooden placard every evening after work, and it was a simple and satisfying task, watching the sum increase one sturdy black numeral at a time.

A few days before the dance, Tom Cat and I took the cattle car to Richland to buy supplies for the party; decorations, streamers, swizzle sticks, and the like. Tom Cat wasn't on the committee but he volunteered to help me when I mentioned the necessary trip to town, and I was happy for the company. I liked spending the committee's money on items that would be used for one night only. The woman at the department store filled up four paper sacks with our requests, and when she placed two of them in my arms I quivered with the furtive existences within, brief, joyous excitement tempered by a swift and certain end. It was a better sort of way to pass one's time on earth, much preferred to the slow drive, the long plateau, the unseen sputtering out. I made a joke to Tom Cat about how I would like to live my life as a swizzle stick, and he smiled and said he knew just what I meant, all that motion, all those hands, but that wasn't what I meant, not at all. Still, I was glad Tom Cat didn't laugh at me the way someone else might have. *Silly Milly. Mad Milly.* Tom Cat didn't see me that way. It seemed like he never would.

With our arms loaded, we crushed in with all of the other Hanford residents who had finished their own chores in Richland. The car smelled of men and exhaust. The passengers watched us as we entered, their expressions ranging from bored to kind to mocking. Two of them rose quickly, offering me their seat, and I accepted the one closest to the doors.

I sat squashed between two large sets of shoulders and arranged my bags at my feet. Tom Cat stood a short distance away from me, eyeing me with a protective air. A couple of other men studied me, too, up and down, dull, unapologetic dog eyes sliding over my curves. I scolded myself for not feeling flattered by the attention.

I was glad to be seated, my legs wobbly and unsure. The throngs of men stood all around me, the rows of shining belt buckles wrapping around me like a cage. The fence of them locked Tom Cat out. I kept my gaze focused on my knees. I thought with longing about how being married must instantly make you less afraid of the foreignness of men. The man next to me grunted and shuffled in his seat, trying to find a more comfortable place on the bench, and his hand grazed my knee. Marriage would involve touch far more intimate than this. I tried to think of Tom Cat's hands on me, tried to feel excited at the prospect, but I felt nothing other than a cold dread.

⚹

The day of the dance, Tom Cat and I agreed to meet in the beer hall and decorate. Beth promised to help, too, but she was tied up at the infirmary for a few hours in the morning, so Tom Cat and I walked to the beer hall just the two of us, chatting amiably over the bags in our arms.

We spent the morning nailing up streamers and cutting paper decorations. We put up signs around the room: STAY QUIET AND STAY SAFE;

SECURITY IS AN INDIVIDUAL RESPONSIBILITY (BE AN INDIVIDUALIST!); UNIT B: WINNER, NO INJURIES FOR 272 DAYS!

From construction paper we cut out crowns for King Safety and Queen Security. I secretly hoped Beth would win. It made sense, her being so beautiful and kind to everyone, and also being a nurse, an emblem of care, but I wondered who would be crowned king. I thought about Dr. Hall and laughed to myself.

"What's so funny?" Tom Cat said, looking up from his work.

"Just wondering who will be king is all."

"My two cents on Gordon Nyer," Tom Cat said. "He'll get a lot of votes."

This disappointed me. I thought of Gordon pushing into our barracks, stealing Beth's green nightgown. Where was the nightgown now? I didn't want to think of it lying in a trash can or, worse, in his sock drawer.

"I don't see why'd he win," I muttered.

"He's got charisma," Tom Cat said. "People like him."

"Well, I don't."

"He's my friend, but I hear you. I guess I'd be jealous if you said the opposite."

The statement embarrassed me, but I didn't show it. "Is he really a friend of yours?"

"Sure."

I was glad he didn't argue the point with any real passion.

"He reminds me of a wolf," I said, "or a dog. Cunning, maybe. Ill-behaved."

It struck me as odd then that I hadn't had a vision of Gordon. I thought of my vision of Tom Cat, the sweet fluttering bird in his rib cage, the early death. For all of my thinking of Gordon, it seemed his future was hidden from me.

"I like dogs, though," Tom Cat said. "I'm a dog person."

"What?"

"You said Gordo was like a dog, but dogs are great."

I laughed. "I guess you have a point there, Tom."

"Would you ever want a dog?"

"And name it Gordon?"

"No, I'm serious. Or are you more of a cat person?"

What sort of person was I? The heron sprang to mind, her beak at my ankle, freeing me from another's sad form of protection. I thought of the coyote.

"Dog person," I said.

"Me, too."

This seemed to solidify something in Tom Cat's mind and he beamed at me. It was so easy to make him happy.

It occurred to me how easy it would be to be his wife. He would dote on me, spoil me. He would be predictable, constant, generous, the opposite of Mother. I told myself I wouldn't grow bored or unappreciative, I would match his steadfastness and affection, even if it killed me. At this last thought I tore the head off of a paper queen I was making for the ballot box.

"Damn it," I muttered, and I crumpled her up in my fist.

Tom Cat glanced up at the large white clock on the wall. He put down his scissors and paper.

"I gotta go change, Milly." He was wearing his overalls from work, and although it suited him, the modesty of them, the sturdiness, they weren't meant for dancing. "You okay here?"

I was already in my simple party dress, so I told him I would stay and finish the few decorations remaining.

"We've made the room beautiful, Mildred," he said, putting his arm around my shoulders.

We stood together admiring the giant, cavernous hallway. It glittered in the low light, soft with candles and streamers and paper decorations.

"It's lovely," he said, "like a room for angels."

He was right. It was heavenly.

Our aloneness in the room became a living, hungry thing. It trembled and opened its dark mouth.

I moved away from him, murmuring good-bye, and he hesitated only a moment before hurrying out the door.

❧

Beth arrived, breathless, shrugging off her coat, apologizing to me profusely for being so late. She wore a long black sheath dress with simple white beading on the shoulders. She reminded me of Anna Karenina, tall and untouchable at the dance where she meets Vronsky. I wanted to be Kitty, or Natasha from *War and Peace*, but I knew that was silly. If I were a character from a Tolstoy novel, it would likely be Sonya.

"You're fine," I told her. "Tom Cat and I did almost everything. I checked on the cooks and they said all's well. Just look at the room! It's so pretty."

Beth agreed, eyes shining. "You've outdone yourself, Milly. Truly you have."

She helped me push tables aside so that people could dance front and center of the big room. The members of the band arrived and began tuning their instruments. Men and women slowly poured into the hall, then more and more swiftly, like a mudflow gathering speed. Before long, I was shouting at Beth for her to hear me, and she shouted at me in return. Bottles were popped open and drinks poured. Women wore pretty gingham dresses or simple cocktail shifts. People wandered by with small plates of hors d'oeuvres, baked beans, cold cuts, rainbow rye bread, a simple tomato salad. A woman squealed in displeasure when she spilled sauce on her yellow rayon skirt. She rushed off to salt and rinse the stain in the outside lavatories. Kathy arrived, asking after one of our bunkmates, and I pointed in the direction I'd seen her go, but who knew where she'd landed in the vortex of people? I felt drunk already, purely from the crowd.

A man I'd never before met handed me a glass of ginger ale mixed

with beer, and I thanked him and sipped leisurely. Mother hated drinking, and Martha enjoyed only a small beer on Saturday evenings. I,
myself, wasn't crazy about the taste. Still, I liked the sensation of the
bubbles on my tongue, the warmth that traced a furry comet's tail down
my throat. Beth grabbed me by my elbow, gripping her own drink, and
declared that she aimed for a wild night.

"Sometimes I love to drink hard and forget about the world, you
know what I mean?" she said to me.

I didn't know what she meant, not exactly, but I could imagine it.
*Good-bye Annie, dear dead sister. Good-bye, Glen, my darling dead husband. Good-
bye, Death, itself. Good-bye, pitiful Me.* Nothing but the calm black waves of
forgetting.

She winked at me and then downed her entire drink in one blast.

I was impressed.

I hugged her with one arm and took a longer sip of my own drink,
but the fizziness made me cough.

The band started up and whoops of joy rose around us. They played
"Swinging on a Star" and "I've Got a Gal in Kalamazoo" and "It's Love,
Love, Love." Everyone cheered when "Besame Mucho" started up. I
found the punch bowl and poured myself a fresh glass.

"Dontcha just love Jimmy Dorsey!" a woman screamed at me as she
wheeled past, spun by her partner in wide, clumsy circles.

"Sure do!" I said, and I did, I loved all of those crooners, almost as
much as I loved Susan Peters and Richard Quine. I was overjoyed with
the success of the night. I took almost full credit. I laughed and danced
in a little circle by myself.

Gordon blustered up, shouting hello to his many friends and receiv-
ing affectionate pats on the back in return. Beth danced with a man
from Unit B; I recognized him from the cattle car.

"I need a girl," Gordon yelled at the top of his lungs, and men
laughed and cajoled in response.

Then Gordon's eyes fell on me.

"Why, if it isn't Mildred Groves from Omak."

"Hello, Gordon," I said.

"You're not dancing by yourself, are you, Milly?" His tone was mocking.

"No, I'm not dancing at all," I said, but I swayed my hips ever so slightly.

He gave me a skeptical look, like I was a child.

I clutched my drink with both hands, right in front of my heart, and tried to shrink back into the crowd.

"Oh, no you don't," Gordon said.

He reached forward and grabbed my wrist. My drink splashed everywhere and I uttered a soft, "No, please, don't, my drink," but then he took the cup from me, swallowed the rest of its contents, tossed it onto the floor, and wiped his palm dry on his good jacket, all while pulling my body into his.

"Lots to grab," Gordon said, clutching my waist. He rested his chin for a moment on the top of my head, leaning over to do so, but I buckled away from him. "You're as shy as a filly," he said. "Milly the filly." He laughed at his own joke. The singer crooned and the band played and he tightened his grip and whirled me in circles.

He was a wonderful dancer. To my horror, I was thrilled. The band launched into "Sing, Sing, Sing," and we surged and rippled.

"You're not as clumsy as you look," Gordon shouted at me, grinning. I'd never seen him so handsome and commanding.

"You're marvelous," I gasped, and he swung me around and then lifted me clear off the floor, tossing me through the air.

"Good night!" I called out with excitement, and I realized I was drunk but also extraordinarily happy, happier than I'd ever felt.

The song ended and Gordon released me. For a moment I felt cold without his arms around me, but I panted and smiled and blushed. Beth came up to us, holding a fresh drink.

"Milly," she said. "You were wonderful out there!"

"Lighter on her feet than she looks," Gordon said approvingly, and then he reached over and pinched Beth on the waist. "You're up next, sweetheart."

"Fat chance," Beth replied, pushing his hand away, but her tone was teasing and her eyes flirted and shone.

"Don't drink too much, Beth," I told her, worried she was behaving in a way that was beneath her, and she rolled her eyes at me. It was a rude gesture, something Kathy would do, not my Beth.

"You sound like my mother," Beth said.

I thought of my own mother. The comparison irritated me.

"Take that back," I told her.

"Oh, Milly, lighten up," she said. "Here, drink this."

She placed her glass in my hand and took Gordon by the arm.

"I suppose I'll dance with this big lug, after all."

Gordon, beaming, seemed to sprout wings right where he stood. They swirled and dipped away from me.

I shrank back against the wall. I couldn't take my eyes off them. They made an astounding couple, she a full-figured brunette, he a rugged movie star of a man. Susan Peters and Richard Quine, I sighed. I liked watching them together. Almost.

But even as they danced, there appeared to be some sort of struggle occurring. He pulled her in close and she fought for space against him. He put his nose up against her ear, whispering into it, and she flinched and moved her head away from his lips. He was too aggressive with her, as he'd been with me, but she was more graceful at countering his moves, while I merely succumbed to them.

I had half a mind to break in and separate them. A small part of me wondered if I weren't jealous. No, not the way you might think. I was more jealous of his proximity to her than hers to him. I shared that closeness with Beth; it seemed unfair that now he did. Mostly I just hated how he mishandled her, flinging her about the way a child would play with an old doll. He treated her like an object when clearly she belonged only to the power of herself.

Kathy came up to me then, touching my arm.

"What are you glaring at, Milly?" she shouted at me over the music. "You're such a sourpuss."

I quickly smiled, showing I was a good sport. "Just thinking about home," I lied.

"Scorching couple, eh?" Kathy said, nodding toward Beth and Gordon.

"He's rough with her."

"She loves it," Kathy said. "Look at her face."

"She's fighting him."

"She's baiting him." Kathy scratched at one of her elbows, her gaze trained on the couple as they moved to and fro. She wore a navy blue sheath dress, almost as simple as my own. She didn't seem self-conscious in the least. "I don't like him, but he's just the thing for some women, I guess."

"I don't like him, either." It was weird to agree with Kathy about something. I felt a strange flush of affection toward her.

"You sure dance with him like you do."

The flush ended.

"Anyway, Milly, Tom Cat's looking for you."

"I haven't seen him," I said.

"He wants to dance with you," Kathy said, somehow both indifferent and mocking. "He was by the ballot box last I saw him."

The ballot box was near the stage. I had labeled it earlier. VOTE FOR YOUR KING AND QUEEN. People had crowded around the box all night, stuffing papers into the opening. I'd fastened a new paper queen and king to it but I suspected they'd already been torn off and trampled by hundreds of filthy feet.

"I'll find him later." I didn't want Kathy to see me as an eager bride-to-be. I wanted to seem as cool and unaffected as she was. "Or he'll find me."

"Sooner than later," she said, and pointed.

There he was, holding a fake flower—a red fabric tulip—in one hand, looking left and right, weaving through the bulging islands of dancers as though in a skiff of his own sobriety. The sight of his sad search bugged me. I didn't like his doggish, desperate, love-stricken look. Need was nauseating. What was wrong with him, that he seemed so singularly bent on my existence?

"I need some fresh air," I told Kathy, and she moved to the side so that I could press by her toward the large open doors. The cacophony of color and body and scent and music and cheering and singing and stomping was overwhelming. Near the edge of the boisterous crowd, my bunk mate Susan, also on the S&S Committee, clumsily gathered up the ballot boxes, readying them to tally. I hurried past her, worried she'd ask for my help. At the wide doorway, I glanced over my shoulder to find Beth: To my relief, she was no longer dancing but off to one side. For a moment I thought she was alone, leaning against the wall and gazing up with a happy expression at the lights, but then someone shifted position in front of me and there was Gordon. She was smiling up at him dopily.

Gordon reached for her face, cupped her cheek gently, and her head rocked against his hand, just for a moment, before she pulled away from him.

Their intimacy troubled me. A few bodies gathered together then, readying for a slow dance, blocking my line of sight. Somewhere Tom Cat searched for me, but I didn't want to be found.

I went out into the night.

Summer approached. I inhaled deeply the dry scent of the Hanford Reach. It reminded me of home, the aroma of the sage, the aria of the crickets stridulating their wings. A few people stood outside. I passed a couple kissing, and I fought the urge to stare. Instead I admired my feet in their new shoes. *How beautifully you danced tonight! We showed them all, didn't we!* I'd sent the old pair back home to Mother with a letter describing how I didn't need them anymore. Surely Martha would suffer from a brief prick of jealousy. I'd sent enough money their way for them to enjoy new shoes, too, but it would be good for them to accept that I took care of myself now, too.

I reached the barbed wire fencing of the women's barracks and pushed open the gate. Usually there was a guard, reading his newspaper, trying not to look too bored, but even the guards were allowed to go to the party tonight, and so the women had to look out for themselves.

Off to the side, barely concealed in shadow, another couple stood necking. I heard the sounds of their kisses and when the woman moaned, a smell hit my nose, earthy, familiar, both sweet and metallic.

It occurred to me that I should turn and flee, but instead I gawked. A memory occurred to me of seeing my father and mother this way when I was very young. Nonplussed, terrified, I'd watched them, transfixed, frozen, before they'd noticed me, and then they separated, crying out in anger and surprise. I was curious and disgusted. It was like they were trying to kill each other. Later Mother tried to explain it to me as "pleasure," but even she sounded doubtful as she said it. *Rare pleasure*, she'd corrected herself, and this was what I said aloud now, my lips mumbling and dry.

"Rare pleasure."

Now the sucking noises stopped. A small hole poked into the fetid warm smell.

"Hey," the man said, straightening. "What the hell is wrong with you? Beat it, lady!"

I stuttered something about the dance but the woman's voice rose with the man's. "Leave us alone, pervert."

I hurried away.

I stopped to catch my breath, leaning against the wall to a set of urinals. The smell was overpowering but I didn't care, I needed an overpowering. Not in the way women let themselves be overpowered, but in the way of the world showing me how small my place was inside it. This was what I wanted, I realized, more than anything, to be rendered infinitesimal. To be someone who wasn't strange or gifted or foolish or wise but unimportant. An insignificant blip. The thought comforted me. I found a star in the sky and held on to it. The woman and man were in love, maybe, the woman was touching the man and the man was touching her. For a moment my vision seemed to split apart, the future unraveling. I could pull a star down and knit it to my chest, or tuck it in between my legs, my womb seared with its heat. I pushed my hands against my temples, urging out the images, the woman and the man, my father with Mother, Beth with Gordon, myself with Tom Cat, myself with Gordon, myself with Richard Quine, myself with Father, myself with Dr. Hall, myself with Beth, myself underwater, myself broken and dead beneath the white bluffs.

The very earth smelled of sex. I knelt and took up a fistful of dry dirt and then pushed my skirt up and pulled my underpinnings aside and stuffed the dirt into me, the soil pressed into the wet warmth.

I hadn't touched myself since I was in Omak. It was so much better here—no muzzling myself on my old bedroom pillow, no Mother down the hall, no sister banging on my door, asking why it was locked. I fit more dirt up into me.

This was what it was like. This was how I would know. *Stuffed up with earth.* I rubbed myself into oblivion and when the waves overtook me I didn't care who I was or who heard me.

A minute later, regaining my sanity and my shame, I fixed my underwear and dropped my skirt, fluffing and grooming. The crickets started up again; I'd frightened them into silence. Relief. I was alone.

I returned to the dance hall, fortified.

Beth was onstage for the crowning—of course she had been elected Queen—and beside her was Gordon, crowned King Safety. Kathy must have found the paper crowns all on her own. The crown looked silly on Gordon, fastened at the back with a bit of taped newspaper. It was a testament to Beth's beauty that her own paper crown looked glorious. The two of them held hands and beamed. They were relaxed, more than a little drunk, and gracious with the adoring crowd. I waved at Beth with both hands and she spotted me and smiled more fully, mouthing my name, *Milly,* and waving with both hands back at me. She pointed at her crown in a jocular manner. *Isn't this a gas?*

I smiled and applauded, and she winked at me but then nestled closer to Gordon.

When I moved, crumbs of dirt fell from me. If people noticed the trail of soil following me everywhere, they didn't say so. It was too crowded, they were too drunk. The earth moved both into and out of me. *I'm of this place and it's of me.*

Tom Cat found me. "Ah, there you are! Finally!"

I wasn't unhappy to see him. The earth moved in me; whatever I did ultimately didn't matter. I relaxed into his grip and gave way to the music, dancing, crumbling. He held me the way a brother holds a sister, at arm's length, adoringly, respectfully. I tried to find Gordon and Beth in the crowd but they were gone.

PROTECTION FOR ALL

The heat wilted away all of Hanford's spring hues. The vibrant petals, the verdant plains and hills, all of the lushness dried up and rusted by mid-July. The heat was heavy, filled with longing, but it wasn't foreign; it was the same heat I'd felt in Omak. I breathed it deep into my lungs when I stepped outside. Others hurried for shade or cover, but I lingered, allowing the waves of warmth to slow me down, to calm me.

※

There was a tension now like a brewing lightning storm all around us. It was July 16. Dr. Hall, unable to concentrate on work, paced the office, eyeballing his telephone all the while.

"I should have heard from them by now," he said. "What's taking them so long?"

I didn't pry. I was patient, I was dutiful. I'd learn the details soon enough.

"That woman," I said instead. "Hazel Dee. Will you marry her?"

He looked up at me sharply, surprised. But then his face relaxed, and I saw he was grateful for a distraction.

"I'm helping her," he said. "Nothing more than that." He sat against his desk and laced his small pale hands around one knee, relaxing there for a moment. "She's a remarkable woman. She's as fascinating to me as my work. I feel I could pour myself into her for a lifetime and never grow tired of her."

Even when waxing romantic he was professorial, didactic.

"And her illness progresses," I said.

Dr. Hall smirked. "I'm always surprised by how observant you are, Miss Groves."

"But how will you help her?"

"I'm a doctor," he said simply.

"But you're not that kind of doctor."

He nodded sadly. "Unfortunately, no regular doctor would be able to help her in any significant way. Not with the disease she has. She's—"

The telephone on his desk pealed. He grabbed for the receiver.

"Yes?" he said into it. "Yes, of course, yes."

He snapped at me and I pulled my chair away from my tiny desk over to his larger one, scooping up my notepad and pen as I went. I nestled in right beside him and he tilted the phone slightly away from his own ear so that I could listen, too.

"Trinity," he said. "From a John Donne poem, I know. I take it from your tone that you're pleased?"

I wrote down the words *Trinity, John Donne, pleased.*

"And the gadget?" he said.

He leaned forward and I leaned toward him, our foreheads touching lightly so that we could both listen to the voice on the other end of the line.

"At 05:10, the twenty-minute countdown began. Two B-29s observed the test to make the airborne measurements. At 05:29:21, the gadget exploded. You should have seen it, Phil. The sand melted into this gorgeous green glass. The mountains lit up like they were on fire. It took about forty seconds for the shock wave to hit us. The ball of fire that came up was like a giant mushroom, then it was a cylinder of white smoke wearing a long, flat cloud for a hat. It was miraculous, unlike anything I've ever seen. The power of this thing, Phil. Amazing, beyond our wildest dreams. I tell you, Phil, we've done it!"

Dr. Hall wasn't breathing. He handed the phone to me and I held it delicately away from my ear, afraid it, too, would explode. The man continued to speak but I heard him only as a distant, mouse-like chirping. I watched Dr. Hall, marveling at his triumph. He pumped his fist in the air and then finally exhaled in one long, relieved whoosh. He hardly made a sound, but there was more excitement contained in him than I'd ever witnessed.

"The product is ready," he said.

He was triumphant, but a rattling sound shook in my ears, and dread dropped into the pit of my stomach like a stone.

Later I would go to the Richland library and ask the librarian to find the John Donne poem for me. She would do so in a tidy manner. I could never be sure, of course, if this was the exact poem they meant or not, but it struck me as likely.

> Batter my heart, three-personed God; for you
> As yet but knock, breathe, shine, and seek to mend;
> That I may rise and stand, o'erthrow me, and bend
> Your force to break, blow, burn, and make me new.
> I, like an usurped town, to another due,
> Labor to admit you, but O, to no end;
> Reason, your viceroy in me, me should defend,
> but is captived, and proves weak or untrue.
> yet dearly I love you, and would be loved fain,
> But am betrothed unto your enemy.
> Divorce me, untie or break that knot again;
> Take me to you, imprison me, for I,
> Except you enthrall me, never shall be free,
> Nor even chaste, except you ravish me.

Break, blow, burn, I would murmur then; I would consider the speaker begging to be demolished by brutal holy love. The men who found inspiration here equated themselves with the merciless God of my mother's youth, the destroyer of worlds. When we brought ruin to others, did we wrongly assume we brought them love?

But finding the poem would occur later.

In Dr. Hall's office now, my eyes darted over the floor. I was anxious that the rattlesnake would appear at my feet or drape himself across Dr. Hall's narrow shoulders. If the coyote or the meadowlark could materialize at a moment's notice, of course the snake could, too. But the sound of the shaking tail faded, and not even a speck of dust floated by, and I told myself it was in my head alone, and that the dread, too, was my own silly conjuring.

Luella entered the room then, walking swiftly over to the desk. Resting her sharp fingernails on the wood slab, she leaned close to hear what was being said. Her face was all urgency and demand, how I might have looked had I wanted something very badly.

Dr. Hall gave her a brief nod and took the phone back from me and congratulated his colleague. I scooted my chair slowly away from their conversation, worried that the hazard of whatever gadget they spoke of would leak through the holes of the transmitter and ooze onto the floor. It would slide lavalike toward me, melting my new shoes, chewing up my bones, setting fire to my eye sockets and hair. I bit into my knuckle until I tasted blood. It tasted like the ashen screams I'd heard from the *hibakusha.*

Dr. Hall hung up the phone and sat back in his chair, exhaling. "Wow."

"Tell me," she said.

He laced his fingers behind his head and lifted his eyes toward the ceiling in joy or wonderment or expectation, I couldn't tell. I stayed in my chair.

One corner of Luella's mouth lifted. "It's a success then?"

Dr. Hall nodded, beaming, his head still leaning back into his hands.

I gargoyled out at them both, glaring, glaring, and soon enough their heads rolled toward me. Luella narrowed her familiar eyes.

"What's the matter with her?" she said to Dr. Hall.

The ringing in my ears, my sweating brow: I knew what would happen. What always happened when I foretold the future, the annoyance, the rejection, the loneliness I would feel in the aftermath. I would be left alone, to withdraw into the monster of myself.

They watched me, waiting.

I wished I could shutter the windows of the office. I no longer wanted to see the control room, its dials and clocks all staring at me like a thousand cold, empty faces. I hated the shoulders of the control room's men, hunkered over their tasks, waiting diligently for the right moment to press whatever button or rotate whatever lever they needed in order to punish and dominate. *Machines, all of them,* I thought. *Thoughtless.* What did they care about what they made? I saw what was emerging from the concrete womb of this place. It was peril itself, a sorcerer that mutated sand into green glass.

The words unspooled from my mouth and there was no stopping them. As long as I had a tongue, the visions would sooner or later surface.

"We're making a weapon that will kill thousands. Tens of thousands. It will maim even more. Children—babies—will suffer and perish. People will drop dead from the sickness it brings. Eyeballs will melt from their sockets. It will affect the land here, too. The very soil around us will give birth to demons."

I glanced at Luella. Our faces mirrored each other in their intensity.

Dr. Hall lowered his gangly arms, resting them now on the desk before him. He leaned forward. "Go on," he said.

Encouragement ignited the power in me. My blood warmed and coursed through its avenues, pushing open gates of awareness that stunned me with their exactitude.

"The weapons will only get bigger and more powerful. What we make will be terrible, but it will be laughable compared to what will come next."

Dr. Hall licked his lips, not in a predatory way but in the manner of a man deeply engrossed.

"We'll all be in jeopardy. Other countries will make the product. They'll use it here against us, right here in the Inland Northwest. Then more. This invention will destroy everything, the planet as we know it. It might not be for another eighty years, but the damage will be irreversible."

For a moment, I thought Dr. Hall was going to stand up and applaud. He hung on my every word, nodding along with it all, harrumphing, the lean ropes of his body tensed, and I could see even the tiny gray hairs of his pointy ears standing at attention. If not for the grave subject matter, I might have smiled, I might have thanked him. My whole life I'd only ever wanted to help, to be believed enough that I made a difference.

Luella perched on the edge of the desk, folding her arms together. She, too, was listening keenly.

My vision sharpened. A cloud receded from my mind's eye, and I peered through a window there into the open sky, the black-and-blue expanse below, the bulbous cloud lifting from the latter to the former.

"After they drop the bomb, the men will look out of the windows of a plane named Mother. They'll see the fires, the smoke. They'll guess then what they've done. Some will celebrate but one of them will mourn. He will realize how those below them suffer."

I was crying. Tears fell freely but I barely registered them, the firmness of my voice belied any emotion.

We convened in the tidy office of Unit B, so distant from everything I was predicting, and yet there we were, at the horror's epicenter.

I closed my eyes. The tears ceased. When I opened my eyes again, Dr. Hall regarded me with an expression of awe. Even Luella's cold eyes snapped and brightened with appreciation.

I've done it.

Finally.

They believe me.

What if my childhood friends had believed me? What if the belief had altered the course of events? What if the girl had warned her mother about the car wreck, and the mother—laughing, reassuring—had in turn convinced the girl that she would drive more carefully, and then, without even meaning to, she did, because the thought was now locked into her subconscious? How much would we improve as a human race if we listened to the warnings given to us? Why was it always easier to diminish and ignore?

I thought of Martha's warnings, of my mother's, of Beth's tying the bell to my ankle every evening. *Everyone thinks she's a clairvoyant,* I thought. *We cancel each other out.*

Dr. Hall cleared his throat, and I straightened my spine and pushed back my shoulders. I waited as though I was about to be anointed. This would be my vindication.

"Goodness," Luella said. "More poetic than I expected. But charming, really."

"Wasn't I telling you?" Dr. Hall said to her. "It's such a loss."

I was confused. "I don't quite follow."

His tone was adoring, but there was none of the profound understanding that I thought I'd sown in him. "I just mean how sad it is that you're just a secretary from Omak. Think what you might have done with a decent education. You would have made one hell of a scientist. You do have an extraordinary mind."

"A dark mind, certainly," Luella said, but not without approbation.

"But these are all things I've seen—"

"These are all very fine hypotheses," Dr. Hall said, "and all worthy of further investigation."

"There is immediate danger," I said. My throat tightened. I felt on the verge of tears again, sobbing uncontrollable, embarrassing tears. "There are human lives at stake."

"Of course, you're right. We're all losing sleep over the possibilities, believe me. And this is why it's so important for us to complete the project, you see, to keep it from falling into the wrong hands."

Luella made a noise of agreement. "You must remember," she added, "we're doing this to *prevent* such disaster, not to cause it."

My voice rose. "But by creating it, it's fallen into the wrong hands already, don't you see? Now that we've done it, others will do it, too."

I didn't say it aloud—I would sound like a Benedict Arnold—but what I thought then was, *What if we are the wrong hands?*

"That is one way of looking at it, isn't it, Miss Groves? I do see the merit in such thinking." He reached across the desk and patted my hand, which lay curled on the desk like a sickly animal. "I'm very impressed with your depth of consideration."

I saw the truth then: They found me adorable, like a pet puppy, an animal capable of learning neat tricks, so sweet and entertaining. If only I'd been born a human!

"The truth is, we still, even after this test, don't fully know what to expect. And you're right: The power is incredibly destructive, and we must be aware of all that it can do. All of us are working hard to make sure we understand all outcomes."

"We are in a war to the death," Luella said. I saw myself too much in her face, but her voice was the opposite of my own, calm, clipped, certain. "It doesn't help to stand around crying on one another's shoulders. We can't waste time asking one another, 'Gee, is this okay?'"

"It will create hell on earth," I said. The droves of walking dead, the ears and noses and mouths bleeding, the children incinerated where they played, organs boiled to sludge.

"It might reassure you, Miss Groves," Dr. Hall said, "to know that warning pamphlets are always dropped on the towns before an air raid. People will be warned in plenty of time."

"It's not always so simple," I said, "to leave."

I left, I thought, *and barely.*

I was holding a pen in my other hand, the hand he wasn't patting in a condescending manner, and when I looked down I saw that the ink had bled all over my dress. I had somehow, during our conversation, snapped the pen in two.

"Why don't you go home early," Dr. Hall said, waving loosely at the stained fabric. He gave a small laugh. "Clean yourself up. But thank you as always for sharing your interesting thoughts, Miss Groves."

"A little more education and you could stop up that bleeding heart," Luella said.

I retrieved my purse from my desk.

"Take care, Miss Groves," Dr. Hall said. "I'll see you early tomorrow."

What bothered me most was that maybe they did believe me, but even then, it didn't matter.

◦×
×◦

I arrived at the barracks bleary-eyed, sand-stained, my hair disheveled, and I wanted nothing more than to creep into my cot and fall asleep. But when I stepped through the doorway I heard voices speaking near my bunk. Something about their tone froze me. I hardly breathed.

"Mildred's sleepwalking again," Kathy hissed.

This surprised me. Was I sleepwalking? I'd had the impression of it, but no waking memory.

"I saw it, Beth," Kathy said. "A couple of nights ago she came in after midnight and she looked right at me but her eyes were as blank as a fart."

Beth said, "I saw her that night, too. I haven't even told her yet. She's seemed so cheerful during the day. I don't think she's even aware she's doing it." Her voice was muffled, as though she held a hand over her face. I couldn't see them properly, the partial wall blocked my view, but I recognized their voices clearly. "She lost my bell, did I tell you? Glen gave that to me. I don't know what to do about her."

I frowned.

Do about me?

As though I were a porcelain doll, cracked. As though I belonged to anyone at all. I remembered when she spoke to our house mother this way, whisperingly, secretly, as if I was a shameful blight on their lives.

"The truth is, Kathy, I've been asked to keep an eye on her. She's been to the doctor for her nerves. She's as fragile as a kitten. They don't want nervous types here, and I worry she's not mentally fit."

"Don't protect her," Kathy said. "It will hurt you both in the end."

"Her options are pathetic. Where will she go after this? Back to Omak? Her mother and sister are awful."

"She shouldn't be here. It makes a mockery of us all. It's hard enough being a woman here, but someone like Mildred gives us all a bad name."

"I wanted to help her," Beth said. "She's very sweet. But I've grown tired, I'll admit it. Sometimes she just sits and watches us all with these wide, unblinking eyes. I'm afraid of what this place is doing to her mind."

I lifted my hands straight out in front of me and spread my fingers wide apart. They trembled violently. I pictured gnawing each digit off and throwing them at Beth and Kathy, and the thought of their horrified screams calmed me.

My own Beth. How could you?

"The next thing," Beth said, determinedly, "and I'll report her. I will. For her own safety."

"Good girl," Kathy said. "You don't owe her anything. You have to take care of yourself."

I floated into the room then, full of witchcraft. I hovered over them both, these two insignificant, churlish women. I glared down at them where they sat on my cot—*my cot*—as though it were their own. I thought of my grandmother, that enormous bear of a woman.

Hexe.

"That's my bed," I said, my voice thrown out at them like a stone.

Beth jumped to her feet. She put up her hands as though surrendering to me, and I could read the fear in her face. My unsmiling mouth confirmed it: I'd heard everything. Kathy moved more languorously, eyeing me warily.

"Milly, what a surprise," Beth said. "Are you okay?"

"Never better," I told her with a cold smile. "But I need a nap. Get off my bed."

Kathy glanced at Beth and then moved toward the door. She said, cheerfully, "Let's get a bite of lunch, Beth, and then go back to work."

Beth looked at me with concern. She took a step toward me but I slid away from her. I undressed, slid into the sheets, pulled the blankets up over my head.

"Milly, I hope you don't think—"

But Kathy interrupted her. "Let her rest. You didn't do anything wrong."

But you did. Everything is wrong.

Beth tarried, pegged to the room by betrayal. I heard her weight shift from one foot to the other, the soles of her shoes gripped by viscous guilt, and I could smell her contrition, a perfume sweet with rot.

"I'll find you later, Milly," she said. "We'll talk and I'll explain it all. Everything will be okay."

Into my pillow, I mumbled, "Leave me alone."

"Milly, listen to me—"

"She wants us to leave," Kathy said, and I heard her footsteps approach Beth, heard the soft noise of her pulling Beth away. "Let her rest. She'll get over it."

I listened to them leave. For a long time I lay very still, breathing in the warm blackness of those blankets, wondering if I could die in this way, suffocating myself on anger and sadness and solitude. Eventually, I fell asleep.

I slept through dinner. I slept through the comings and goings of the other women in my barrack. I woke briefly with a sense of someone leaning over me, smelling of a lavender scent that I recognized but no longer adored. I turned away from the silhouette. I was fully alone now. Solitude offered its own comfort, a lesson I learned over and over and over again. I went back to sleep.

RAIN OF RUIN

On August 6, as I scrubbed my armpits clean in the sink of the portable, I heard women outside shrieking and hollering.

I dried myself off quickly and hurried into my blouse, shoving my nightgown and curlers into my messenger bag. I caught the eye of another woman changing there, and she, too, was hurrying, alarmed.

"What on earth is going on out there?"

With a rising sense of panic, we hastened outdoors to see what horrible thing had befallen us.

Outside was our house mother, Mrs. Berry, her face wet with tears. I was relieved to see she was smiling.

"We've done it!" Kathy shouted, sprinting past me as I squinted into the summery morning light.

Women celebrated, embraced, and hollered, pouring outside the barracks with cheerful whoops and screams.

Others wandered around as I did, dazed, asking, "What's going on? What's happened?"

Mrs. Berry waved a paper in the air and whistled loudly, and I approached and touched her arm.

She whirled to face me, her cheeks ruddy with excitement. "Mildred, it's incredible! Just incredible!"

She snapped the newspaper under my nose.

The church bell began to toll. We could hear the men whooping, too, from their side of the camp.

I peered at the headline in the *Villager*.

IT'S ATOMIC BOMBS
President Truman Releases Secret of Hanford Product
News Spreads Slowly, Surprises Everyone
Jubilation and Satisfaction Follows Revelation of
Product Manufactured Here

Richland was about the last place in the country to hear the news of the atomic bomb. As in other parts of the country it was the housewives who first heard the news over their radios and broke it to their husbands in a flurry of telephone calls which kept the switchboards humming.

"Atomic bombs," I said numbly.

Something quaked in the distant field of my vision, a phantasmagoric figure that fluttered and twisted with a dangerous, frenetic energy. I smelled the burning flesh beneath her shroud and dreaded her approach.

"Truman released a statement this morning," Mrs. Berry said. "We dropped one today. Japs didn't know what hit 'em!"

The figure at the edge of my vision trembled and inched forward.

"Those who walk in darkness," I said, trying to stifle the rising panic in my throat.

"Mildred, you okay, honey? You've gone white."

"Lady in the dark," I said, and then the figure was before me, hooded, faceless, draped in black tatters. She hung in the air like a stinking stygian sheet. I pushed my fingers forward but the fabric parted, dissipated, at my touch.

"Are you talking about the Ginger Rogers film?" Mrs. Berry asked, nonplussed.

I opened my mouth to yell for help and the figure flew into my throat.

My cheeks bulged, my eyeballs. My gut swelled with her acid and stench.

I looked at Mrs. Berry in panic. My nose started to bleed.

"Mildred, are you having allergies?" Even in my frenzy, I saw Mrs. Berry as a ridiculous woman, kind and always missing the point. She put a hand on my shoulder and pulled something out of her pocket. "Here, no biggie."

She pressed a handkerchief to my nose and held it there while my eyes watered. The dark figure in me fought and punched. I tried to swallow her but I couldn't. My gut churned.

"Get back," I managed to say, and then I was heaving, choking with horrible retching sounds.

The vomit hit the ground, black, chunky, steaming, and splashed onto Mrs. Berry's legs.

"Ow!" She swiped at her shin, more shocked than angry. "It burns!"

The syrupy black gunk shuddered on the ground. I knelt down in front of it and in the liquid's taut black velvet lifted a hundred tiny faces, agonized, screaming in pain. They emerged like so many bubbles, lifting, writhing, then going flat again. The vomit shuddered and then dissolved like an oil back into the earth. Mrs. Berry stared at the ground where the faces had been, gasping almost as wretchedly as I was.

"What in the Sam Hill did you eat today?" she said.

The blood dried in my nose. My stomach settled. I slowly returned to myself. I asked Mrs. Berry if her legs were okay.

She bent over her shins, examining them. "Huh. Look at that. Right as rain. I thought I was burnt, but I guess not." She sucked on her big lower lip, marveling. "That was like hot coffee coming out."

"What was the name of the place?" I asked her.

"Huh?"

"The place in Japan?"

"Oh. Truman said it was a military base. A place called Hiroshima."

"A military base?"

"That's what he said."

Relief. There couldn't be that many civilians in Hiroshima, not if it was a military base.

"He'll drop more if they don't surrender," she said proudly.

"More bombs?"

"He promised them a 'rain of ruin.'"

Off to the side of my field of vision, it was happening again, the shuddering figure drawing herself back together, humming, waiting to pounce.

"I'm sorry," I said. "I'm really not feeling well."

"Go to the infirmary," she advised. "And stay away from black coffee. Seems to bother your stomach. Add milk to it next time."

I assented with a grunt, even though I hadn't yet taken coffee or eaten breakfast. There had been nothing in my gut except for the phantom.

I stumbled away from her, lacing through the celebrating crowd. I spotted Kathy and Beth talking excitedly to each other near our barracks's side door, but I ignored them. The squirming shadow-figure followed me at a distance.

At work, Dr. Hall smiled and rose uncharacteristically when I entered. He seemed happy to see me.

"You've heard," he said.

"Yes."

"How does it feel? Now that you know?"

I hesitated. He sat down in his chair and motioned for me to do the same.

"It's a good thing, isn't it, Miss Groves? We've won a major battle, you realize. And I'm not just talking about Japan and Germany. I'm talking about the race we were in, scientifically. We've created the atom bomb first, and this means we can use it to protect ourselves and all good nations. Imagine if it had fallen into the hands of Hitler, as we feared for so long!"

"Hitler's dead."

"There will be other Hitlers."

This was obvious to me. "And what happened to the military base?"

"You mean where it was dropped today? Hiroshima? We don't yet know. We're waiting to hear the reports. There's never been another bomb like this, so I'm eager for news."

"Eager," I said. "Yes."

I felt sick.

"Miss Groves, I know you've expressed concerns about the product. But as our general said, 'This will be the bomb to end all bombs,' and I hope that's true. Our hard work is for the global good." He explained Japan's refusal of the Potsdam Declaration. "We gave them every opportunity. Truman warned them, if they didn't agree with our terms, they would face utter annihilation."

"Will they surrender now?"

"If they don't, Truman will drop another atom bomb. I can't imagine the war will continue after that."

Off to the side the coat hook shuddered. It was the phantom again, vibrating with terror. She wanted me to notice her. She had a message for me. I strained to listen.

It was the humming sound. *Hir. O. Shi. Ma.*

It hovered closer. I kept my mouth sealed. I didn't want to swallow it again, couldn't feel her writhing inside of me.

Hir. O. Shi. Ma, the figure hissed, and then I was the figure, also hovering, but not here in Unit B, but in the sky far above a town. Peninsulas of land stuck out like toes into a large bay, and a river wound through attractive buildings. The whole map of urban space thrummed with life.

I landed with a thud back in Dr. Hall's office.

"It's a city," I said. "Hiroshima. Why would President Truman call it a military base when it's a city?"

"Miss Groves, I'm sure he wouldn't say it was a military base if it didn't have—"

"You knew," I said. "You knew all along it was a city. They told you on the phone that day, about the target."

"I wasn't told much of anything, Miss Groves. Targets were mentioned but not Hiroshima."

"It's all true," I said. "Everything I told you. The town destroyed, the people mutilated beyond recognition. I told you and you didn't believe me."

"I listened to your hypotheses with much interest, Miss Groves. We'll see as the reports come in whether or not—"

"I've *seen* it," I retorted. "They are *facts*. We are killing everything by making this bomb and one day they'll bomb us here, just like I told you. Someone will bomb us. Our grandchildren, our great-grandchildren. And *that* bomb will be thousands of times more powerful than this one."

Dr. Hall grew cross. "Did you have so much to say during the Tokyo firebombing, Miss Groves? Hundreds of thousands died then and you protested nothing. And what of the millions the Japanese have killed in China, Korea, Malaysia, Indochina? You have a narrow view of humanity. This is *war*."

I was quiet. My foot tapped anxiously against the floor.

Dr. Hall wiped at his face. I had upset him. I was glad to see him rattled.

"Listen, Miss Groves," he said shakily. "Go home for the day. Emotions are high. I understand your point of view, I do. It's the point of view of a compassionate human being, and surely the world needs more of those. But please don't fool yourself: You've willfully participated in the creation of this bomb just as I have. Voicing your opinions about it now is too little, too late."

"I warned you," I said. "I told you all of this and you ignored me."

He waved me off. I could see from his face that he'd closed his mind to me. I was a woman, unpredictable and shrill. He muttered something about me nearing my menses.

I gathered my purse and light scarf. The trembling figure was gone from its post near the coatrack. I had said what I needed to say. I was free to go.

"Talk about it with your friends. You have a right to feel proud of your work here, Miss Groves."

"I don't have any friends."

I heard Mother in my voice as I said it.

"I'm sorry to hear that," he said, and he really did sound sorry, as though my friendlessness was worthier of his attention than the massacre of an entire people.

I took the cattle car back to campus, but other people had also been let out from work, and the beer-drinking and carousing irritated me. I tried to walk outside, by the river, but the heat shrank my spirit. I returned to the barracks. I read a penny book mystery and napped fitfully. I rose to eat alone in the mess hall and then returned, again, to bed. All around me rose the excited chatter of the women, my roommates, all of them exuberant, prideful, about the bomb. I hated that I couldn't fall asleep. I craved erasure.

Finally, haltingly, I dozed.

Later in that long dark night I snapped awake to find myself sitting on top of a rocky cliff overlooking the Columbia River. I was mid-conversation with the heron. I was happy to no longer be in the barracks, and I was even happier to have someone to speak to, even if I could never decode the *aufhocker's* intentions.

The product, the heron said.

She had been repeating this to me for several minutes now, waiting for my response, but I was only now awake, the word resounding, vibrating, in my left ear.

"They've killed civilians," I told the heron. "The Japanese will surrender now. Dr. Hall says I'm part of the success. He says I should be proud."

The heron squawked; it was an ugly, lonely sound.

I asked her where the wind had gone.

She beds down behind the mountains. The more she rests, the stronger she becomes.

It was strange not to feel the wind's warm, strong body against me. I found myself missing her, although most of the Hanford residents would be pleased. When she was absent, they played late evening games of baseball and picnicked outdoors rather than in the loud airless mess halls. The children chased one another, shrieking in pleasure when they got caught.

Without the wind, the night sky was polished to a fine sheen, cloudless, be-glittered with stars. It was a new moon and the stars, liberated, breathed deeply.

I shut my eyes. There was the sound of the river, washing, washing, *Washing west in Washington State.* I was drunk with the present and future.

What fine shoes you have, the heron said.

"Oh yes," I said, and I wiggled my feet. Usually I'd been barefoot during my wanderings—I wondered now if putting on the shoes had been my idea or the *aufhocker*'s. "I ordered them from the Sears Roebuck catalog. Do you know," I confessed, laughing, "I once wondered if I took this job just so I could buy these nice shoes."

They're divine, the large bird opined.

The rattlesnake slept on my lap and I petted her gently. I worried at first that she would soil my nightgown, but she was as dry and clean as an old bone.

I won't see you for a long time, the heron said.

"Oh?" I was surprised. "Are you going somewhere?"

She tossed the long cord of her neck. *You are.*

"I'm not sure why you bothered me all this time, anyway," I said.

"Empathy at a distance is a luxury." You were chosen for your empathy. You were chosen for your distance.

"You could be talking about anyone," I said.

We thought with your visions you could influence change. We thought you'd make the right choice and destroy the product. But how wrong we were. You are doing what they all do. You are the same as them. You've become part of their engine, the machine of men's rule.

I didn't take the heron seriously; she annoyed me. Did she really think I could have listened to the coyote and followed all of his hurried, rabid instructions to destroy Unit B? Did she really think anyone would have allowed it? I would have been caught too easily, men crawling all over the walls like greedy spiders. I wanted to believe we were creating something good, something that would save us all. . . .

"How irritable you are tonight," I said. "Maybe it's a good thing I won't be seeing much of you."

But I didn't mean it. I was frightened by the prospect of leaving. Hanford was my home now. I'd watched it unravel others but it had only tied my knots tighter. Back in Omak, I'd lost sight of myself. I'd watered myself down with self-hatred and inhibition. This was the only place I'd ever truly known myself. I'd succeeded here. I'd become a working woman, a patriot.

Hadn't I?

The heron's words made me doubt myself.

I couldn't return to Omak. Not now, not ever.

Someone will join us tonight, the heron announced, and I waited for the scores of wounded and dead to tumble down the slope of Rattlesnake Mountain.

But it was only a lone man.

He came down the embankment toward me, swinging his big arms, a graceful figure, athletic, muscular. He walked like a dancer, with a slight lift in each step.

The tinnitus in my ear whined.

It was Gordon Nyer.

I rose to my feet, unsteadily. The rattlesnake dropped away and slithered swiftly into the darkness. The heron flew over the shadowy sagebrush toward the river. My gaze returned to Gordon. There was nowhere else to look.

He treaded toward me in his work boots. "There you are," he called. "This is no place for you."

Gordon grinned. It was not at all friendly. For a moment I confused his face and the heron's face, his eyes with the yellow death eyes.

"I've been sent to fetch you," Gordon said. "Beth said you weren't anywhere to be found. Beautiful night for a stroll, isn't it?"

I tipped my face. The sky curved in a cupola, containing us like a glass cloche.

"Others are searching for you," Gordon said. "Tom Cat, Kathy. Beth, too."

"I'm fine," I said. "I took a walk."

Gordon eyed me up and down, his gaze catching on the tiny bows of my summer nightgown. He followed the curves of my body down to my new shoes and then back up to my chest and face. He was amused. "If I squint, you look a bit like Rita Hayworth."

His grin showed the big, dull kernels of his teeth.

I was flushed in my lace and bows, overexposed. I'd thought about a man seeing me this way, after we were engaged, after we'd been married, but not now, not like this, in this ceremony of darkness.

"What did you do with the green nightgown?" I asked him.

"What?"

"Beth's nightgown. The one you took from her nightstand."

"Maybe I still have it," he said. "Maybe I don't. Maybe I had some fun with it, if you want to know."

I frowned in disgust.

"Does it bother you, that I took it?"

"I don't care about Beth now."

"No? I do. I like her a lot." He pushed his hands into the pockets of his trousers and kicked a stone toward the river below us. The heron hunted in the waters there, purposeful, strong. "I'm going to marry her."

I laughed in revulsion. "Good luck," I said. "She'd never marry you."

"What if I told you you're wrong?"

"Then you'd be a liar."

"But you *are* wrong, Milly. She's already agreed."

"I don't believe you."

I started to walk forward, brushing past him, but Gordon seized my arm, high up, just beneath my armpit.

He put his face close to my own. I smelled beer on him, and cigarette smoke. Also the overwhelming male musk of him, the woodsy, dank scent of shot buck. I remembered my father dressing those bucks in the old shed behind our house in Omak. I'd watched every moment of the gory ritual. The intense sights and smells had amazed and dizzied me.

"You don't think I'm good enough," he said.

I didn't say anything. It was true: She deserved better. He was handsome, but he was vain and coarse. I wanted to hate Beth. I wanted her to deserve him. But she didn't. I felt deflated by my perpetual love for her. It made my hate stronger.

"What's the matter with you?" Gordon said, and he grabbed my shoulders and shook me, short and violent so that my teeth rattled. "Cat got your tongue?"

"Let go of me," I said. "I don't want you touching me."

I wasn't being coy. I was incredulous. But he must have been insulted, because he shook me harder.

"You're lucky any man would touch you, let alone me."

I searched for the heron. The river was empty. Where had she gone? My loss of control shamed me. This was my place, I thought. I belonged here just like the desert creatures and the river. No one would dare hurt me here.

"I want to go home," I said.

For a moment, Gordon relaxed his grip. I stepped away from him, turning my ankle on a sharp stone, but I didn't cry out. I held my ground.

"I don't understand you at all, Milly," he said, and he watched me with focused intent, as though I were a deer he had sighted in his rifle. He was quizzical, more confounded than upset. "You flirt with me, you walk around at night half-naked, then you act like you're too good for everyone. You know what I think? I think you're bananas. You belong in a loony bin." He waited a moment. A thought occurred to him. "Mad Mildred," he said, and laughed. "No one will ever believe a word you say."

I stiffened at the familiar moniker. "Leave me alone."

"Mad as a rabid dog. I saw you up here talking to yourself, petting your lap. You looked like a lost little kid. You're bats."

His tone wasn't rude, just matter-of-fact. I didn't argue with him. I just wanted to return to the barracks, to my cot, to Beth.

"She won't marry you," I said. "You're nothing. If you weren't a man, you'd have no power. You don't know what real power is, and you never will."

"Mad Mildred. No one will believe a thing you say about me."

He outstretched his fingers. An invitation.

The gesture alarmed me.

The idea of my safe place fully shattered. Who had I been fooling? I could have died out here. I could have been maimed, killed, by any number of things.

My confusion momentarily froze me.

The sharp lines of his face came together into a mean snout. A wolf, but there were no wolves here, they needed trees, forests. Panic unfroze me. I pictured the deer, their strong legs, thighs firm and big like my own. I gave a shout and then turned and sprinted, leaping, bounding, away from him. I was the deer, wild-eyed, startled, gasping for breath. I ran on my four legs over the rocks and sagebrush, scrambling down the sandy banks to the river, and I heard Gordon cursing, loping behind me. There she was, the heron, wading near the river's edge, stabbing her beak into the water and spearing a toad, which she choked back in one foul motion. She was interested in her survival just as I was in my own. I fell into the river near her and splashed wildly, and she flew into the sky. I meant to swim for my life, to allow the river to separate me from Gordon by pulling me downstream. I had a head start and felt certain I could outswim him. But then his hands encircled my ankles and he pulled me roughly backward. He grasped my hair and shoved me under the water and held me there while I thrashed. Then he lifted me up for one breath, only to dunk me under again. I flailed uselessly. He dragged me facedown by my thighs onto the bank, cutting my forehead and chest against the earth, and then he rolled me over and pulled up my nightgown. I blinked the water from my eyes and sputtered, "No, please." I was strong—years of lifting Mother and housework had made me muscular and able. I struck him and kicked and he yelped in pain. He pushed me down by my clavicle and then his hand encircled my throat.

"Be still, damn it," he screamed at me.

He lifted up a rock and held it over me, panting.

He brought it down on my skull.

I was a tree hit by lightning. I swam through a flash of lights and pooled blackness and a pain both distant and engulfing. The view from one of my eyes burst and went dim.

I spoke to him but not with words, only with blood.

He was on top of me then, tearing my panties aside. Near my face lay my shoes, though I had no memory of taking them off. He couldn't fit in me so he spit on his hands and rubbed between my legs, pushing and forcing himself. His face flickered, the coyote's face one moment, Gordon's next, then Tom Cat's, Beth's, the great blue heron's. My unwillingness deepened the pain. The rattlesnake snaked into me, biting and shaking and splitting me in two. It hurt not there but everywhere and I groaned. *If only the wind would come and wipe all of this away.* The heron stabbed at my mouth with her beak. I coughed blood. Gordon spit it back at me and stared down at me with cold, satisfied eyes, triumphant.

I rolled my head to one side and vomited.

Gordon drew his hands away from my shoulders and backed off, finished now. My body emptied. Flesh, then liquid. It was over. I lay as if dead, not sure if I was in a nightmare or a vision.

Don't be the future, don't be the past. Be nothing.

I would waken soon beside Beth, her arms wrapped tightly around me, and I would relay the whole nightmare to her and we would laugh about how real it had all seemed. She would tell me that everything she'd said to Kathy was a lie, and she'd make fun of Gordon for talking about marriage, and all would be right again. We would start over.

I gave a strange sound like a laugh now. *Beth, Beth, beautiful Beth! What an awful thing I saw.* It was a guttural, low sound that turned into a hoarse scream.

"You tell anyone about this, I'll kill you. I'll go to Omak and do the same to your mom and sister. You know I will."

My eyes had almost fully swollen shut, but I could just make out the thick shape of Gordon working at something above me. For a moment I wondered if his arms were lifted in prayer, but then came the bloody rock, his arms dropping again. I relaxed into the blackness of the impact.

UNDERWORLD

Kathy above me, speaking.

Confusion.

Why is she being so nice to me?

I moaned. *Leave me alone. I need sleep.* A tooth fell into my throat and lodged there. Kathy rolled me onto my side and I coughed and swallowed the tooth. I couldn't see well, but I recognized her voice.

My mouth was filled with dirt and prairie grass and blood.

"God, Milly. Oh, shit. Milly, can you hear me?" Then, yelling, "I've found her! Over here! Come quick!"

When the invisible man lifted me, no more than strength and purpose, something jostled in my face and resettled. Not in my face. Behind my face. Two lonely stars frowned down at me, spitting their weak light. Almost dawn. The pink blood of it on the horizon. I could see only in blurry streaks.

Kathy spoke to me violently, walking beside me where I floated. "Stay awake, Milly, stay awake. We'll carry you to safety."

A wraithlike spider stitched a black web over my field of vision. The web closed in around me with a slight scratching sound.

HEADLINES

There was a rattling of papers and in my half dreams it rasped like the rattlesnake's tail. My eyes flew open. I tried to cry out but there was no sound.

I was in a large white room, lying on a cot with a thin cotton blanket drawn over my legs and torso. Between the other beds, wearing starched uniforms, nurses bustled, some of them cheerful and chattering lightly, others businesslike, wiping people down, removing bed pans, frowning over an injection.

A hospital. I was dead but undead.

"Milly," a voice said, and my eyes focused painfully on the woman sitting to my right.

Beth.

She held the newspaper open in her arms and stared at me with a shocked expression.

"Milly, you're awake!"

I tried to speak to her but my mouth was broken. I drooled, instead. I looked at her with a panic-stricken expression. I could feel the words in my head but I couldn't express them.

Beth hurriedly folded up the paper and rested it on my legs, leaning forward with her normal compassionate exigency.

"Don't worry yourself, Milly. You've had a terrible blow. Your skull was fractured. The fog is normal. You've been in a coma for a few days now, Milly, but you're on your way to recovery. Try not to worry or think too much. You need to heal."

I glanced down at the newspaper headlines. With difficulty I read,

PEACE!
OUR BOMB CLINCHED IT!

I looked up at Beth, startled.

They surrendered.

"Such good news, Milly," Beth said tenderly. "We've won the war. Isn't that marvelous?"

I took up the paper and tried to read more, but when I focused my eyes a wretched pain spread through my head and down the back of my neck.

Beth took the paper from me. "Milly, you need rest. No reading. No papers. No thinking, for that matter."

Next to me on the side table was another newspaper and I pointed to it, and then to Beth.

"Okay," she said. "If you want me to. Because it's happy." She took it up and read it. "This is older, more than a week ago. I saved it for you. I'll just read you the headline, okay?"

The words floated on the backs of my closed eyelids, fully capitalized, thick and black: *NEW ATOMIC BOMB LOOSED ON JAPAN.*

"We dropped another one, Milly," she continued. "On a town called Nagasaki. The first bomb, you know, they named Little Boy, this second bomb was called Fat Man. Isn't that droll? It was made of our plutonium. Hanford's own! It was too much for the Japs. They surrendered just a day ago, on the fifteenth. Everyone is over the moon with our work here."

Over the moon. Buried in moon stuff.

I closed my eyes again. I wanted to lie down fully, but my bed was locked in an upright position, perhaps so the blood wouldn't collect in my face and brain.

"Those . . ." I tried to speak but the words were muddled. "Poor . . ."

"Milly, don't strain yourself."

"Peep—" I couldn't say the word *people*. My eyes remain closed, but the tears flowed down my cheeks, anyway.

My hands were locked together above my waist. Beth cupped my hands with her own and I concentrated on their warmth. She seemed to understand why I was crying.

"A small group here has protested," she said. "They made some signs and marched around but they were threatened and booed. I suppose it was horrible there, for the Japanese. It's good of you to think of them."

She bent fully at the waist and put her head in my lap. She heaved a giant pained sigh, but I couldn't tell if she was crying or not.

"Oh, Milly, I'm sorry, I'm sorry. I didn't mean to hurt you. If I could take it all back, I would."

Later, I awoke from a dream where two rattlesnakes clung to my breasts, dangling from the soft flesh by their fangs. *I saw her once. Hop forty paces. Defect perfection.* An electrical charge from their venom shot up my spine. I stood straighter, taller. I absorbed the pain and was more formidable for it. *Power breathes forth.*

"Mildred Ferret Face Groves," said a sharp voice above me.

I didn't want to hear that voice. I stared at the corner of my bed instead. I daydreamed over and over a scene involving the heron in which she was a fish and I was a river, indifferent to her passing through me. I flourished the more she flailed—soon she would be dead while I swelled, swift and coursing to the fey ocean.

I'd been fumbling with such reveries since waking. They were useless. I was no river, indifferent and purposeful. I was the dirt, the land, stuck and passive, poisoned by men.

"Weasel Brain," the voice said, more tenderly this time, and I slowly dragged my eyes away from the bed corner.

Mother.

Martha's face floated there, too, so that the heads formed two large, wavy-haired orbs, regarding me with desolation and wonder.

"What have they done to my girl?" Mother cried, bringing a knuckle to her lip. "Poor Ferret Face. They've wrecked even your plainness."

"Oh, Mother," Martha said, touching my arm. "It's just bruises and scabs. She'll look better soon, you'll see."

"Her left eye, though. That eye is broken. The doctor says they'll replace it with glass. It's like your aunt Edna's eye, Martha, after she was kicked by that mule. Of course, we all know Aunt Edna deserved it. She was a brute to animals."

"Why?" I managed, and they leaned forward.

"What was that, Mildred?" Mother said, in a kind voice I hadn't heard from her since I was a child. "Can't you speak up, dear?"

"Why here?" I asked again.

"We took the bus from Omak once we heard you woke up," Martha said. "We've been so worried. Did you know it took them more than a week before they notified us? What's wrong with these people, Mildred?"

"Richland is a hideous place," Mother agreed. "Government types are numskulled puppets."

I was pleased to see them. I had half a mind to rise from the bed and loop arms with them and show them around the Hanford site. How proud they'd be of me! But I could hardly sit up. The doctors said it would take several weeks to remind my body of how to move, how to walk, how to speak.

I closed my eyes. I wanted to sleep in my childhood bed.

"They say you were muddled with," Martha said in a low voice, glancing around at the other patients. "They say you were muddled with *down there.*"

"You could be pregnant," Mother said matter-of-factly. "It's a possibility."

"With twins even," said Martha, and our mother scowled at her.

Beth never spoke to me of such things. It was easier with her to pretend that nothing untoward had happened. She had given me a bouquet from Tom Cat, saying that he sent his prayers for my healing and that he wanted to come visit me. I shook my head frantically, *no no no no no.* Beth had made shushing noises at me until I calmed down and then promised me she would relay the message. "You're not ready," she said. "And that's okay." And only once she mentioned Gordon, saying he felt "awfully sorry" for me, and the words hit me like a nightmare, visceral, full-bodied, the smell of blood and pounded meat, *tell her tell her,* but I couldn't tell her the truth, it would make it too real, I'd relive it all, the scabs would tear off and I'd be vulnerable and sick. Maybe Beth wouldn't believe me. And in my broken brain the whispered threat issued again and again, *You know I will. Kill you. Go to Omak. Your mom and sister.* I felt myself split in two just as I'd been on the riverbed, the heron's beak murderously stabbing my mouth. *You know I will.* Tom Cat and Gordon were men who expected things of me both good and gruesome, and when she mentioned them I moaned and turned away from her. Beth got the message. She stopped bringing them up entirely.

"Martha, why don't you go fix your hat?" Mother said irritably.

"I'm not wearing a hat, Mother, you said at the motel that it fattens my jowls, so I—"

"Go to the restroom, dear," Mother ordered, and the stridency of her tone sent Martha scurrying.

"Did he . . ." Mother ran a hand through the air just above my face, and I felt a small cool wind from it, her familiar scent, the baby powder she patted into her armpits. "Did he do this to you, too?"

I nodded.

Mother's face firmed with anger.

She leaned over me. Having a purpose, she was more lithe and agile than I'd seen her in years.

"They said you were in your nightie. They said you were wandering around mostly naked. Why would you do this, Mildred? Not even you are so dumb."

I clutched Mother's coat sleeve. My mouth worked. "I. Saw." I couldn't explain. *I saw it all before it happened. All of it. The bombs. I deserved this.*

My eyes filled with tears.

Her brow wrinkled. Then she put a palm on my forehead and its cool plumpness calmed the fever in me.

"You brought this on yourself. I've always told you, Mildred, *you can't trust men*, and yet you waddled right into a pack of them. But it's over now. The doctors will fix you up and then you'll return to Omak. You know what they told me years ago about you, after you pushed me into the river?"

I stared at her, my mouth working.

"They said I needed to occupy your mind. So I overdid it, Milly. I became a layabout, a sickling, a needy old maid. I half-believed it myself. But I don't think that helped you at all. When you return, it will all be different. I'll care for you. *You'll* be the old maid, the layabout."

A loud whimper rose from my chest, exploding from my mouth and nose. *A performance?* Her needing me to bathe her, to wait on her hand and foot, to clean up her bathroom messes, was all for *my* benefit?

A month ago, I would have hesitated to anger her, given how much I had told her that I shouldn't have. She could have reported me, she could have caused trouble for me then. But now the whole world knew our secrets, so what did it matter?

"If only," I told her, lowly, with much effort, "you'd died."

If only I'd killed you at the river.

It wasn't eloquent, and I worried for a moment that it wouldn't be an adequate message, but she drew back from me, putting a hand over her heart, registering the venom of my words. I enjoyed the pain they caused her.

"If only I'd killed you," I said.

It was the most complete sentence I'd formed in weeks.

Martha returned then, her hair combed into ringlets around the saucers of her ears. She was in a huff for being so rudely dismissed, but then she saw Mother's face, and my own, and she balked.

"What's this about? What's happened now?" She looked frantically between Mother and me, reading our tense faces. "Mildred, are you returning to Omak with us or not?"

Mother had already risen, was taking up her purse and cane. "No, she's not coming with us. We've done enough for Miss Mildred Groves here. We don't owe her a thing. It's your fault, Mildred, but I'm still sorry it happened."

She began to walk for the door but then turned back to me and said, "I'm not saying I've made the best choices. But one day you'll see how we women are the only ones looking out for one another."

As Mother went through the door, Martha turned back to me with a sad, reproachful look. "Why'd you have to do that? You're always so selfish. All she does is talk of you, you know. You never stop to think of the pain you cause her." She put her hand on my arm, lovingly. "I don't want to leave you here, but it's for the best."

From the hallway Mother hollered Martha's name.

"Good-bye, Mildred," my sister said.

"Good," I managed, exhausted, and if I'd had my full mental capacity, I would have added, *riddance.*

FIENDSHIP

"Go. Away."

This is what I told Kathy when she came to visit.

Kathy cocked her head and snapped her fingers in front of my nose. "Mildred, don't be difficult. Stop feeling sorry for yourself."

"Don't," I told her, but what I meant was *I don't.*

She shook her head at me, scowling in her mean way. "Just listen for one damn minute, Mildred. It's not all about you, you know."

Why was she so angry with me? What had I ever done to her? I lay on my stomach with my right ear on the pillow, watching her with my face tipped to the left.

She reached forward with a surprisingly kind movement and drew a coil of my hair behind my left ear.

"It's awful what he did to you. It happened to me, too, Mildred. An older boy when I was young. I loved him. He was my very favorite cousin, until . . ."

She rolled up her fists and stacked them one on top of the other on the edge of my mattress, resting her chin atop them. We could look each other in the eyes this way, although from my angle she looked tipped onto her side like the queen on a chessboard, less mean, less threatening.

"Men get away with everything," she told me.

My eyes filled with tears.

"I. Want. To," I said.

"What's that, Mildred?" She moved her fists away and lay her head on its side so that we looked at each other directly. How awkwardly she'd contorted her body, I thought. It was the kindest gesture I'd ever seen from her.

"Die," I said then, shutting my eyes tight so that the tears fell thickly, all at once.

"I know," she said. "But you can't."

"No," I said. I didn't mean die. "Kill."

"Oh. That, too. Me, too."

"Gordon," I said.

Kathy sat up. "Gordon?" A thousand furies flitted over her expression. "God, Mildred. Gordon! Really? But he," she stopped herself here, took a deep breath. "No. Never mind that. What a snake. I never liked him, you know. I see him with Beth now and again, but no wonder he's lying low. You'll have to just do your best to avoid him."

I didn't like hearing this about Beth. "Yes," I managed.

She breathed deeply for a minute. "You can't kill him."

I knew I couldn't. The only person I could harm was myself.

"You need to forget," she said. "Forget and move on."

"You. Forget," I said to her, brow furrowed. It was an argument, a retort.

"I don't know what else to tell you," Kathy said, and she sounded sincerely regretful. "It's easy to give advice. Harder to live it."

AUTHORITIES

The next day a few men came to speak with me about "the incident." They called themselves the authorities. I saw no badges or identification, but they looked well-groomed and each held a pen and a tablet of paper, so I believed in their importance.

"Why were you out there in your nightgown?" one of them asked.

"You know a young woman should not be alone outside of the barracks. We've given multiple warnings about this."

"The behavior itself was promiscuous."

"You weren't meeting anyone? There wasn't a secret rendezvous?"

"A swimming date at the river?"

"Are you Catholic? Would you like a priest? For a confession?"

"A minister, then? A man you can trust?"

"Was this your first time?"

"Your head injuries could be explained by a bad fall."

"Have they checked you for pregnancy yet? Too early?"

"Did you enjoy any of it? Did you indicate enjoyment in any way, shape, or form?"

"Of course your memory is shaky. Given the injuries."

"This wasn't your first time out there."

"Are you sure you weren't wanting this to happen?"

"We've known about your hysteria for several months, Miss Groves. People have been monitoring you."

"How do we know you didn't do this to yourself?"

"Would you say you enjoy the attention your 'episodes' bring you?"

"Is it true you were sleepwalking prior to what you call 'the attack'?"

"Maybe you dreamed this?"

They fell silent, waiting for my response. I watched them with throbbing eyes from where I lay on the cot.

"Only," I began. I thought of the *hibakusha*. I thought of the glass and metal impaled in the baby's skull. "Expect. The. Worst."

They looked at each other, one of them smirking incredulously. "Well, that just about explains it, eh, boys?" He reached out and squeezed one of my toes, which hurt terribly, sending a painful shock to my brain. "Rest up. Heal up. Put all this behind you."

My response slurred together into a garbled curse.

When they left, I realized they'd never asked me the most important question: *Who did this to you?*

I wouldn't have named him, anyway.

You know I will. Go to Omak. Your mom and sister.

I shouldn't have cared about them now—Martha, Mother—but stupidly I did.

PARALYSIS

Autumn passed in an unpredictable weather pattern of confusion and triumph.

There were days when I could hardly grasp the instructions I was given (*squeeze your hand, tap your toes, sit up straight*) and days when something lost became, again, automatic. There were days, too, when I slept and dreamed. I dreamed of Japan, of the great blue heron, of Dr. Hall, of Stanley Johnson. I dreamed of the tortured and immolated children of Auschwitz. I dreamed of twins stitched together at their spines. Before my eyes the duo grew foul and rotted and died. The things we've done to the children of this world—slavery, brainwashing, exile, genocide—do any other creatures harm their children in this way? These deviances built our own nation, they've built all of the civilizations of men. I awoke with the certainty that none of us deserved to be alive, myself least of all.

One evening, in the middle of the night, I awoke to a snuffling noise at the foot of the bed. The coyote was there, the heron's yellow eyes boring out at me from his protuberant face. He licked my bare toes with a pitying look, ears low, tail sagging. I kicked at him, hissed at him to leave. He lifted my shoes—Susan Peters's shoes—in his mouth. They were filthy, caked with dirt. I remembered the last time I'd worn them and cried out. A nurse came running and the coyote slipped away, under the cots of my bedfellows.

The next day an aide presented the shoes to me, polished to a fine sheen.

"Let's try walking in these today, shall we?"

I shook with rage and frustration. "No," I said. "They aren't safe."

I spoke even now, months later, with hesitation. I could handle short words but nothing else.

"I love these shoes," the aide said, admiring them. "So fashionable. Where did you find them?"

Outside, it was snowing. Every morning they told me the date but the information slipped through the new holes in my skull. I couldn't keep track of the simplest details.

"Susan Peters."

"What's that?"

"Susan Peters, the actress," I said again. "Her shoes."

"How funny you should mention that," the aide said, smiling. She put up a finger, indicating she would return in a moment. She left the shoes sitting on the edge of my bed. I didn't want them there. I pushed them onto the floor with my feet. They clattered onto the linoleum. Maybe the floor would open up and swallow them whole.

The aide returned with a newspaper and cleared her throat.

"Listen to this," she said. "'On January first of 1945, Spokane-born actress and Hollywood 'Girl Next Door' Susan Peters went duck hunting with her husband, Richard Quine, and was accidentally struck in the spine by a discharged bullet. After a year of hospitalization, doctors say she is paralyzed from the waist down. Peters remains plucky even in the face of her mother's death this December. She promises to continue acting, even if from a wheelchair.'" The aide looked up at me. "Something else, huh? She's had a horrible year. And we always think stars have it all."

I tried to sit up. The aide saw me and reached forward, but I batted her hand away. I struggled into a seated position and managed, slowly, to swing my legs over the edge of the cot. The aide tried to help me but I pushed her away again.

"Why are you weeping?" she asked, putting a hand on my back.

I wanted to stand and walk into the lavatory where I could be alone. The effort of it was too much. I brought my hands up to my eyes, covering them, but even the darkness there swam and dissolved, and before me unfolded all that would happen to Susan, all of it: her forced cheer, the cancellation of her contracts, the pathetic attempts at acting, the isolation, the divorce, the sanatorium, the electric shock therapy that triggered an even darker depression, the anorexia, the bronchial pneumonia, the terrific release of death.

For a moment I *was* her in that last second of life, etiolating into exultant erasure. I wept tears of gratitude even as a headache implanted itself behind my eyes, the worst headache of my life. Over the next months, I became more and more acquainted with the power of these headaches. My visions took on a more focused strength, and so did the pain.

"Don't cry," the aide said. "It's only an actress."

"A person," I protested. "All of these discarded persons!"

She congratulated me on formulating such a long, eloquent phrase.

AN UNEXPECTED GIFT

Daily, as I improved, a nurse's assistant, usually Joanie with her carefully straightened hair, would hand me a cane and take my arm and together we would walk outside, a five-footed, two-headed beast, slowly circuiting Richland Hospital's courtyard. I relished the fresh air. The hospital air was sterile, its aroma grotesquely clean, bones scoured in bleach, but outdoors I inhaled the scent of the earth and its snowy richness. Inside the lights flashed faintly at all times, just enough to make me think I was losing my mind, but the light outdoors, thin and cold, was stable, omnipresent. "Let's go around again," I would beg, and the assistant, especially if it were Joanie, would usually comply. It was an escape for her, too, from serving the cafeteria slop and straightening sheets and scrubbing shit from bedpans. We looped around and around again, and each visit to the courtyard served to deliver a part of me back to myself, my brain and limbs remembering one another again, finally. Before long, I abandoned the cane. Spring was coming; the creeks and rivers swelled with melt. My feet were steady, even on the ice. But now I had a limp, a noticeable one, and after a few weeks of no improvement I realized my ambulation was as good as it would ever be. I struggled to accept this, what had been done to me, and I tried to grow accustomed to dragging a reluctant part of me along, but I could never shake the sense that there was a corpse attached to me now, hindering my movement. My own corpse, presumably. The old me from before Little Boy and Fat Man, the one Gordon had bludgeoned to death.

One day when Joanie and I rounded the bare hydrangeas, their branches finally relieved of snow, I heard a familiar, warm voice calling, "Mildred Groves! I'm so happy to see you!"

I looked up from the glittering walkway and there was Tom Cat hurrying toward me, a sporting figure in his sturdy winter coat and good boots and hunting cap. I was genuinely happy to see him. Joanie no longer held my arm during the walks, but we walked close together for companionship, sometimes with our elbows touching. We separated now and I waved at Tom Cat, smiling. Joanie moved away from us, providing space for us to speak privately.

Tom Cat stiffened at the sight of my face. The rest of me must have looked the same, hidden as it was beneath a winter parka and a long wool blanket, wrapped around my hospital gown like a skirt, but my face was changed, one eye dead and unblinking, the nose busted and healing in an angry, crooked line. There were other scars and lacerations, too. I was Mary Shelley's monster, stitched together with parts that didn't match.

"Oh, Mildred," he said, and I was grateful for the pity in his voice, the awareness of loss. But when he reached forward to take up my hand, I yelped and pulled away from him.

It hurt, being touched by a man. The pain slammed deep in my organs, like someone had plunged a butcher knife into my bowels. I struggled to catch my breath.

"I won't touch you," he said. "I shouldn't have done that."

He waited with me, hanging back, and I could see how he battled against his instincts, how he longed to put his hand on my shoulder and pat me comfortingly, how he sensed that this would only intensify my agony.

"I'll never not feel it," I said, and he seemed to understand, and sadness flickered in his eyes, not just pity for me, but for himself.

When I regained my composure, he said, "I brought you a gift."

We began to walk, side by side, toward the hospital doors. I was feeling the chill now. I looked forward to getting inside.

"Oh?" I couldn't imagine what the gift would be. "How kind of you, Tom Cat."

"I wanted to visit you for so long, but Beth told me you weren't ready. I hope it's okay I came today."

"It's good to see a friend," I told him, and I was relieved that I actually meant it.

"I think of you all the time. I've written to my mother and sisters in Tonasket about you. When I told them you'd been involved in an accident—"

I stiffened. *An accident.*

"—they all gave a little money and bought something for you. It isn't much, but I thought it might cheer you, even give you some guidance. At the very least, it will let you know we're all praying for you."

He brought out a prettily wrapped gift, handing it to me, and I sank onto a little stone bench near the hospital entrance to open it. Joanie lingered nearby, no doubt curious about the item. It had been a long time since anyone had given me a gift, and I remembered my childhood, the excitement of a birthday party when I got everything I wanted, including a handsome stuffed bear.

I unwrapped the present while Tom Cat settled himself on the other side of the bench, shining at me.

It was a Bible. They'd paid money—good money, I knew—to inscribe the front of it in gold leaf, *For Our Friend, Miss Mildred Groves.*

I looked up at Tom Cat, and he read the question in my eyes.

"I know, I know," he said timidly. He reached up and scratched his ear beneath his red hunting cap. "It's a common gift for newlyweds. I hope that doesn't make you uncomfortable."

I considered what all of this meant: that Tom Cat had expressed his interest in marrying me to his siblings and mother; that they had liked and supported the idea; that Tom Cat wanted to marry me now, despite what had happened.

"This is so kind, Tom. I'm really touched."

He scooted closer to me, sensing my awe, and said, lowly, desperately, "Tell me who did this to you, Milly. You don't deserve this. No one does. Tell me who did this and I'll speak to them personally."

He cracked his knuckles. He sought more than just conversation.

I closed my eyes against the tumult of rising tears. I was overcome with the goodness of some people, when the rest of us were so terrible.

Part of me wanted to tell him, to see if he could, in fact, enact the revenge I craved, but another part of me knew that Gordon would overpower him, destroy him in an even more violent way than he had destroyed me.

"Tell me," he said, in the same breathy tone of, *I love you.*

"I don't remember." I felt exhausted by the request. *Stop asking me for things, Tom Cat.* "But please thank your mother and sisters from me."

I hugged the book to my heart. I didn't think I'd ever open it, feeling like religion was a distant planet I never wished to visit, but I cherished it, nonetheless. I saw it as a gift from a past life, a relic of hope that no longer lived in me. I didn't want to marry Tom Cat now, no matter his intentions, but it warmed me to know that I was adored, that I'd been close to whatever dream this country tried to foster in young girls.

Tom Cat reached his hand up as though to stroke my hair but then remembered himself. His palm hovered beside me, shaking slightly at the edges, a fragile dragonfly, and I leaned closer to it as if it were a warm fire, something I admired but understood I could never touch.

CONGRATULATIONS

Just after the New Year, Beth visited me in the hospital and stood beside me nervously, jostling from one foot to the other. I rested in a rocking chair, reading the paper. The staff urged me to sit there instead of in my bed, just to shift my muscles from one position to another, and I enjoyed it, even if the rocking chair was so close to my cot that I brushed my knees against the sheets as I rolled my heels to and fro. Reading no longer hurt me. They offered me sewing materials and knitting needles but I refused them; I only wanted the newspapers. I was trying to find any information at all about the *hibakusha*, the people I knew intimately from my time at the river, but there was only a small snippet about a Hanford scientist being sent to Hiroshima for research.

Not to help them, I thought, *but to study them.*

At one point someone brought me a paper from New York City. I saw one line in it that alerted me to the presence of the dead but not the survivors.

The United States Strategic Air Forces reported yesterday that 60 percent of Hiroshima and 40 percent of Nagasaki had been destroyed. "The destructive power of these bombs is indescribable," the broadcast continued, "and the cruel sight resulting from the attack is so impressive that one cannot distinguish between men and women killed by the fire. The corpses are too numerous to be counted."

The bombs were declared a success. Of course they would be. The destruction of anything was a success, so long as the perpetrator was an empire of men.

I wondered about Dr. Hall. How did he feel about it all? Was he ecstatic? Remorseful? Knowing him, I figured a mixture of both. He never visited me, but he did send a card, *Get well soon*. The actress Hazel Dee signed it, too. She had stamped the card with a kiss, and the red pucker of her lipsticked mouth reminded me of entrails. I could smell her perfume when I opened or closed the card. I gave it to a nurse to throw away.

Now I absently took Beth's hand. I loved her and hated her both. There was no need for hello or small talk. I continued to read but eventually grew impatient with her fidgeting.

"Why are you such a nervous Nancy today?" I asked her querulously.

"I brought someone along with me," she said. "My fiancé."

"Fiancé?" I dropped the newspaper and rose from the rocking chair. She held my elbow to steady me. "Who in the world?"

She gazed excitedly out across the hallway, over the white cots and IV bags and quiet patients and busy nurses. She lifted a hand and beckoned a dark figure from afar.

I followed her gaze.

I didn't think she was capable of it. I really didn't. I was sure she had rejected his proposal.

I was wrong.

I was wrong because he was a man who knew how to be charming, perfect, when it suited him; he could turn his violence on and off like a switch. He knew how to trick a woman he admired, even a woman as brilliant and kind as Beth, and he'd been patient in his courting, precisely manipulative.

Aufhocker. Shape-shifter.

Gordon sailed toward us. Gordon's body, at least. Huge, towering, dressed in navy suit trousers, a crisp white shirt, a thin navy tie. He was trying to make a good impression. In his big fist he gripped a heart-shaped box of chocolates. For me, I presumed. But it was his countenance that terrified me.

It was the decapitated buck I'd seen more than a year ago at the river, its head shoved over Gordon's face and throat. The blood from the beast's neck marred the fabric of his otherwise clean shirt. *Did Beth iron his clothes?* The dead eyes grinned out at me as Gordon advanced. Through the gaping stag maw, behind those blunt teeth, I could make out Gordon's nose and smiling mouth. It was a hideous mask, evil and crude. It moved stiffly atop Gordon's person like a papier-mâché puppet.

I backed away, pressing my spine against the cold hospital wall. I clawed at the plaster, whining.

"Milly," Beth said, alarmed. "What's wrong?"

Be still, damn it.

My speech had improved in the last several months. It wasn't normal yet, and I suffered terrible lapses from time to time, but I had regained almost full capacity of my vocabulary and syntax. But now I was trapped. The buck floated toward me, stuffed atop this man's powerful torso, and I bellowed.

You know I will.

"Stop him," I tried to scream. "Help!"

You know.

No words came out. I was as hoarse as if I had laryngitis. I began to sob. Beth grabbed me and tried to hold me close but I gnashed my teeth at her and pushed her away.

"Someone help us," Beth cried.

The buck came forward and hung over me with his dead eyes glinting, the mouth within the mouth issuing clucking and shushing noises.

The callused fingers stroking my arms were familiar and I shrieked as they brushed my skin.

I will.

He was holding me, too, now, whispering to me gently through the buck's ugly straight mouth, and I buckled and screamed. It was Gordon's voice. I buckled and fought with revulsion and confusion.

"Why is she acting like this?" Beth demanded, desperately, eyes wild. "What's wrong with her?"

"I'm a man," the buck said in Gordon's voice. "And look what a man did to her."

Two nurses were on hand now, pulling the figure of the buck-man away, pulling at Beth.

You know I will you know I will you know I will you know I will you know I will you know I will your mom and sister you know I will you know I will you know I'll kill you.

"What did you say to upset her?" a nurse said accusingly to Beth.

"Nothing! I wanted her to meet my fiancé. But when she saw Gordon—"

I shrieked so loudly the room shook. Footsteps descended from all directions, an earthquake moving toward me.

"Get them out of here," someone said.

Hands took hold of me, pushed me onto the cot, strapped me down. Someone shoved a wet rag between my teeth. I shrieked deep in my throat. A nurse administered a shot of something to calm me down.

"We don't want you to hurt yourself," she said.

I looked frantically at all of the serious faces crowding the bed. No Gordon. No Beth. Whatever was in the shot worked quickly. My body relaxed. I was in the water of the big river, steered by a peaceful current.

"You can't bang your head on the wall like that again," a nurse scolded me. "You'll undo all the good work we've done."

The crowd dispersed. I was okay. I didn't remember slamming my head against the wall, but my head ached.

The words came easily now, shaken loose by physical pain. "Is he gone? Did he leave? Where is Beth?"

"They left together. She was very upset. That was no way to treat your best friend, you know. And no way to treat your rescuer."

"My rescuer?"

"That man. The man that was with her, the fiancé. He and a young woman found you." Kathy, I remembered. "He was the man who carried you here safe. You would have died in the sagebrush without him, your brain was bleeding so profusely. He deserves a parade, that one."

"A parade," I repeated.

I laughed and sobbed uncontrollably.

PUSH OFF

Joanie put my small suitcase on the edge of my bed. "There you are," she said. "All packed."

I wore my good shoes, but I noticed now how loose they were, how my feet slid and seemed unable to find purchase. I'd lost weight and muscle, even in my feet. I couldn't look down at my legs without remembering Gordon and the river.

"It's time I leave," I said.

"Godspeed," Joanie said, and then embraced me. "We'll miss you, Mildred. Take good care."

I took up my suitcase and bid the nurse good-bye. She asked me if anyone waited for me and I told her yes, of course, that Beth herself was coming, and she said, "Oh, isn't she just the loveliest?"

The truth was, I hadn't told Beth. I hadn't told a soul about my departure. I wasn't sure what I wanted. There was no place for me to go. Hanford, with all of its flaws, had felt like home to me, but now that home was broken.

Nonetheless, when I left the hospital, I walked through the hills of Richland in the warm spring sun with my eyes on Rattlesnake Hill.

. . . when it all becomes too much.

I made up my mind where to go. If I walked at a good pace, I would get there by midnight.

At one point a bus filled with men pulled up alongside me. The driver wrenched open his door and said to me, "Heading to Hanford? Get in, we'll drive you there."

"No thanks," I said. Who knew if Tom Cat was on the bus. Or Gordon Nyer. The thought of seeing either of them crumpled me. "I'd rather walk."

"Suit yourself."

The bus accelerated and covered me with a fine dust. It didn't matter. The wind was terrible, anyway, and I clutched a kerchief in my fist so I could wipe my eyes clear.

I was made of wind and dust. I could have floated clear to the ocean. *This is where.*

The most beautiful time of day here was when the sun had mostly set, and all of the bare hills turned the fiery color of gemstones. I'd left my suitcase in a patch of sagebrush some miles back. It'd grown too heavy. I'd walked the crossing to the northeastern side of the river, my target the White Bluffs. My pretty shoes wore giant blisters into my toes and heels. Given my hospital lacuna, I hadn't walked this far in months, but it was good for me to ache, to hurt, to move.

It was, I assumed, my last day here. I was ready to become what I had seen: the broken body on the earth below, the organs spilled like garnets and rubies all around me, the transformation to a new or absent selfhood.

I arrived after the sun had set and the stars had risen and the wind had quieted to a mere stiff breeze. I walked to the very edge of the cliff face, still huffing from the climb, and then went down on my hands and knees. Beneath my palms, the eerie white sand was warm and comforting. The Columbia slid smoothly south, the currents like deep green scales on a leviathan's spine. On her shore the waters frothed and separated and Fat Man's ghosts came out of the waters and stood watching

me with their melted, eyeless faces, their heads and shoulders covered
in dark ash, waiting.

This is where you must jump when it all becomes too much.

I stared down at them. I wasn't far from them here, but there was
still this distance, myself looking down on them from this white cliff.
And the distance from here to Japan, to Germany, was even larger. It
occurred to me that the distance from one human being standing beside
another was just as incalculable. *It is happening to someone else, but not to me.*
From that dark gap in our imagined spaces, indifference was born, and
cruelty, and murder.

I can leap over that distance.

My legs felt strong enough, even now. One leap and no one would
ever know anything else. My secrets about Gordon and Hanford and
my own complicity would be over. I would never have to leave, never
have to expect anything else of myself. I was so sick of expectation. Nauseous with memories and hopes. The sand, the water, the wind, the
snakes, the furred creatures. If I rotted here, they would take me over. I
would become part of them, still moving beneath the starlight. It would
be a more graceful existence.

I wiped my eyes with my wrists and they came away stained with
tears.

I turned away from the cliff. I could feel all of the eyes of the dead
on me and I thought, *What else could I have done? I talked about you, I did.
I warned Dr. Hall. Do you think you can blame me? I love you as I love myself and I
hate you in the same way, too.*

I took ten paces. I meant to pivot and run and leap, aiming for the
river. I would sprout wings mid-flight. I thought of my little suitcase,
alone out there in the wind and sage, my few clothes in it, the Bible from
Tom Cat's family in Tonasket, no finery, just modest objects of everyday life. I felt I owed those objects an apology.

I swiveled, facing the river again.

This is where you must jump when it all becomes too much.

There would be a rush of clean air. A moment of terror, an

attempt to scrabble against nothingness and rise again. An impact. The scattering of glittering wet stones. And then . . . silence. The perpetual hush.

I closed my eyes, tensing my legs.

"Please don't do that, Milly," a voice said.

I opened my eyes and turned.

There was Tom Cat.

"Beth found out about your discharge. We've been looking for you all day. Please come home with me, Milly."

I pulled my eyes away from him, back to the starlit canyon.

"Leave me alone, Tom."

"I'm not going to hurt you," he said. He moved toward me then, and when I glanced at him I sensed the dead meadowlark in his rib cage, fluttering. *Let me out.* "Beth begged me to search for you. She said you've come here before."

"Tell Beth I love her."

"She's worried for you. She loves you, too."

"She feels sorry for me."

"She's your friend. Like me. I'm your friend, Milly." His voice grew thick with emotion. "I wrote to my mother about you again. I want to be with you. Please."

I stood at the edge of the cliff. One great leap and I'd be free of pity, of visions, of weddings, of everything. The wind licked at us warmly. She whispered to me, *Soon soon soon.*

"Come on, Milly," he said. "I'm not going to let you do this."

"Leave me alone," I said again, and I tensed my legs, readying myself.

He gave a cry then and lunged for me, pouncing, just like a dog would, and I tripped, shouting. He caught me around the waist and pulled at me, and for a moment I mistook him for Gordon, waltzing with me at the Safety and Security Dance, and I twirled with him like I would with a lover, even resting, briefly, head against his chest, and then, recoiling, the pain of his touch everywhere outside and inside of me, a branding iron pushed into my womb, my ovaries, the rattlesnake entering me, striking out, the hot sticky venom. I cried out in agony, slipping from his grasp.

"Don't *touch* me," I screamed, and I hated him and everything I'd ever wanted from him: marriage, children, status, companionship, joy.

I wheeled around and shoved him, furiously. He windmilled his arms, then sailed backward off the cliff and into the starlight, mouth gaping, brow lifted in astonishment.

Solemnly, trembling with rage and strength, I watched him, not yet fully aware of what I'd done.

He seemed to hang there in the firmament, suspended by our espoused shock and regret, time slowed in horror, and I cried out and stretched my arms open to him.

Come to me!

But he plummeted, howling in terror down the cliff's carapace. My eyes shot elsewhere, to the Big Dipper, large enough to hold an entire city of dead bodies. My mind squalled.

Scoop me up, scoop up everything in the river, clean up the whole mess of us.

There was a crack, the splitting of a rotten melon, and when I gathered my courage and looked over the edge I saw Tom Cat's broken body slamming against the rocks and spilling into the river, his rib cage cracking open and the organs pouring out like ripe fruits all around him. The meadowlark fluttered to life, lifted from the wreckage, and flew west across the water.

Murderer.

The dead in the river came forward to huddle against Tom Cat, to fawn over him or feast on him, I couldn't tell. I crouched down in the sand. They dragged his corpse and ruined organs deeper into the current. The big muscle of water flexed around him, pushing him smoothly south. He would eventually see the ocean, I thought; I likely never would. I turned and limped down the hillside. I ignored the snake who coiled in the grass, rattling its sorrow, and when I witnessed dirty fur keeping pace with me in the underbrush I quickened my stride and kept my eyes on the eastern horizon until there was nowhere left for an animal to hide.

Murderer.

My desire to jump had vanished after seeing Tom Cat fall. It was as though he had taken my place in the falling. It was not that two wrongs do not make a right, but there was a relief that something horrible had happened and I was solely, directly responsible for it. *I'm as awful as I've always assumed.* I had something of my own now to regret deeply, a new awful secret, and it was my responsibility to ferry the weight of such a secret now. To exist—painfully, regretfully—was to apologize.

I walked and walked through the night. I found my little suitcase right where I'd left it. At dawn I accepted an offered ride on a passing cattle car. In the eye of a storm of loquacious men, I sat filthy and quiet. In Richland, I prowled the streets for most of the morning. Eventually I entered a simple brick building facing the park and gave some cash to an elderly landlady for a modest apartment. It was no more than a small room, really, with a kitchenette and a shared bathroom down the hall. The landlady asked what I did for a living and I told her I worked at Hanford. She lowered my rent by half.

"So proud of what you've all done over there," she told me. "We really creamed those Japs, didn't we?"

"I suppose we did," I said, but there was no joy in my voice. There was no emotion at all.

I was so tired.

A rattlesnake hissed.

Murderer. Murderess.

I left my suitcase closed and packed on the unwashed floor and collapsed on the bare, stained mattress. I slept like that in my clothes and shoes for almost a full day and night, waking occasionally in a confused sweat. The next morning I washed myself in the shared bathroom down the hall, dressed slowly, and ate breakfast in a nearby diner.

Full of pancakes and syrup and black coffee, I took the next cattle car to Hanford to see Dr. Hall about my job.

ENDLESSNESS

Dr. Hall had never visited me in the hospital, but the moment I arrived in his office he rose to shake my hand and then turned to his new secretary and, without apology, dismissed her. She left fighting tears, wrangling her coat in her hands, and he called after her to see Human Resources, to say that he'd sent her. I felt sorry for her, but not enough to help her. This was my place. Murderers Inc. Dr. Hall pulled out the chair for me in front of his desk and when I was properly settled he returned to his own seat, facing me.

I wasn't dead. I was returned to the space I was meant to inhabit. There was no place safer and more secure than this office. From here we attacked the world. Nothing could get in, only out.

Even as I thought it, I understood how mistaken such thinking was. I was keenly acquainted now with vulnerability.

"Miss Groves, you've returned right when we need you. We're upping plutonium production."

I stifled a laugh. Of course we were! *More plutonium. More bombs.* I thought of Tom Cat, his trip to the ocean. *Washing west in Washington State.* How long of a journey would it be?

"Yes," Dr. Hall said, watching me carefully. "Yes, I'm worried about it all, too. Many of the physicists are leaving the program, Miss Groves.

It turns out your hypotheses were true regarding this weapon. It's difficult to feel proud of something that's waged such destruction, though I'm certainly in awe of it. Do you have any new thoughts regarding our continuation of the program?"

I shook my head, *No*. For a short time, I was free of visions, although in a few days I would begin to dream of babies born with ruined, deflated heads. I would dream of pink tumbleweeds and radioactive crocodiles loosed into the Columbia and chemicals with names like iodine and xedone released en masse on populated areas. I would see men in suits exploring farmlands in the dead of night, plucking at radioactive materials in the earth while the farmers and their families slept unaware in their modest homes. I would envision the premature deaths of my colleagues, including Dr. Hall, who would die of a rare stomach cancer, and of Gordon, too, who would perish, miserably, of a cancer of the blood.

It was coming. It pushed at us like the great Hanford wind, like the Columbia River herself.

"No," I said, and for that day, that week, I wasn't lying. "I've seen nothing."

Dr. Hall was silent for a long moment, his head turned thoughtfully to one side. "I remember you said something about the pilots. That's what strikes me. You were right about it, what you said. Did you know that the pilots who dropped the bomb had no idea what they carried? They felt the aftershock in the air from miles away, after flying to safety, and when they returned later to the city they saw a thousand little fires merge before their eyes and create one enormous fire. It was worse than the Tokyo firebombing. One of the pilots cried out and put his hands up against the glass."

"He must have been terrified."

Dr. Hall nodded sadly. "He knew what it meant for the people below. A powerful moment, to be sure." He pushed his glasses up onto his forehead, revealing his tired, swollen eyes. "I feel horrible for wishing that I'd been there to see it. But I wish it, nonetheless."

Dr. Hall's glance returned to my face, tracing from chin to crown the unfamiliar crookedness of my nose, the half-closed eye with its new glass eyeball, the craggy dent in my forehead. He gazed at me with a look that was almost tender.

"I'm sorry for what's happened to you, Mildred."

I let out a little sob of surprise. "The power of men," I said.

I thought of the power I had over them, too. *Poor Tom Cat. If you played by their rules then you could win,* I told myself, as if, by killing a man, I'd taken up their mantle.

"Farmer's not pleased, of course," Dr. Hall said, and I realized that we'd sped beyond the subject of my battery. "He thinks it's an abomination. He wants to shut the entire program down. Even Einstein's with him. The very men who started all of this! Some people shirk all responsibility once they achieve any sizable goal. They don't realize what this could mean for the safety of the world. They don't realize that if we can do this, just imagine what we could do next."

"Maybe they worry one will be dropped on us," I said.

"Yes! That's exactly why we need to up production. To prevent that very thing. The Soviets are already hard at work on their own weapons. Someone has leaked plans from our facilities here. There will always be new enemies, Miss Groves."

I thought about how stupid humans were, how uncreative. "New secrets," I said.

"Necessary secrets."

I took up a tablet of paper. On it was the scrawl of the other secretary, the one who had just been fired, and I noted her shorthand's lack of sophistication.

Dr. Hall handed me one of his fancy pens.

"A gift," he said.

It was a beautiful pen, squat and firm in my fingers. I told him thank you.

With practice, I hoped, I could shut off my mind, the sluicing waters of thought. I would trust in the work ahead of us. I heard some workers passing by in the hallway behind us. Tom Cat, I thought, and then shuddered.

Gordon.

I straightened in my chair, keeping my back to them, showing them the rigid rod of my spine. I controlled this body, at least up to a certain point; it was mine alone to keep strong despite what others might do to it.

the indifferent passageway of the river

the bodies it carries

the river the river the river

Dr. Hall said, "Start here."

TRUE LOVE

I ran into Bethesda on a Saturday, just as I was completing my morning exercise. I was breaking in a new pair of shoes, and I was pleased with them. They were brown cow-skin wedges, nothing special, "everyday shoes" as the clerk had called them in the department store. They were similar to Luella Woods's pair, and I remembered all that cleaved us apart and together. The shoes were boxy and plain but comfortable. I'd thrown Susan Peters's shoes out only the week before, and I hadn't felt a hint of regret hurling the curse of them into the large green Dumpster behind my apartment building. Unlike my mother's shoes, the new shoes allowed me freedom, and unlike Susan Peters's shoes, they allowed me to disappear. I could feel the weight of them with every step, but it was a gratifying ponderousness, as though they gave my journey import.

Normally I started my walk on Washington Avenue, where my apartment was, and then I curled south toward the river, where I sometimes encountered a deer or a pheasant staring back at me in terror from the tall grass, and then I ambled back north to the business district and capped off the event with some mindless window shopping. This day, however, I turned the corner onto Flager Avenue and froze.

There was Beth, statuesque, graceful, standing on the corner as though waiting for someone special. She concentrated on the sleeve of her coat, fussing with a loose string, and her auburn hair fell around her face in pretty ringlets. A red purselet hung from her wrist and she was dressed attractively in a blue kick pleat skirt, simple black pumps, a long brown coat. She'd clearly come into town for some shopping, and for a moment I wondered if I could turn and slip away before she spotted me, but she sensed my presence in that very moment and looked up, her face splitting into a happy smile.

At first I was relieved that she seemed okay. She was as radiant and beautiful as ever. But when she grabbed my shoulders and pulled me into her, hugging me too hard, I whiffed a noxious odor on her breath. It mingled grotesquely with the sharp scent of the witch hazel she used to clean her face. I drew away from her, feeling as though I might gag. She likely had a dead tooth.

"Milly, why haven't you come to see me? Haven't you received my letters?"

I'd received them, five or six of them, and, sitting on my bed in my small apartment, I'd run my fingers along the edges of those clean white envelopes. I'd thrown all of them away unopened. I was afraid of the phony sentiment inside. She hadn't bothered to find me in any real way, she'd only written things down. If she had mentioned Gordon or Tom Cat's disappearance, I would have screamed so loudly and unstoppably that I'd be kicked out of my new building. This paranoia wasn't even born of guilt, but of boredom with the whole subject. I felt I would shatter at the very tediousness of those emotions.

"No," I said. "I haven't received anything."

"I got your address from the payroll women," Beth said. "I was so surprised to hear that you were living alone. I don't blame you for wanting to live off-campus, after what happened to you, Milly, and after Tom Cat's disappearing and all. But we could have gone in on an apartment together."

"I like being alone."

Part of me wanted to apologize to her. Something else in me growled, *The fact is I've grown sick of you.*

But truthfully I was as in love with her as ever. Her voice was warm and tender and sincere. It occurred to me that the cold things she had said about me were likely no more insidious than simple venting, as we all did about our loved ones when life became dull or difficult. She hadn't meant to hurt me any more than I had meant to hurt her.

"I figured you would move in with Gordon soon," I said, and I nearly slapped myself for saying his name, baffled at my own needling curiosity. "When is the wedding?"

"Yes, well, we have plans to move back to Seattle. I'll head over there first, I've already found a job. We'll marry in a year or so."

I waited a moment, silently studying her face, those damp, kind eyes, the long lashes, the shining hair that looked its very best when swept up from her jawline, pinned neatly into a nursing cap. I adored her familiar composure, her shoulders round and strong, her chin lifted, controlled.

And yet her breath tinted the very air around us with the stench of offal. Something was amiss.

"He's been so moody lately," she confided. "Nothing I can't handle, of course, but goodness, it's draining."

I was silent. I wanted to tell her. I did. But what if she didn't believe me? Maybe it would turn out okay for her in the end. Maybe he loved her enough to treat her well. I knew this was ridiculous. How heavy was the burden of my own bitterness, sick of being disbelieved, sick of giving warning.

"I don't know why I'm telling you all of this, Milly," she said. "I know you don't like him. It's just so easy to speak to you."

"I hate him," I said then, and the finality in my tone made her lift her eyes to mine and the dark openness in them showed me the truth I hadn't let myself consider.

I withdrew from her. "You know."

Her face fell. "Know what, Milly?"

She was a phony. I recognized that tone of hers, the voice that commanded sweetness even as she judged you.

"You know what he did to me and you're still marrying him."

"Milly, have you gone mad?"

Mad Mildred.

"What an ugly, shallow grave you've dug for yourself," I told her, wickedly, coldly, with the voice of Mother.

"He said you were crazy. He said you'd try to pin it on him. He warned me about this."

Her eyes were two bright fireballs in her face but the death smell from her tooth wafted out at us. One small, tough nugget of her body guessed all that had happened and suffered for it. She brought a hand to her mouth as though to seal in the stench.

"He did this to me," I said, motioning at my face, then at my lower half, "and you know what I did because of it?"

She shook her head. She didn't want to know. She wanted the conversation to stop. She moaned and put her hand against her jaw: the rotting tooth was hurting her.

I was angry, mostly at myself. *Someone hurts us and we turn and hurt someone else.* You couldn't take anything back that you did in this world, not really, not at all. All of our wrongs were connected.

"I killed Tom Cat. I shoved him off White Bluffs. I imagined he was Gordon as I did it."

She brightened with the excitement of such a tale, but then she shook her head. "He said you were crazy, Milly. God. To think I defended you."

She relaxed. She didn't believe me. It didn't matter what I said now—future, past, present—none of it was believable. By uttering it, I stripped it of its reality. I hated my tongue then, my mouth, my lungs with their thoughtless automatic breathing.

She reached forward and touched my arm and I felt all of her pity there.

"I love you, Beth," I told her, and I said it firmly, for the last time.

"I know you do, Milly," she said affectionately. "Not that it does us any good."

She invited me to lunch but I demurred, as I'm sure she suspected I would. "I have a terrible headache," I said, and it was the truth.

"You know, I worry about you mostly at night," Beth said. "Are you sleepwalking?"

"I'm not," I told her.

This was also true. As far as I could tell, I'd never so much as risen from my bed and walked to the bathroom. I slept like a sunken stone the whole night and rose in the morning as though crawling from a thick viscous pool, gasping for breath, relieved to be freed from the soundless nothingness of slumber. But it was true that my waking visions—though rare now—were more excruciating than ever. The ensuing headaches crippled me. I reeled with a pain so intense that usually I vomited. *With great power comes great pain.*

"Don't be a stranger," she told me.

But I was.

⚫ˣ
ˣ⚫

When I next heard from Beth it was by post. This time I read the letter. She was in Seattle. She'd started a job on Cherry Hill at Providence Hospital. She asked me to write to her. She asked me to visit. If I wished to start anew, I could share an apartment with her and a couple of other girls. She wouldn't marry and move in with Gordon for another year or so. She assured me that I could find a swell secretarial position in the city. The change would be good for me, she wrote, but I knew that being with her, as much as I wanted it, would very well kill me. I would stay in Richland and continue to work at Hanford, which seemed like the only place I was meant to be, demons and all.

I never wrote her back. Rather, I did, but I never posted it. Now and again I sat down and filled an entire sheet of paper with my regret and grief. I asked her questions like, *What if he'd done this to your sister*

Annie? and *Would you forgive Annie if she killed a man?* They were letters that would have upset her tremendously; I decided that sending them would be too deliberately cruel. I'd said enough to Beth. She would now decide alone her own limits of allowance and forgiveness.

I wondered about her future: marriage, children, the drudgery of being a dutiful housewife. There was a time when I wanted those things, too, not because I was born that way, but because they were beaten into me by the man-made world. I didn't deserve or desire them now. I hated the thought of what happened behind those closed doors. My marriage to Tom Cat had been bloody, violent, and mercifully short. My children were the things I consumed every day: a loaf of bread, a pitcher of milk, a cup of coffee enjoyed at my small, round kitchen table. When I used up those briefly cherished things, I purchased new ones. My house was a cheerful one, filled with these small relationships. The only person I could fail was myself.

I thought of my dead father, how I'd once overheard him say that he wished to be entirely alone: no children, no wife, no job, no responsibility. I asked him, *But what would you do then?* He replied with a simple answer, "I would garden." He said he would feel a joy so serene that it wouldn't even matter to him if he was happy or not. When he died, I hoped in a faintly religious way that he was given his own garden plot in heaven.

By now Tom Cat might have reached the ocean. In the gardens of the deep sea his soul swam and twirled. Other souls gyred there, too. Bubbles issuing from their dead mouths, they spoke of those who had wronged them and of those they had wronged. They confused the details, the perpetrators, the victims.

In this nebulous underworld they found peace.

THE WALL

Guilt does not disappear with age, but it does mellow. There are moments, of course, that shoot up from the earth like fireworks and send you to your knees, but with time these detonations weaken and fade more quickly. You're used to them now. You endure them. You plod forward and time, like the river, washes away the intensity and dulls the sharp edges. Your identity merges with the identities of those harmed. The bodies you imagine floating downstream become your own.

If Gordon felt guilt, I never learned of it. I did my best to avoid him. He'd been transferred from Unit B and worked instead at one of the new reactors being built. Beth was already in Seattle and I heard from Kathy that he planned to join her soon. I was relieved. I hated that I might run into him in Richland or be trapped on a cattle car with him. Somehow, I went several weeks without ever seeing him. Nonetheless, there were times when I was forced to complete a task at one of the other reactors, and I journeyed to these places filled with a suffocating dread.

On a warm Tuesday, carrying papers to a DuPont manager at the new F Reactor, I paused in the foyer, my movements slowed as though I were caught in an enemy's lasso.

I sensed him there before I saw him. Despite a dizzying sensation of needing to run, I turned, scouting. There he was, leaning against the concrete wall.

He spoke to another man, but he watched me with his one good eye, unblinking. For a moment I worried that he might beckon me over or jog up to me. How would I respond? My hands spasmed. I spilled my papers everywhere. *There are so few secrets now.* "Our bombs clinched it." I swallowed a scream; I worried I'd be mocked and chided and called a liar even as he attacked me, fucked me. A few men loitering nearby hurried to help me with the scattered papers, but Gordon gazed at me placidly, as though he'd never done anything wrong. I was confused. He'd done it, hadn't he? I put a hand against my forehead.

My heart beat wildly. I remembered the meadowlark that had been trapped in Tom Cat's rib cage.

It happened.

"Are you okay?" a man asked, gently taking my elbow and helping me to my feet. I leaned for a moment against the man's arm. The muscles thrummed with his masculinity. I hated him for it. I pulled sharply away.

He handed me the file and messy papers. I stammered at him to leave me alone.

"I'm just trying to help," he said.

I glanced again at Gordon, whose good eye regarded me emptily from over the shoulder of the man he spoke with, and I wondered where my glass eye pointed, if it listed to the left like his own. *Dark Twin.* How like him I was now; he'd broken me to be like him. He and I, damaged, damaging, would only ever see half of the truth.

I hastily arranged the papers into the folder and rushed away.

I wish I'd killed Gordon, and not Tom Cat.

It was the only time I allowed myself to think it.

❂

Instead of returning to Unit B, I took an early cattle car to Richland. I phoned Mother from a pay phone there, still clutching the file, now dirty and crimped, to my chest. I was upset, weeping. She couldn't understand a word I said.

"I only have one daughter now," she told me. "I'm not interested in your tears."

"I saw him, Mother," I said. "I saw him."

She was silent for a long moment. Then, "I suppose I don't have to ask who."

I cried into the mouthpiece and she allowed it.

Eventually she cleared her throat. "Mildred, that's enough. Shoulders back. You have a life to live. Choose to be strong. That's all strength is, a choice."

"Yes, Mother," I said. I shook myself, straightened my spine. I was grateful to be told what to do.

"And don't wait a full year to phone me again, Mildred. I'm not long for this world. Your silence is killing me."

I wanted to explain to her, *I didn't want to be a murderess. It's not who I am. But I am one, we all are here, we—*

She hung up.

It was a type of forgiveness, more than I deserved.

THE BASIC POWER OF
THE UNIVERSE

After seeing Gordon, my visions intensified.

When they dropped over me, I crumpled in pain. The heron perched right on top of my head, squeezing my skull with her claws. Her full power throbbed through me, filling me with the sense of this place and all I had done wrong here. I grew intimate with the soil, the sickness already taking place inside it, the roots drinking their poison. I breathed in the venom with the plants, I absorbed the particles, drew in the iodine through my stomata and then out, exhaling. I was relieved when humans plucked me from the earth, cooked me dead, ate me, drained me finally of the pain only to absorb it themselves. When cows pushed at me with their big lips, churning me up in their many stomachs, I filled their fat udders with creamy poisoned milk. In the end I became the diseased children and diminished adults, pain-stricken, querulous, thinned out by cancer until I was no more than the bony leg of the heron, weak and fading. Only then did my visions release me, lifting away, and I stumbled back into myself, grimacing, groaning.

You had a chance to stop it and you failed.

There is more than one type of murderer.

I had become them all.

One evening, as a cruel joke, the vision transformed me into Tom Cat, all of the disparate parts of him, an organ licked up by a coyote, a pelvic bone caught in a tangle of weeds, the head and neck and torso, still whole, rolling bloated and silty beneath the river's surface. I could see now beyond death herself, could peer into the afterlife, the infinite, and it troubled me, the lack of peace there. No peace for Tom Cat, none for me. And yet as I inhabited his mangled ephemera I saw nothing of anger or terror, only a persistent disinterested pull toward something ahead of myself, a lazy wish.

When I came to again, having blacked out on a dock overlooking the Columbia, this remaining gentleness of Tom Cat's almost ruined me.

I hated myself and my gift. I was a demon.

The muscles in my neck and jaw throbbed. My skull seethed. I was familiar with these headaches now, but there was no getting used to them. It was bone-deep agony, pain so intense I was afraid to blink.

My stomach revolted. I vomited into the water.

One of my last visions was the coldest, the loneliest. I was a girl, young, eleven or twelve, recently orphaned, torpid with grief. I stood on a soap box surrounded by doctors. I didn't speak their language. None of my own people were there. I was trembling, afraid. The room was chilly; I was dressed in underpants and a thin cotton tank top. They examined the burn scars on my face and right arm, shined flashlights in my eyes, put their rough hands on my jaw to open my mouth, prodded my tongue with a blunt wooden stick. I gagged but they didn't apologize or draw back, only murmured and peered. They bent me over and pulled down my underpants and stuck something in my asshole. A translator told me they knew about my diarrhea, they were curious if it was still happening. I nodded. My insides had been boiled by Fat Man, and I hadn't been able to eat or shit normally since.

The translator told me to rise. My breasts had recently started growing, and I was embarrassed that my nipples eyeballed through the white
fabric. Exposed and vulnerable, I tried to sink my shoulders, but they
tapped me on the back of my arms, on my spine, to make me tall again.

A doctor said something to me, motioning, and I turned my head
to one side so they could look into my ear. Straight black hair fell into
my eyes and I whimpered. Somewhere in the city were my parents, dead,
and I wanted to cry out, to call for them, to leave this bare, mean room.

The doctors pushed and prodded. They loved my scars, they cared
for them, they spoke to them more than they spoke to me. They wrote
down loving words about the scars, about my asshole, my pain, in their
tidy clipboards. They didn't see me, but they saw and admired what
they'd done to me.

As the young girl, I could almost see Mildred, the seer back in Hanford, who convulsed in the prairie grass, whites of her eyes blaring, hair
clasped by sage.

I am in a vision, but I might not return from it.

The keenest of my memories *not my memories her memories* reared. My
father, *her father*, struck down by the fireball, begging for someone to kill
him, begging for me *her* to kill him. My *her* mother lying a short distance away, already dead. I hovered over my *her* father, unsure of how to
help him, *Dadē, ⅄˥⅄˥, Papa, my arms and face are on fire, too, Dadē, I need help,
too,* he'd taken on most of the burns, shielding me *her* at the last moment.
He writhed, *Kill me, Kill me,* it was like he was trying to crawl out of his
own skin. And then he did. I watched him crawl clean out of it, like a
snake sloughing old cells, unaware of my future solitude *his daughter not
me not me please not me,* unaware that I would be stared at and studied and
objectified by American doctors curious about what our bombs had
done to them all, aware only of the blistering agony and of its sudden
release. He glistened at my feet, dead.

Her feet. Not yours. Mildred, don't disappear. Mildred, come back.

I bucked. I could feel the girl trying to keep me inside her, *Don't leave me, I need you, Whoever you are, I'm alone,* but I crawled, crawled like I'd seen her father crawl, right out of her. I came apart, away from the young girl, shrieking, to find myself collapsed on a deer path in the Hanford steppe, only a few yards away from the Columbia.

What hour? What day was it?

My mind reeled. I was still the young girl, I was not yet myself. I pushed my palms into my eyes, coaxing myself to return, and I did, hesitantly, petulantly.

I worried that I wouldn't be able to return from the next one.

I tried to breathe. *It's Sunday,* I remembered. *It's almost lunchtime. You took a walk. You were in a good mood. You skipped a stone in the water. You heard the heron's wings—*

The bird emerged then from the water, so tall on her piston legs, her feathered body like a torpedo aimed at me. *How powerful you are now,* she said, *to lose all sense of self.*

I didn't respond. I breathed. The pain was already edging in, my stomach was already roiling. I retched and retched, sobbing. My throat was ulcerated from the vomiting. Too many visions now, too big, too out of my control.

I wanted everything to end.

There, there, the heron said with her yellow death eyes. *In one way or another it will all be over soon.*

ATOMIC SHADOWS

After weeks of silence, of secrets, of going about my diurnal tasks with a numbness that almost felt like contentment, it became clear to me that Tom Cat's spirit was lodged in the glass of my left eye. When I reached into a cupboard for a fresh wash-cloth, the glass eyeball went hot, and there was a view of salmon, pummeling upstream. Or when I drew a circle around a mistake in a letter Dr. Hall had written, the heat sparked, and there was a hawk, its talons digging into a bone *once a piece of me*, its mouth tearing at the marrow. Another day I pulled down my underpants to find that I'd started my period, and, annoyed, mopping myself up with toilet paper, my vision in my right eye went black, and instead of the cramped stall, my own blood, I saw thunderclouds overhead, lightning, felt rain on my face. Tom Cat was showing me his worldview, in real time, maybe, or what had already passed or was coming for him. My tongue and throat swelled. He wanted to talk through me, he wanted to live through me, too.

I thought of Gordon's own glass eye, and I wondered who lived in his, an abusive father, a tense mother, a parent's friend who had touched him when he didn't want to be touched? Or just an emptiness he was born with, a disregard for human life? I reached up to feel the glass, and the eyelashes brushed my fingertips but the eye didn't wince or shut anymore, and I could tap against it even if the sensation made my head hurt. For that last season at Hanford I was discomfited by the ghost that lived in this cavey socket, nestled there like a sleeping bat, carried along with the rest of me from task to task as though he were my constant unwanted pet.

Good night, Tom Cat, I said, and through the glass I heard a voice answer, *Good night, Milly.* It was the closest I would come to a marriage.

One morning I took the cattle car to work and midway to the reactors it sighed and sputtered and rolled to a stop. There was a flat tire. The bus driver told us not to fret, he'd have us going again in half an hour, tops, and he allowed us to rise and stretch our limbs, telling us, "Don't wander too far."

The men let me disembark first. Then they noisily followed me, laughing, heaving down the cattle car's steps so that the vehicle groaned and shifted. They alighted on the soft, soundless prairie. They lit their cigarettes and filled the peace with their big voices and laughter, teasing one another, kicking at sagebrush, testing one another, but I ambled away from them, pulled as I always was to the Columbia River. Their voices faded behind me and I was grateful to be alone.

But as I hiked down into the gully I was overcome by a sense of unease. Someone had followed me. I glimpsed a movement to my right: a shadow, no more. Almost simultaneously, to my left, another shadow. I heard—and looked for—the heron's great wings. Then a shadow behind me. In front. I went very still, the way you're told to if a bear attacks: *Play dead, maybe it will go away.*

Shadows splayed all around me, the shadows of children, the shadows of grown men, the shadows of hunched old women, canes and all. They swarmed thickly across the clumps of wheatgrass and fescue, limbs churning, as alive as they were featureless. They glided across the ground like figures across a movie screen. They were not the *hibakusha*: These were the dead. They gestured to me gracefully, *Come with us*, and frightened, I obeyed, worried that if I turned and ran, their dim hands would fall on me and steal the color from my flesh, from my uterus and liver, from my heart and lungs, flattening me until I was no more than a black slip of paper.

I followed a deer trail to the water, the shadows buttressing me on all sides, falling across my sensible shoes, my stockinged ankles. The path was steep and scabbed with rock; I slipped, dirtying my skirt, and slipped again, cutting my palm. I pressed on, beckoned by the graceful, diaphanous hands.

I finally reached the bank, my shoes caked with silt. The shadow of what must have been a small boy pointed into the water. I leaned over, hardly breathing. I expected to see Tom Cat floating there, outing me, finally. Or maybe it would be Gordon, springing from the water to grip my arms and pull me under. I tensed my body to recoil, to run.

But there was nothing. Just the water, pewter, thin and cold. A few minnows darted frantically below the surface.

I relaxed for a moment, chiding myself for my nervousness. I was safe. It was daytime. The worst had been done to me. No harm could befall me now.

I heard the heron's voice. Her beak like a dagger against my shoulder.

There's a way to stop these visions. There's a way to never tell anyone anything again, to never be disbelieved. Look closer.

I reached down and touched the water. Beneath the surface was a rusty old knife. I gripped it with purpose, wonderingly.

I wanted, more than anything, to be free of myself. I took up the knife.

A thin line of light flared on the horizon.

The water tore apart. A bolt of lightning hurtled me backward onto my haunches. There was a sound like ten thousand buildings being ripped in half, so loud in my ears that I screamed. My head collapsed with pain. Disoriented, I recalled Dr. Hall's description of the thermal flash, how it temporarily blinded anyone who saw it. I reached up and touched my head and shook with pain. The shadow people gathered around me, flitting together and apart like so many crows. For a moment

I saw the figures as they had looked when alive, and they were beautiful, vivid, filled with blood and life and longevity, and then death recaptured them and they collapsed into shade.

A voice then, calling to me from the cliff. The shadows panicked and dispersed. The sun shone brighter, the river blued. The crushing pain in my head faded into a large, general numbness. My face was sticky and wet and I leaned over the river and washed it with my right hand. When I turned, I saw a man waving his arms at me from atop the bluff: The tire was fixed, or very nearly. It was time to depart.

I limped up the bank. It was easier going up than down, more steady if harder on my lungs. My mouth felt heavy and full and tender. I lost my footing at one point and pivoted forward, catching myself with one hand. In the other hand, my left, I gripped something wet and warm.

Panting, sweating, I stopped on the hillside and stared at my left hand, uncomprehending. What did I hold there? I remembered the rusty knife, and then nothing but light and sound and pain. But this wasn't a knife. It felt like one of the frogs heron liked to catch, slimy, alive. It must have been placed there by someone during the thermal flash—another of my visions, maybe—perhaps by the shadow of the boy, or by the heron, herself? A dumb joke. Where was the knife now?

I tried to open my fist to look at the object but my fingers held fast. *Not yet.*

My knuckles were stained with what looked like rust. From the knife, maybe. Whatever I held appeared to be leaking.

Another shout from above, more urgent this time.

I couldn't miss my ride. I swallowed mucus and river water—silty, muddy—and noticed how senseless my mouth was, how I couldn't taste a thing. I hurried up the path, urging myself to remain calm, and when I reached the cattle car I shoved my leaking left fist into the pocket of my cardigan and took my seat without meeting anyone's eye.

"What were you doing down there?"

"Your dress is filthy, honey."

"Ha! And those shoes! Filled with mud!"

"She's part mermaid."

"Doesn't look like she'd swim well."

"Bet she can float! Plump little lady like that."

"I like them plump."

"Leave her alone, you Marys. She looks like a good Christian girl."

"She looks like pudding and pie is what she looks like."

I glared into my lap. Dots of the liquid began to leak through the knitted cables of my mustard-colored sweater.

A knife. A heart. An organ. A dead mouse. A mutilated bird.

A five-point buck edged out over the embankment and stared warily at the bus for a few moments, twitching its ears, its eyes as black as sleep. The bus coughed to life and the buck pivoted, plunging down the gulley toward the river and out of my line of sight. One of the men started talking about hunting and then all of them started gibbering about it, who shot what and where and how, and they forgot about me for the rest of the ride.

I was grateful for the fuzzy numbness in my face and skull. For once there was no sensation at all.

I entered Dr. Hall's office only slightly late. He was irritated that I wasn't on time, and I didn't bother to explain the flat tire. He loathed explanations, anyway.

He grumbled at me but didn't look up from his desk. I took my seat across from him and with my free hand took up his schedule. Normally we began with my recapping yesterday's work, and then we discussed the plans for the day, but I found that when I went to speak, my mouth refused to open. The numbness was so pervasive that my lips didn't seem to register my mind's commands, as though a wire between the two had been cut.

After another long moment of silence, Dr. Hall's gaze lifted from his paperwork. Irritably, he asked, "Miss Groves. Are you waiting for something?"

My mouth trembled with effort. I hoisted my clenched hand, stained reddish brown now, and held it in front of his face.

"What's gotten into you?" he said. "Are you ill?"

I rose to my feet, humming a moan through my closed lips.

You did it! You made it stop forever! Well done!

His eyes widened, taking in my sordid dress, my torn stockings, my muddy shoes, my face mangled and swollen.

"What in God's name is wrong with you?"

I willed the hand to open. By then its contents were of no surprise to me.

Dr. Hall lifted from his chair, bending over the desk to peer into my palm, and then he recoiled, his face paling with revulsion. "Is that your . . . ?"

I tried to say what I thought had happened. The rusty knife, the blast, the shadows who must have held my mouth open. I couldn't recall who had done the sawing.

"Mildred, how did you—"

He rounded the desk and came to put his hand on my back. For a moment I thought he was comforting me but then I realized—he was urging me to my feet. He was prodding me toward the door, away from his office and its view of the control room. In the control room of my heart, the fire started, the warning lights flashed, the dials crackled.

I would leave Hanford, permanently now. I almost welcomed the change. Where I would go next was a mystery to me. It would become my new home and I would do my best there. I would become the most decent version of myself, I would hush and recede. I thought of Susan Peters and her lovely shoes, of the end I had seen for her: the divorce, the sanatorium, the isolation and death. She was a star and I was a paltry, insignificant thing, a woman, no more, no less. If she could endure it, surely I could, too.

"We need to get you to the clinic," Dr. Hall muttered, pushing me down the hallway. "We'll get some ice for . . ." he trailed off, as though worried about alarming me. "This is a nightmare."

Nightmare? Salvation. Now it won't matter.

"There must be some ice somewhere," he said. "Come on, hurry up."

A small crowd had gathered, watching us, perhaps noting my blood-stained dress and hands. I continued to hold my tongue in my fist, and the joke of it nearly made me laugh—*Hold my tongue!* I considered dropping it in a wastebasket. What did I need it for now? Surely it was of no further use to me. Dr. Hall's glasses were askew on his narrow face. He perspired in terror as he guided me stupidly toward what he thought might help me. Nothing could help me now. I was beyond help. I no longer wanted or needed it, but fear delighted me, as though I finally had power over all of them.

A few other men gathered around us, whispering to one another about me. They all waited for me to say something. They wouldn't touch me until I allowed it. What a weird respect they showed me when I no longer wanted it.

"Where is there an ice box?" the doctor asked urgently. "We need ice!"

That old familiar sense of levitating returned to me, and I floated above them in that gray-green room, their faces upturned to me in awe as though searching the sky for a sign—a benevolence, Santa Claus, a bomb, a beginning, an end.

Whatever spring had been set on my jaw was released, and my mouth flew open. From it flowed the shadows of the dead and the river water, choking and black, and then my own reddish-brown blood, fragrant and spiced with iron. I sprayed their upturned faces and they recoiled in horror, but I couldn't stop, the water kept coming. I swept down the flooded hall, letting the sick current wash me out of the metal door and into the desert and the light.

Nothing waited for me there, only the big, empty expanse of the Columbia plateau.

A magpie flew by and I dreaded that it would speak to me, but it ignored me. I was no longer a vessel for the words of the *aufhocker*. My glass eye, too, sat hollow in my head; Tom Cat no longer lived there. I'd destroyed the very organ that gave me power to house them.

Summer approached. Soon the heat would become unbearable, but I relished it now. I plopped down in my wool skirt in the middle of the barren field, not far from the reactor. Now and again I leaned over to spit a mouthful of blood onto the sagebrush. I picked absently at the mud on my shoes. I pulled the cheatgrass one seed at a time from my stockings. If I continued to pretty myself, to preen and to pluck, I might look half-decent by the time the vehicle from the clinic arrived. They might allow me some paper and a pen so that I could write to them in my excellent cursive, *If possible, please, I'd like to be near the ocean.* I admonished myself to stay docile and patient.

As far as they know you've been a good girl. They might very well give you what you want.

WESTERN STATE

After all was said and not said and done, I was left with no more than a third of my tongue. The surgical team had tried to re-stitch the organ back into place, but it was too late: The rusty knife's cut had been too sloppy, the incision too uneven; I'd ridden on the cattle car with the muscle through the desert and the heat; and Dr. Hall, brilliant man though he was, failed to find any ice. According to the surgeon, they'd wrestled with it for a good hour, and then decided to just "leave well enough alone."

"We can't risk infection," the surgeon explained to me as I lay recovering from the anesthesia. "But we stopped the bleeding, and it should heal successfully now."

He recommended only a soft diet, or else I might choke and die.

"You can have cranberry sauce and mashed potatoes at Thanksgiving," he said, "but no turkey."

The nurses laughed at this and in my grogginess they sounded like the possessed squawks of the heron. I breathed deeply through my nose. Moving my mouth at all in those first few weeks was too painful.

"With patience and work, you'll be able to speak again, but I can't promise it will be easy. There will be certain sounds you won't recover, and I'm sorry about that."

I shook my head. They'd shorn my hair since I came in, to make it easier for the surgery, I guessed, or maybe to prepare me for the transfer to the sanatorium, where my womanhood would be mocked and tortured. I liked the open feeling around my ears, bare now to the sky. I clutched his forearm, shaking my head more desperately.

"Miss Groves, are you telling me you don't want to speak?"

He tensed as if to argue with me, but then he sighed, perhaps remembering what I'd done, perhaps sensing my reasons for it.

"Regardless, you need to learn how to drink and chew properly. Silence is perfectly fine, but drooling is inelegant."

His tone was playful and all around him the nurses smiled with their pretty, flirty lips. I thought of Beth and darkened, pinning my shoulders inward and ducking my head. The surgeon patted my leg compassionately before he turned for the door.

He was a kind man, and good-looking. My old self might have compared him to a movie star, Gregory Peck, maybe, but I was through with all of that now, that silly, starstruck sweetness. If the world wanted nothing but our bombs and our Hollywood, then they could have them. I was through with all of it.

Martha was right. I'd been naive. When I felt a little better, a week or so post-surgery, I wrote her to say so. I apologized. She wrote me back almost immediately, saying how right I was to do so, that she was pleased to see me embracing the Christian spirit, and then continued. "We're looking forward to your return. But without a tongue you won't be of much use to me. We need a babysitter who can really scream at the children." I smiled, but I knew I wasn't returning home, and I'm sure Martha knew that, too. Still, it was nice to think of my nieces and nephews. I'd almost forgotten how special it was: I was an aunt. It was a role I decided then and there to cherish. I figured my brief stint as caretaker had begun with Mother and ended with Tom Cat, but maybe that wasn't necessarily true. I promised myself that I would order each child a toy from the Sears Roebuck catalog, and I kept true to my promise, and Martha later wrote to say the children were "pleased as punch."

It was a small gesture, but it felt life-affirming. I hoped they would let me place such orders from wherever I wound up next, but likely they would not. I made arrangements to forward all of my savings to Martha.

The good surgeon tried to keep me with them in Richland for as long as he could. He knew where I was going even before I did, and he guessed at how exactly terrible a facility it was. As the days passed, I began to worry that I would be sent inland.

I wrote a note to the surgeon: *Can you please request that I'm placed somewhere west? I'm longing for the ocean. . . .*

He read the note in front of me and then told me he would look into it.

"Some of the nurses here have trained in such places," he added. "They can be . . . unkind."

I was touched that he wanted to warn me. I gestured for him to give me back the piece of paper. I scrawled, *I belong there.*

The surgeon liked me. He wanted to protect me, as he did all of his patients. But I didn't want protection, only the silence I'd violently gifted myself.

Right before they transferred me to Western State Hospital, Bethesda sent me a letter from Seattle, telling me that poor Tom Cat's body had been found not far from Umatilla, Oregon, spotted by two teenagers smoking cigarettes near the shore ("they were probably necking," Beth added, maybe to make me smile, as if anyone could smile thinking of Tom Cat's passing). Tom Cat was badly bruised and shattered, she wrote, and it was generally assumed that he'd fallen from a cliff near Hanford and then rolled into the river. Some parts of his body were still missing. It was common knowledge among his friends that Tom Cat took leisurely hikes in the evening, and he'd once confided that he thought about jumping. He'd mentioned that to me, too, during one of our friendly conversations on the cattle car. "Not out of any desire to die," he'd hurriedly said, "but out of this intense curiosity." Perhaps due to his innocuous, ill-fated statements, no one made the connection between his disappearance and my reappearance in Hanford. They might have privately called me Mad Mildred, just like I was called at Omak's elementary school, but they didn't think I was capable of murder.

Beth commented on my confession briefly. "I think, Milly," she wrote, "that you really do believe you killed him, even if you didn't, but maybe then again you did, figuratively, I mean, by not loving him the way he expected. But I admire it really, how you didn't cave to him. You've always been stronger than me in that way, even if you couldn't see it."

The statement was strange to me, as heavy with regret as it seemed. *She's unhappy with Gordon*, I thought then, but if this were true, it gave me no happiness. I recalled that awful stench emanating from her insides. She knew the truth, whether or not she could admit it to herself. The rest was just a choice.

She was a murderer, too. All of us at Hanford had, in one way or another, guided the plutonium into Fat Man. Now 110,000 deaths were on all of our hands, the death toll rising day by day. Little Boy and Fat Man had been very patient with the killing. The radiation continued to pluck people off as the days passed. And not just in Japan, but soon here in the Northwest, too. There would be three-eyed salmon and cancer-infested trout. Then would come the little girls and boys, paralyzed mysteriously in the middle of what had been an active childhood, and the doomed babies born with undeveloped brains and skulls. Then the sterility, the miscarriages, one after another after another after another. There would be a rash of heart attacks, of stomach cancers, of dementia, of thyroid cancers and dysfunctions. There would be hundreds of red crosses placed on the Hanford Reach Death Map.

And they would struggle to contain the waste but it would be too much for them. It would leak and continue to leak fifty years from now, seventy years from now, a century, until an attack, a "rain of ruin," fell on us, too.

All of this was old news to me, the future I'd conjured when my visions were sharp and my tongue useful. Such old news, but it nonetheless squatted on the horizon, waiting for us to catch up to it, as we assuredly would.

Tom Cat's Bible had so much of it wrong. God didn't put men here to tend the garden. He put them here to destroy it.

All I did, all I've done, all I'm doing. All I haven't, can't, won't do.

※

It troubled me that Tom Cat hadn't made it to the ocean. Maybe he and I were never meant to see it, being, as we were, from the Inland Northwest, cloven from the surf by the ponderous Cascades.

I wondered now why I hadn't confessed Tom Cat's murder to the authorities. Maybe because I was scared. Maybe because I was angry. Maybe because I would never be believed in anything I said to anyone, so what did it even matter? I'd killed him because I'd become one of them, but I was through with all of that now. Tongueless, rudderless, my rules were mine alone.

Beth had included the address for Tom Cat's family in Tonasket, if I would like to send them my condolences. From the Richland hospital, I mailed to them the Bible they gave me, including a simple card with a lone blue iris on the front of it, a flower that smelled to me like death, the only card they had to loan me in my ward. In the card I wrote,

> *I'm so sorry. It should never have happened. He was very loved. Thank you for the lovely gift but I'm returning it to you. I can't take it where I'm going.*
>
> *Yours truly,*
> *Mildred Groves.*

It was far from a confession, but it helped.

※

In my last days at the Richland hospital, I sat around with my eyes closed, doing little to nothing, tunneling inward. It was easier now to forget the world.

How easily we trick ourselves into negating our empathy.

It's happening far away so it won't happen here. It's happening to someone else but not to me. It's happening to the forsaken but not to my family. It's happening in my mind's eye but not in my neighborhood. It's happening in a novel but not in real life. It's happening it's happening it's happening.

Just before Christmas, they transferred me to Western State Hospital.

⁂

When I wrote to Martha and Mother from my new home, I told them that I had a tidy room with a small window and a view of the ocean. I wrote about how thankful I was to be here, and not at Eastern State Hospital near Spokane. I marveled over the greenery of this place, with its rain-swollen trees and salty, fish-smelling air; I exclaimed over how healthy it was for me to be in a different environment. I told them, too, about the movie star I'd seen here, Frances Farmer, who asked me if I'd ever had a broken heart. My letters were long and happy and false. Martha wrote me back every few months, and I embarrassed myself by crying over the monotonous news of her children, of Walter's promotion, of Mother's latest illness and recovery. Even the sight of Martha's horrible handwriting affected me poignantly. I teared up even before I opened the envelope.

In truth, there was no window, no ocean view. But I could smell the brackish water always, and if I strained, I could hear the slaughtering sounds, the tortured beach thrashed by waves. I both longed to go to the water and cherished the distance. I feared what the ocean might return to me: my voice, my visions, all of those rotted murdered Japanese bodies, Tom Cat's missing femur, picked clean by teeming life.

I didn't deserve to see the ocean now, to dip my toes into her or taste her salt. But I glimpsed her breadth from the knoll where the nurses' aides sometimes took us for fresh air, a long slab of gray tucked between the green shrubs. I considered this my own small triumph.

I heard from Kathy now and again, too. She wrote to me not infrequently, even though I rarely wrote her back. Her letters were full of complaints and humor about her new life in Portland, Oregon. It made me laugh that she worked in a pediatrician's office; she once told me she hated children. She was living with another woman there, and seemed happy, at least as happy as Kathy would ever allow herself to be. I appreciated her letters for their detail but also for the way she always signed them,

> Yours, darkly,
> Kathy.

I could hear her wry voice in those slanted letters. Now and again there was a postscript, always the same:

> Those men do not define us.

In the end, Kathy was the only one at Hanford who I felt really cared for me. Because of what we shared, the mutual darkness, we trusted each other. It might have been the only true friendship of my life.

It had been a torture to be treated well at the Richland hospital, and I was grateful to be at Western State now, where little kindness was afforded to us women. To think I'd once thought of jumping off a cliff! Since I'd killed Tom Cat, the idea had become laughable. By doing an act so horrific, I'd shocked myself awake. Gordon had annihilated me but I'd pushed all of that annihilation onto someone else, an undeserving person. I was exactly like the men who ruled over us, vengeful, destructive, indiscriminate. To survive in this world, I simply had to give myself over to that masculine way of thinking. It made sense to me now, the dropping of the bomb. *Here, take this, pass it along, it doesn't matter where it goes next.* Now that I'd cut out my tongue, I'd stripped myself of my grandmother's powers, the powers of foresight and warning. All people wanted was a cudgel. Force wasn't the only power, but it was the only power people recognized.

I could write, I found, and I enjoyed writing, but my narratives were only figments, never visions. I could write pages and pages and never uncover the future. But I wrote, anyway.

I didn't start this. I'm a part of it now but it's not my fault. This is the plot of men.

In my wing there were only women. The doctors appeared with their devices and threats and we hated them openly. The nurses were even worse. Women treating women horribly is perhaps the most humiliating punishment of all. Compared to the others, I was left mostly alone. The pretty ones, the loud ones, the impossible ones, were prodded and bedded and beaten. Some complained of the rats and of the food, which looked and tasted like vomit. I tried not to frown at these bellyachers or appear too condescending.

What do you expect? This is womanhood, boiled down.

Some of the patients believed in their improvement, that they still had a chance at a normal life. They spoke wistfully of a boyfriend on the outside, or of a job they hoped to return to, as if any employer would have them after this.

There is no normal life.

The treatments, mundane, sometimes horrifying, served only to distract us from the hopelessness of it all.

Even then, surrounded by blank white walls, my mind wandered to the people lost across the sea, rivers I helped vanquish, the carcasses immolated. If I settled my ear against the thinnest flesh of my wrist I could hear the hollowness of those dry creek beds. *Don't worry,* I mouthed soundlessly into my veins. *My death will come, too.*

Some of the women nodded at me respectfully when I passed. More than one asked for permission to touch my knuckles or my shoulders or my short dark hair, as if prodding my features might transfer protection to them.

Witch, they took to calling me, and there was reverence in their voices, even desire.

They read my silence and glowering as a sort of power in and of itself. They were envious of the even way I handled the prosaic wretchedness of this place.

Only now, encased in silence and ignorance, did people accept me for what I truly was.

How long was I there? Three years? Five? I stopped keeping track of time. I'd learned to be fully present. It didn't matter what was happening. A doctor fingering my cunt, grunting as he peered into me. A nurse smacking me across my throat with a ruler, ridiculing me for my dark expression. The sight of an over-drugged patient slipping into a coma, and then into death. I stared at everything, observing, not judging, this miracle and tragedy, this pain and beauty. I moved slowly down the hallways so that everything liquefied and there was no more than the weight of my bones, the small white ghost of my nose constantly floating before me, such an unappreciated loyal companion, the sound of my breath, the ice of inhalation, the fire of exhalation, the support of the dirty pine floor beneath my slippered feet, firm and forgiving.

I awoke one morning in my cell, realizing that one of my roommates, a girl no more than seventeen, lay moaning at my feet. I half-rose and absently stroked her hair. Dawn was peaceful now. My mind was preternaturally quiet, my sleep undisturbed. Without a proper tributary, my prophecies dried up and perished.

I loved the women here because of their collective innocence.

My roommate mumbled into my knees about what they'd done to her. I comforted her as best as I could, with pats and humming. If I could speak to her, I would tell her not to fight, to curl up, to wait and stay small.

When the wall of man's watery hatred hits you, don't struggle. Go limp.
Float like the dead.

Let yourself wash up wherever it takes you.

I tried to push these thoughts from my palms into her skull and the girl fell silent under the pressure of my hands.

The door scraped open then, and a raspy nurse's voice said, "Mildred Groves. Someone's come for you."

The girl started whimpering again, upset with my departure, but I brought a finger to my lips and she quieted.

I rose and put on my robe and slippers and went into the dim hallway. I had no things I cared about, so I left them behind. I figured they were transferring me to a different place. Or maybe to a clinic where there would be new shots, a different procedure. They liked to experiment on us. I was indifferent. The nurse motioned for me to follow.

"You have a visitor," the nurse said. "Hurry up."

I was surprised. I cracked my knuckles. No one had ever visited me here. I worried it would be Beth, maybe with Gordon *oh God not Gordon not him I'll kill him*, maybe with their child. A few years ago (two? three?), she'd written to say she was pregnant. After that, the letters stopped. I suspected why but I hoped I was wrong: that Gordon had revealed his true self to her. I remembered what the heron had said to me, *Eventually we must become who we are.* Once Gordon fully owned her, there would be no reason to hide his sadism. She was now too ashamed, I worried, or too beleaguered (*too injured?*), to reach out to me. I hoped she'd gathered enough strength to get out of there before his wrath affected the baby.

What if Gordon's here?

I suddenly couldn't breathe. I walked so slowly that the nurse turned to yell at me, "Stop dawdling, Mute! I haven't got all day!"

I nodded but did not quicken my pace. I waded through the liquid cement of dread.

We went down two flights of stairs and through a locked gate, then down the long hallway that led to the building's foyer. There she stopped, gesturing at a sitting room off to one side, a room I'd never before entered.

"Go on," she said. "Your guest is waiting."

She turned and left, and I thought, *Unsupervised?* They hadn't let me do anything without being watched.

I went into the little room.

It wasn't Beth.

It's not Gordon.

But I was shocked, anyway.

It was Mother.

I hesitated, standing in the doorway, staring at the thinning hair of the small woman seated before me, a woman who I'd never before thought of as small. She'd lost a fair amount of weight. She hadn't heard me enter. She stood primly with her hands clutching the patent leather purse on her lap. She wore her driving gloves. I could make out her thick thighs in their simple dress, the sagging, deeply wrinkled skin of her arms. I smelled the clean scent of the chipped soaps she used for the laundry, and I fought the urge to embrace her, to bury my face in her neck.

I came forward and put a hand on her shoulder.

She jumped, and then half-turned in the chair. Her eyes saw me and softened. She made no movement to rise, but she reached up and squeezed my hand tautly, with such strength that tears sprang up in my eyes. I sank into a chair beside her and we entwined hands.

"Mildred, you swamp rat, you look awful."

I reached up and touched my short hair. I hadn't looked in a mirror in years; they didn't allow mirrors in our wing, because of the ways we women hurt ourselves with them, but I saw myself then as Mother saw me: pale, turgid, mussy-haired, riddled with lice, a bloated beast with one swollen, bloodshot eye.

I shrugged at her as if to say, *What does it matter?*

"You need a haircut. I'll see if Mrs. Brown has a good lipstick for you. You could use some color on your cheeks. Here, try dragging this through that bird's nest." She opened the latch on her purse and took out a comb. I accepted it and then pulled it through my hair, reluctantly, wincing at the tiny shrieks of the tendrils tearing.

Mother watched me, satisfied.

"You'll look like ten bucks in no time."

When I finished, I handed the comb back to her. She considered it a moment, holding it away from her with thumb and forefinger, and then dropped it into a wastebasket.

"Let's go home," she said.

My eyebrows raised in horror.

"I've already signed the paperwork, Mildred. I asked for your things but they said you have very little, except for these shoes." She motioned below the chair, and there they were, as if they'd been waiting for me all of these long years, my sensible shoes, the ones I'd purchased during my final, failed attempt at a normal life in Hanford. "Put them on. It's time to leave."

I shook my head. I made the motion of a pen writing on paper, and my mother sighed.

"What now, Mildred? Can't you leave well enough alone?"

But she rummaged around in her handbag once more, bringing out an envelope and a pen. She handed them to me and I could feel the warmth of her curiosity spread as I scribbled. It took me a good few minutes to write it all down. I could hear the cuckoo clock ticking on the wall in the small room, the room with only soft chairs and no hard-edged surfaces. They couldn't trust us with anything.

Finally I finished, read it over once, and handed it to her with a look of entreaty.

Mother read the letter, her lips forming the words in a whispery way I'd forgotten about in the time I'd been gone. The sound of it filled me with memories, a sudden rush of love dazed me. I leaned against her shoulder as she read. It, too, was thinner than I'd remembered. *Is she ill?* The cuckoo clock burped out a little wooden bird. It chimed the hour and stiffly swatted its wooden tail, reveling in its freedom before being sucked back into its coffin.

When Mother finished reading, she pushed me gently off her and groaned to her feet. She rose clumsily, her knees clacking. She was aging, she was shrinking, she was turning into a delicate cricket.

"Well," she said, tearing up the letter into tiny shreds, "time to go."

She eyeballed the wastebasket where the comb lay but then seemed to think better of it and shoved the jagged pieces of envelope into her purse instead.

I winced. Those little shreds of paper were all miniature white tongues. If they flew back together they would form the bulk of my own truth.

I could no longer cry out in terror. I pursed my lips and steeled my gaze.

"Up and at 'em," she said, as if my words meant nothing.

She plucked at the sleeve of my robe, trying and failing to tug me to my feet.

I huffed through my nose and folded my arms over my chest. I wasn't going to budge for her, not now.

"This is your one chance at leaving. I've been negotiating this for months. If you refuse, God help you."

God help me, I thought, and I closed my eyes.

I heard a shuffling noise, the clatter of purse and keys. I opened my eyes, thinking I'd find Mother with her arm cocked back, ready to swing her purse at my head like a mace, but to my astonishment she was on the floor before me, kneeling with her hands stitched together in prayer.

"Please. Mildred, get up. Come with me. We want to take you home."

I blinked at her, rattled, embarrassed. I had never before imagined my mother in this position, beseeching me in any earnest manner. This had to be an imposter, a wolf in her own clothing, maybe even Gordon in disguise. I wiped a hand over my face.

"Whatever that note was, Mildred—a confession, an apology, a fart written in ink—forget it. You need to come with me now."

I pointed at myself, widening my eyes for emphasis, and I mouthed at her emphatically, *MUR. DER. ER.*

I wanted her to understand fully what she wanted, who it was she wanted to ferry home to Omak.

She flung her arms up in frustration. "Every mother is a murderer, if you think about it. For the love of Lucifer, get up, you dimwit. We're heading home."

I rose to my feet, mountainous, cumbersome, heavy with all of my long years of loss, and she half-dragged me, half-limped with me, out the door of that little room. She carried my sensible shoes beneath one arm, pulling me along with the other.

If I hadn't been so stunned, so confused, I'm sure I would have refused her and stayed. But Mother had sprung this on me so suddenly that I wasn't sure what was up or what was down. Omak now seemed as good of a place as any to spend my remaining days. It was her plan, of course, to startle me into obedience. She knew me too well.

We passed the front desk with its frowning long-faced nurse and its bizarre statuette of a girl kissing a satyr. The morning light streamed in through the foyer's east-facing windows, and the effect was inviting if overwhelming.

When one of the orderlies attempted to assist Mother with the door, reaching for the small of her back as though to press her through the portal, she snapped at him, "Keep your hands to yourself, Bub. We're murderers. You don't want to mess with us."

He gave an uneasy laugh and swiftly backed away.

Walter's car waited in the long, circular driveway, and, of course, Martha waited in it, too, the engine humming. She waved at me nonchalantly from the driver's seat, as if I was just returning from a quick trip to the hair salon.

When Mother pulled open the front passenger door, Martha said, "Took you two long enough."

I raised a hand in greeting, mouthing with difficulty, *Hi Marthie.*

She was fatter, more handsome, and calmer-looking than I remembered. It was a relief to see her. My eyes watered with emotion.

"You sit in front," Mother told me, standing back and gesturing at the roomier chair.

I ignored her and snapped open the back door.

"Suit yourself, Ferret Face," she said, and I could tell from her voice that she was grateful for the better seat. Maybe she even thought I'd given it to her out of kindness, out of a sense of daughterly duty, and it was fine with me if she cherished the gesture.

But it was the backseat I wanted. From there I could watch the world spin to us, I could witness whatever was coming next, the suffocating greenery of Western Washington, the spindly waterfalls striping the Cascades, the opening up of the prairie lands, the muscled, burnished fists of the canyon, the disinterested gray serpent of the Columbia River, the dry, colorless sagebrush steppe, the dip into the valley of my home-town with its neat square houses and its sunsets the color of shame. I could watch and watch and watch with no visions unspooling, only the landscape, the future as unknowable as the meaning of it all.

From the backseat, I could watch, silently, without terror or judgment.

I could watch without anyone watching me.

REFERENCES

Voices of the Manhattan Project, http://manhattanprojectvoices.org/.

Daughters of Hanford, http://www.daughtersofhanford.org/.

"Native Americans Begin 'Ceremony of Tears' for Kettle Falls on June 14, 1940," by Cassandra Tate, March 16, 2005, HistoryLink.org, Essay 7276.

"Mourning Dove (Christine Quintasket) (ca. 1884–1936)," by Jack and Claire Nisbet, 8/07/2010, HistoryLink.org, Essay 9512.

Hiroshima, by John Hersey, published originally in 1946, available to read on the *New Yorker* website.

"Exhibit Chronicles Hard Life for Blacks at WWII Hanford," by Annette Cary, published in the *Tri-City Herald*, February 27, 2016.

"It is an atomic bomb. It is a harnessing of the basic power of the universe. The force from which the sun draws its power has been loosed against those who brought war to the Far East." Statement by President Harry S. Truman Announcing the Use of the A-Bomb at Hiroshima, August 6, 1945.

Atomic Frontier Days, by John M. Findlay and Bruce W. Hevly (University of Washington Press, 2011).

"The Night the 'Little Demons' Were Born," *Spokesman-Review* article, July 28, 1985, by environmental investigative journalist Karen Dorn Steele, who cracked open the secrets of Hanford's deleterious effects on the local environment.

ACKNOWLEDGMENTS

For the writing of this dark book, I'm grateful for the thorough, excellent, necessary edits from my agent, Julie Stevenson, my editor at Henry Holt, Caroline Zancan, and my endlessly discerning and supportive husband, Simeon Mills. Thank you to the incredible team at Holt, including Kerry Cullen, Austin Price, Declan Taintor, and designer Meryl Sussman Levavi. I also want to thank Elizabeth Conway, Kris Dinnison, Lisa Heyamoto, Aileen Luppert, Ed Reese, Greg Reese, Gayle Terry, Karen Dorn Steele, J. Robert Lennon, Megan Fadeley, Andrew Gerhardt, Shann Ray, Sarah Ruppert, Kevin Taylor, John Smelcer, Mpho Tlali, John Paul Shields, Alexis M. Smith, Colin Sorenson, Sandra Patricia Cano, Rob & Kisha Schlegel, Jeremy N. Smith, Crissie McMullan, Lisa Stisser, Astrid Vidalón, Jess Walter, Ellen Welcker, Ryan & Kim Yahne, Maya Jewell Zeller, my grandmothers Itha Anderson and Jessie Shields, and my parents, especially my mom, who all in some specific way inspired and/or encouraged this novel's shape and content. Thank you, too, to friends, family, my writing group here in Spokane and my colleagues at the Spokane County Library District, compassionate humans, all.

And to my children, Henry and Louise: I love you. You (all children) deserve a beautiful world.

ABOUT THE AUTHOR

SHARMA SHIELDS holds an MFA from the University of Montana. She is the author of the short-story collection *Favorite Monster*, winner of the Autumn House Fiction Prize, and the novel *The Sasquatch Hunters' Almanac*, winner of the Washington State Book Award. Her work has appeared in *Slice, Catapult, The New York Times, The Kenyon Review, The Iowa Review, Electric Literature*, and more. Shields has worked in independent bookstores and public libraries throughout Washington State. She lives in Spokane with her husband and children.